LAST THINGS

E. J. MYERS

LAST THINGS

E. J. MYERS

A NOVEL

MONTEMAYOR PRESS

MONTPELIER, VERMONT

For information contact:

Montemayor Press
P. O. Box 546, Montpelier, Vermont 05601
Web site: www.MontemayorPress.c om

1 3 5 7 9 10 8 6 4 2

Library of Congress Cataloging-in-Publication Data

Names: Myers, Edward, 1950- author.
Title: Last things / Edward Myers.
Description: First edition. | Montpelier, Vermont : Montemayor Press, [2017]
    Identifiers: LCCN 2017013348 (print) | LCCN 2017018414 (ebook) | ISBN
    9781932727258 (e-book) | ISBN 1932727256 (e-book) | ISBN 9781932727241
    (paperback : alk. paper) | ISBN 1932727248 (paperback : alk. paper)
Classification: LCC PS3613.Y468 (ebook) | LCC PS3613.Y468 L37 2017 (print) |
    DDC 813/.6--dc23
LC record available at https://lccn.loc.gov/2017013348

For Rabbi Tamara Eskenazi
in gratitude for the many decades
of our friendship

O Lord, help me to be pure,
but not yet.

—St. Augustine

LAST THINGS

E. J. MYERS

W hy had he stopped? Later, when Frank thought over what had happened, his decision made no sense. He had driven past dozens of accidents over the years without pulling over, since the circumstances hadn't needed or allowed any other response: they were just fender benders, or the conditions were too hazardous for him to stop, or he had encountered the scene so abruptly that he'd simply shot past—no chance to slow down—or else, like this time, he had become aware right off that emergency personnel were already present. Just east of the Genesee Park exits, traffic had abruptly slowed. Frank's car and all the others ahead, beside, and behind him crawled along for two or three miles. He had assumed that an accident must have caused the bottleneck. This was a notoriously dangerous stretch of I-70, a long, steep descent from the mountains that fooled even experienced truckers. A well-marked emergency ramp offered an opportunity to bail out, but drivers sometimes missed that one chance or deluded themselves about their brakes holding up. Frank figured that a truck had gone off the road. The sight of red-white-blue flashers ahead confirmed his suspicions. What a surprise, then, to creep along in the column of vehicles and arrive at a far worse scene than what he anticipated. Not a jack-knifed semi but four cars strewn about on the highway, on the shoulder, and even beyond the guardrail. Frank had never seen such a terrible accident. *"Qué carajo,"* he muttered, then corrected himself with the more appropriate *"Dios mío . . ."* Approaching the wreckage, he spotted several Colorado Highway Patrol cars, three ambulances, and a fire truck. Why, then, should he have felt any impulse, any responsibility, to pull over?

He recalled later how two insights had struck him at that moment. One was the severity of the crash. The scene was a mess—four vehicles, the first and second being a car wedged halfway under a panel truck, the third an SUV lying belly up, the fourth a sedan shoved against the railing; broken glass, car parts, and passengers' belongings strewn a hundred yards along the highway; and a dozen bystanders now clustering together a dozen yards from the wrecks while a state trooper kept them away from the rescue personnel. The other insight was Frank's awareness that he happened to be garbed in a black suit and a Roman collar. Why had he chosen to keep wearing his clericals after the conference had adjourned? It's true that he always felt obliged to dress the part when interacting with other priests at an official event, but he had no reason to stay attired like that after the sessions ended and all the other participants left Breckenridge. Had he been too impatient to change clothes? Just eager to get home as quickly as possible? Now it was too late. Frank found himself acutely aware of the image he presented while creeping down the highway in full view of the motorists whose cars crowded around him on all sides. Aware, too, of feeling obliged to play the role he was costumed for . . . to offer solace even though he had none to offer.

Frank eased out of the right lane and pulled over. He was now ten or fifteen yards downhill from the accident scene's lower edge. In the rear-view mirror he saw the jammed-up highway traffic and, beyond the shoulder, the commotion of the rescue effort currently under way. Starting to tremble, he remained in the car for several minutes; then he forced himself out and walked uphill.

A trooper stopped him before he got within twenty feet of the nearest ambulance. "This is a restricted area," he said. "Go back to your car."

"My name is Francisco Ochoa. I'm a priest."

The trooper sized him up. "Wait here." He walked over to the ambulance and spoke to some medics partly visible near the back of their vehicle.

Frank considered retreating. He felt conspicuous—out of place and foolish, just a paunchy, middle-age guy in a black suit and a ring-like collar. Better to leave.

The trooper came back, said, "Come with me," and led Frank to the far side of the ambulance.

There he found a woman and a man, both attired in EMT uniforms, near a gurney cart. The thirty-something male, dark-haired and muscular, stood to one side. The woman—also thirtyish, pretty, auburn-haired—stood next to the gurney. The person on the cart lay wrapped in a sheet with only her face exposed. The female medic held a plastic bottle in one hand, a piece of bloody gauze in the other. She appeared to be cleaning the patient's face.

"Can I help in any way?" Frank asked as he reached them.

"Not really," said the male medic.

"All right—I'm sorry to bother you," Frank said, relieved, as he turned and walked off.

"*Wait,*" the woman medic told him, and, after a moment's hesitation, she left the gurney to catch up with Frank. "We have a deceased patient who appears to be Catholic."

Some noises distracted them: another team of medics wheeling a stretcher toward their ambulance, the patient crying out in pain as they passed. "Coming through," said one of the medics.

The woman pursuing Frank now showed him the object in her hands: a purse. "We found this in the car." She opened the bag, poked through the contents, and presented Frank with a wallet. He took it hesitantly. The driver's license revealed the owner's name: Bethany Willams. Not Williams: Willams. The photo showed a pretty woman laughing. He found other pictures, too: a sandy-haired man, also smiling, and two girls, the younger one around six years old, the older maybe nine or ten, each of them grinning as they posed for their school photos. The medic now reached into the purse again and pulled out a rosary, the beads clicking in her hands. "See what I mean?"

"I do."

"If you could— *You* know."

No way around it. "I'll be back," Frank said reluctantly. He left, walked back to his car, opened the door, and removed his travel bag. Inside was what he called his oil-and-water kit.

He felt both unnerved and relieved by how the situation was taking shape. This task would be easier, surely, than coping with a grievously injured accident victim. Yet on returning to the ambulance, the reality of the situation hit him harder than he expected. A dead woman! Thirty-five, maybe younger. Reddish-blonde hair, gorgeous green eyes, the eyes in fact still open, the lids just a little droopy . . . The sight of her—a human being who had been alive and thriving just an hour ago—punched him in the gut and left him reeling with nausea.

"Okay, do your priest thing," the male medic said.

The woman scolded him: *"Tyler."*

The guy turned and walked away.

"I apologize," she told Frank.

"No need."

"I'll leave you in peace."

Frank felt uneasy when she, too, walked off. He was alone with Ms. Willams now. Not the situation he usually faced when administering this sacrament! Parishioners' homes or hospice rooms . . . Men or women much older than this young accident victim . . . Yet he would do what needed to be done. He placed both palms on the woman's forehead—she was still warm to the touch, he noted uneasily—and he said quietly, "May the Holy Spirit be with you." Then he took out his vial of chrism and a piece of cotton, opened the bottle, and daubed the oil on her forehead. "Through this holy anointing," he said, "may the Lord in his love and mercy help you with the grace of the Holy Spirit." He pulled the sheet back to expose her arms and hands so he could daub oil on her palms. Then, struggling to remember the words, Frank spoke the final prayer and ended, "We ask this through Christ our Lord." He was half-aware of people around him throughout this sequence of actions—the movements of medics and troopers; the departure of two emergency vehicles, sirens shrieking; and the activities of the two EMT's as they gathered up their equipment and stowed these items in the ambulance on Frank's left.

Finished, he signaled hesitantly to the female medic.

She walked over.

"What a terrible tragedy," Frank said.

At first she didn't respond. She seemed aware of him; she wasn't ignoring his words. Too busy to comment? Or perhaps too affected, too moved, to get the words out? "That's the right word for it," she said at last. "Terrible."

"I admire what you've tried to do."

"Oh?" She looked weary and distracted. "Nothing we did made any difference."

"You gave this poor woman a better chance than I did."

"Which was?"

"The usual thing I do for someone who's *in extremis.*"

"Last Rites?"

"It's now called Anointing of the Sick. I suppose the softer name avoids alarming people if they're conscious . . . and, who knows, maybe avoids sending them over the edge."

The woman chuckled uneasily at his comment. "This woman— what's her name again? Bethany!—really did go over the edge." She gestured toward the embankment slanting away from the shoulder while watching Frank with her unblinking gaze.

He quickly grew uncomfortable.

She said, "I hope I haven't offended you."

"Not at all."

"I'm so punchy I'm babbling."

"I'd hardly call it babbling."

"I'm—" She looked close to tears.

"It's understandable that you're upset."

At that moment the male medic walked over. If Frank read his expression right, he looked annoyed or surprised to find Frank still chatting with his colleague.

"We're having this deep theological discussion," the woman told the other medic, then giggled abruptly. At once she said, "Tyler, this is Father—" And to Frank: "I didn't catch your name."

"Francisco Ochoa. Please call me Frank."

"Tyler van Dyne."

The men shook hands. Frank noticed the embroidered nick-name on his dark green EMT jacket: *Dyne-o-Mite.*

Frank asked, "And you are?"

"Laurie Anders." Her jacket showed more plain-spoken embroidery: *Laurie.*

"Glad to meet you both. I appreciate what you've done."

"Not one of our better moments," Tyler said.

"I don't think *they* would see it that way. The people you've been helping."

Tyler didn't respond—he just stood there as if daring Frank and Laurie to make the situation less uncomfortable.

"Thanks," Laurie told Frank.

"I should be thanking *you.*"

"We better go," Tyler said abruptly, turning to the ambulance at his back and opening its two rear doors.

Laurie told Frank. "I appreciate you stopping," she said. "This is a dangerous scene, but you stopped anyway."

"I'm supposed to offer comfort," Frank said. "That's the theory, anyway. It's more than I usually succeed in doing. Though it's true that my natural habitat is much less dramatic than this place."

"You're a parish priest?"

"A campus chaplain."

"I see. Anyway—thanks."

"You're welcome."

"Let's go," Tyler said, now insistently.

Laurie turned to the dead woman and carefully folded the sheet over her face.

Frank watched briefly, then walked back to his car feeling relieved to have performed his duty and desperately eager to be somewhere else.

I

ICH UND DU

1

The view. The view.

Settling in at his desk, Frank stared out his fifth-floor office window at what he saw beyond: the campus below, tidy and unblemished, trees and lawns and well-kept buildings; the neighborhood sloping gently downward to the west; Denver and its suburbs spreading out to fill the entire Platte Valley, then angling up again toward the blue-purple contour of the foothills; and the Rockies beyond, the higher peaks already radiant white with autumn snow. At this hour of the morning, almost nine, the mountains weren't a separate substance from the early October light illuminating them.

He stared for a long time. Like a daydreaming schoolboy, Frank couldn't restrain himself from imagining how much fun he could be having out there. Snowshoeing up the Homestake Creek trail. Having a lunch of schnitzel, sauerkraut, and beer at the little Czech restaurant in Georgetown. Exploring the gimmicky shops on the pedestrian mall in downtown Boulder. Browsing in a bookstore and, if he found a book worth a closer look, settling into one of the comfy chairs to read for a few hours. Whatever. Almost anything would do. Anything that involved not working on Sunday's sermon. Not preparing notes for tomorrow's meeting with the Interfaith Advisory Council. Not completing paperwork on last week's counseling sessions. Not checking his agenda to see which students would show up today. The harder he tried, the harder he found focusing on his tasks.

Fatigue? He hadn't slept well the night before—early on too many nightmares, then a long period of pre-dawn wakefulness. The culprit: probably the accident three days earlier. Not that Frank had forgotten about it already, but he had somehow succeeded in nudging the memory to the edge of his awareness for a day or two. Not so surprising. Even someone claiming insights into psychological processes could be swept away in the currents. Wasn't that the whole point? The routine drive down I-70 had turned into something altogether extraordinary.

"Father Frank?" The intercom: Serena's voice.

"Yes."

"Mike Mullen to see you."

"Right."

He glanced at his watch: nine already. Mike Mullen? He couldn't recall who that might be. What a great way to start the day: lost in reverie, he had let his first appointment catch him by surprise.

Mike Mullen turned out to be a sophomore showing now up for his third counseling session. The kid was a blond, brawny young man whose frat boy grin toggled back and forth with a stunned, almost blank expression. Attired in shorts, T-shirt, and flip-flops, he was tanned, buff, and handsome. This kid was surely an electromagnet whose intense male energy pulled girls and women toward him at random. A more sexually confident young man would be hard to imagine.

"Hi, Father," Mike said on entering the room.

"Good to see you." Extending his hand to shake, Frank winced at the force of the boy's grip. Handshake as dare. Handshake as warning shot.

"Thanks for seeing me."

"I'm happy to be available. Have a seat."

They sat facing each other and, following some chitchat about the pending ski season, they soon revisited the topic of their earlier sessions. Frank was happy to be available, but he found the boy's situation depressing all the same. Having joined Sigma Chi Whatever, Mike had gotten fully involved in his fraternity's raucous party scene, much of which involved drinking massive quantities of alcohol and having casual, almost random sex with one or more of the numerous girls hanging out among the frat brothers on any given evening. Not unusual, this scenario—the mainstay of social life at a ski school like Rocky Mountain University. He also realized that nowadays, preachy admonitions wouldn't go far in restraining this cool dude or anyone else. What to do, then? What to say? Given his role as pastoral counselor, Frank's concern was the emotional and psychological damage he could detect in a relatively thoughtful kid like Mike, who had come to the Center not entirely sure of his own motivations for seeking help but growing aware of his own discomfort. Mike felt especially troubled by a recent incident. A communal drink fest had prompted him to have intercourse with Kaylie, a sorority girl who was herself so drunk as to be almost unconscious at the time of their coupling. Mike himself could only dimly recall what had transpired. The aftermath hadn't led to accusations from the girl—whether of date rape or anything else—and Kaylie had, in fact, made her lusty intentions known earlier, as well as her explicit consent to act on them. But Mike rightly felt troubled by this incident. He had sought pastoral counseling unsure of what nagged at him but conscious of a still, small voice whispering to him all the same.

After discussing these events for a long time, Frank said, "Look. There are lots of issues here, and we can explore them in the fullness of time. But here's my question today. Did your experience with Kaylie provide a satisfying sense of intimacy?"

Mike glanced at Frank, his expression neither hostile nor receptive. "Meaning—'cause I banged her while she was out cold?"

"And while you were more or less comatose, too."

Mike didn't seem to resent the jab. "Of course not."

"What's your sense of this relationship?"

"*Sense?*"

"Your feelings about its substance. Its nature."

"Father, you and I both know the answer."

Frank waited.

Mike looked at him for a moment, then away.

After a minute or two passed in silence, Frank asked, "Mike, what are you feeling?"

The boy shrugged.

"At this very moment."

Another shrug.

"It's fine to feel whatever you're feeling. I'm not judging you."

The silence continued. Frank fought the temptation to glance at the clock on the bookshelf. Only two hours had passed since breakfast, but his stomach was already rumbling. A plate of *huevos rancheros* for lunch would offer solace. Or *huevos revueltos con chorizo*. The session would end in ten minutes . . .

Dead silence.

Frank wouldn't ordinarily have nudged an undergraduate toward insight by recommending a book to read, but he decided to play that card. He had learned during the two previous sessions that Mike, despite his frat-boy appearance and manner, was relatively literate for an RMU sophomore, and he was on the verge of changing his major from business administration to psychology. Knowing this background prompted Frank to try an unusual gambit. "Have you ever heard of a writer," he asked, "named Martin Buber?"

A look of bewilderment bloomed on Mike's face. *"Boober?"*

The kid surely imagined a porn star, maybe a transvestite stripper. At once Frank added, "It's spelled B-U-B-E-R. He wrote some remarkable books about spiritual issues. He wasn't Catholic—in fact, he was a Jewish theologian." Frank went on to describe Ich und Du, and he commented on Buber's beliefs about human relationships, including the quest for relationships that might truly lead to an authentic encounter between I and Thou. "So . . . that's something to consider."

Mike nodded blankly.

"You might find this book interesting."

"I'll give it a try."

"I'm not saying it'll address all the issues we've raised, but might shed some light."

They chatted for a while about other aspects of the situation; then Frank let the session fizzle out. Mike eventually picked up on what Frank hoped had been his clear but not too-pushy signals that their time was up.

"Thanks, Father."

"You're most welcome."

The boy administered another palm-crushing handshake as he left Frank's office.

Sitting again, Frank swiveled in his chair and gazed out the window. He felt as blank as the blue Colorado sky. A quick look at his watch: nine fifty-four. It wasn't the intensity of counseling sessions that exhausted him, he told himself. It was the effort to swim upstream like a salmon against the torrent of his own fraudulence. *Ich und Du,* indeed! By what right could he lecture this young man about authenticity in human relationships? About a satisfying level of intimacy? Frank wasn't bankrupt enough to bang stupefied coeds, but what gave him the authority—

"Frank?" Serena again.

He stole a furtive glance at his watch. "Yes."

"Ms. Anders to see you."

"I thought my next appointment was at eleven," he stated into the intercom. "Are you sure about this?" For a moment he sat there feeling cornered. Ms. Anders. He couldn't recall anyone named Ms. Anders. "All right, send her in."

He recognized her at once: the EMT he had met at the accident scene on I-70. Laura? Lori? An attractive woman—thirty-five or so, slightly plump in an appealing way, what Rabbi Miller would have called *zaftig.* Bosomy torso altogether elegant in her satiny dark green top. Firm hips whose curves were appealingly evident in her tight jeans. "You!" he exclaimed, trying to sound cordial, even jocular.

"I'm so sorry!" she exclaimed. She stepped in cautiously, lingering in the doorway, an odd reticence in someone surely accustomed to pulling people out of car wrecks or entering their homes to examine their sick and injured bodies.

"Don't be sorry," Frank told her. "Please come in. I'm just . . . *surprised.*" He stood, walked around the desk, reached out. Firm handshake. She seemed to relax. Lovely hair—a rich, multi-hued honey blonde. She had worn it braided while on duty the other night, a single rope that had extended down her back almost to her waist; now liberated, it fell around her shoulders like a cape. "Please have a seat."

"I'm sorry to bother you."

"It's no bother."

"I'm not even Catholic."

"That makes no difference." He couldn't help wondering what brought her to the Center. "Tell me your name again?"

"Laurie."

"Right."

"And you're Father Ocho?"

"Ochoa. Please call me Frank."

"Father Frank."

"No, just Frank." He motioned toward the chairs opposite his desk. Stepping closer and sitting, he gestured for Laurie to do the same.

She looked around at his office: at the shelves full of books, at the Asian and Latin American folk art on the walls, at the photos, at the knick-knacks from his travels. Perhaps she felt puzzled, as so many people seemed to be, by the multicultural, multi-religious mish-mash, by the limited presence of specifically Christian art, but she didn't comment. She stared for a moment at the *sumi-e* prints near the window and at the Majapahit-era *bodhissatva* in a shadow box. She glanced, too, at the weavings and pottery and metalwork that Frank had purchased in Mexico, Peru, Indonesia, Ghana, Thailand . . . He had always enjoyed first-time visitors' bewilderment as they viewed his collection. "I want to thank you for the other evening," she said.

"No need for thanks," Frank told her. "I can't even recall what I might warrant your gratitude."

"What you did for that woman."

"The anointing."

"You talked with me afterwards."

"That's hardly heroic."

"It helped me."

"I'm glad."

"It was a bad situation."

"So bad I'm still shaking!" He forced a laugh.

"What a mess," Laurie said flatly. At once she added, "It upset me, too. And— If I'm not being too presumptuous, I want to talk with you about something that's, I don't know . . . that's maybe related."

"I'll be happy to. I'm just surprised you tracked me down."

"You said you're with a campus ministry, so I called a bunch of colleges till I found the right one."

"An EMT sleuth!"

She smiled. "I thought maybe you'd help me figure out something."

Frank motioned for Laurie to continue.

"I hate my job," she said. "I'm sick of it. It's the worst job in the world."

"And why is that?"

"People say, 'Oh, Laurie—you're so lucky to do what you do. You get to help people!' Right. I help Joe Schmoe, he either lives or dies, and I leave the scene. I help Jane Doe, she lives or dies, and I move on. I help Susie Smith, she lives or dies, and I move on. There's the next person and the next, and after that the next, and then the next and the next and the next." Her voice lacked any sense of agitation. She might have been referring to customers at a grocery checkout line.

"Isn't there some degree of satisfaction in what you're doing?"

"It's the same satisfaction I'd get from an endless string of one-night stands."

"I guess I wouldn't have thought of it quite that way."

"I can't stand it any more."

"How long have you been an EMT?"

"Almost fifteen years."

"That's a long time. Especially in a stressful line of work."

"Maybe too long."

"What do you plan to do?"

"I really think I'd better quit."

"Fair enough. Have you considered what's next?" Almost

without thinking, Frank settled into what he called PCM—Pastoral Counseling Mode.

She ran her fingers through her hair, grasped the whole mass at the back of her neck, then released it, a gesture that surprised Frank and unexpectedly prompted a shiver of delight. "Something. Anything. Something . . . different. Something that's not in the health field."

"Maybe in business?"

"Maybe, but not a job that's too people-oriented."

"You seem like a people person."

"A people person who's sick of people!" she blurted out. She hesitated for a moment, as if taken aback by her tone of voice, before continuing. "Maybe I should go sell plants."

"Plants?"

"You know—house plants, garden supplies, stuff like that. 'Cause, yeah, I'd have to interact with customers, but it wouldn't be so intense. At least my customers would be healthy. I'm tired of dealing with sick people and dead bodies! I want to see things thrive and grow."

"Fair enough."

"Something else: plants don't accuse you of incompetence after you knocked yourself out to save them. Plants don't throw up all over you. Plants don't swing punches. Plants don't *sue* you."

Listening, Frank grew more sympathetic but also baffled—sympathetic, because he grasped that such intense, risky work would take a toll; baffled, because what he had seen of Laurie's performance at the accident scene clearly showed her concern for other human beings. Why, then, such anguish and fatigue? Maybe post-traumatic stress, the chronic variant of the disorder. If so, even PTSD apparently hadn't damaged her ability to care. "Look," he said, "it's not my role to tell you what to do. On the contrary, what you say makes sense. But here's what concerns me. What if you leave this difficult job, a job that rightly causes you some distress, but you end up in a line of work that's—arid."

"I'm not worried about arid," she tells him. "I'm worried about what's wet."

"Wet?"

"I'm worried about getting so soaked with other people's pain—not waterlogged, but *pain*-logged—that I'll stop caring about what anyone is going through. People's crises already seem like just problems to solve. If someone goes into cardiac arrest, I go through the motions, do compressions, zap him with the AED, get that ticker started. If a toddler pulls a hot saucepan off the stove and scalds herself, I slap on the wet soaks and haul the kid off to the E.R. If some motorists smash into each other, I collar 'em, board 'em, and haul 'em off. If an asthmatic teenager has respiratory distress, I ventilate her. Whatever. I deal with everyone's accidents, illnesses, calamities, attacks, and crises. I do it well. I help them. You better believe it—I help these folks! But I don't really care what happens afterwards. Not any more. Why? Because I'm too heavy, I'm saturated, I'm pain-logged from too much pain, I'm sinking just like waterlogged wood full of too much water."

Frank struggled to find words that might console her. "You've seen so much."

"I can't unsee what I've seen."

"True, but you can ease the stress."

As he prepared to ask more questions, Laurie interrupted him. "We took care of this couple at an accident scene. They'd been driving down I-70 in a vintage convertible, they'd rolled it, and the car skidded upside-down for five hundred yards down the highway with the couple trapped underneath. When the rescue team arrived and flipped the car, we discovered that the friction against the road while the man and the woman rolled around under the passenger compartment at sixty miles per hour had not only stripped off all their clothes, it had skinned them alive. They were—*peeled*. There was nothing we could do for them. They'd suffered severe head injuries, too, broken bones, stuff like that. We treated them for shock, bundled them up, and transported them, but they both died before we reached the hospital."

Frank didn't know how to respond. Saying, *Well, you did your best* would sound worse than patronizing—simply idiotic.

"Another time I showed up at an accident where an eighteen-foot truck went off U.S. 6. It turned out that twenty illegal aliens were riding in the cargo box. The truck shot down the embankment ten or fifteen yards and smashed into Clear Creek. The river isn't deep, so nobody drowned, but everyone apparently died on impact. We found a huge pile of bodies inside the cargo box. All smashed together up front. Massive trauma. Every one of 'em was dead. Except that while we tried to get the bodies out of the truck, which was tipped steeply forward, we heard a cry. A baby's cry. Believe it or not, one of those immigrants' kid had survived the crash. So I was thinking, 'Wow, it's a miracle!' We worked fast to get the bodies off and rescue that baby."

"Wonderful," Frank said, relieved to see at least one ray of light in this otherwise dark tale.

"Later, once we got the baby to the hospital, it turned out she'd been smothered by all the bodies heaped on her, she'd asphyxiated, and she'd suffered massive, permanent brain damage."

Frank waited, nodding. What could he do but acknowledge Laurie's anguish?

"Speaking of babies—or toddlers, actually—here's another incident. A hiker at a local state park went into an outhouse near the campground to relieve himself. While he stood peeing into the hole in the boards, he heard this whiny noise. Like a child whimpering. He zipped his pants and went outside to see if maybe there was a lost kid out there. But there wasn't. So he figured maybe he'd just heard the wind. He went back into the outhouse and started to pee again. And he heard that same sound: whimpering. He couldn't believe it, but the noise seemed to be coming from inside the latrine. So he left and got a flashlight and came back, and he shined the light in, and there, down in all the piss and shit—pardon my French—was a little girl."

"She'd fallen in?"

"Of course that's what everyone thought. So once he called 911 and our squad showed up and we got the kid out—which was a bad-enough ordeal, believe me—and the sheriff's deputies arrived to talk with the girl. She was about three years old. After calming her down, they asked how she'd got down there. 'How did you fall into the toilet, Sweetheart?' And she said, 'I didn't fall. Daddy put me there.'"

"You can't be serious." Something deep inside Frank's gut shifted in revulsion.

"I'm dead serious. She said, 'Daddy pushed me in the potty.'"

"But why?"

"Maybe *you* can tell me why. You've got deep insights into good and evil, right?"

"I certainly don't!"

"No?"

"Sorry." He pulled his pockets inside-out to reveal their emptiness. "Search me."

"Hmm—I could've sworn you guys had deep insights into good and evil."

"The only insight I have," Frank told her, "is that whatever evil exists in the world, whatever its origins, human beings have the capacity to resist and to ease the pain it causes. You EMTs, especially, are at least trying to ease some of the pain. That's more than most people do."

"Yeah," Laurie said, "we're all generous, good-hearted, and ready to serve the weak and vulnerable. Like some guys I heard about recently. Two EMTs in a neighboring county picked up a college girl who'd collapsed at a small-town bar. She was totally intoxicated—couldn't walk unassisted, could barely talk, and kept passing out. She'd bumped her head, too, and cut her forehead. So the EMTs figured on taking her to the regional E.R. Only first they went for a little ride. They drove into the woods on a deserted back road and parked in a secluded area. Then, with little Miss Drunk-on-Her-Ass out cold and conveniently secured to the stretcher—they'd strapped her wrists and ankles to the rails with four-point leather restraints of the type we sometimes use on belligerent patients—the benevolent EMTs took turns raping her."

He shook his head in disbelief.

"Every word I'm telling you is true."

"Such a violation of trust."

"Sort of like priests and choir boys."

"Listen," Frank told her abruptly, "I would never, ever defend what some of my confreres have done. It's beyond comprehension. Beneath contempt."

"I didn't mean it that way. I don't mean to sound so—accusatory. I'm just saying that all kinds of people violate other folks' trust. Including EMTs."

"I don't know what to say."

"You don't have to say anything. I'm just telling you what I've seen and heard."

"That's why I don't know what to say."

"And that's why you don't have to say anything."

He couldn't make sense of what she was telling him, but that wasn't what troubled him, or at least wasn't what troubled him most. Something else did, too, something beyond the tales themselves. Frank felt more and more exhausted by this conversation—disheartened by Laurie's tales suffering and cruelty, sickened by the details of what she faced while trying to help other people. Maybe this was what bothered him most: that her tales were somehow a relief, or at least a strange distraction, from what he heard at the Center day in day out—students' anxieties about grades, their roommate problems, the *sturm und drang* of adolescent sexuality, the squabbles with parents, the late-teen angst of every imaginable sort. Yet he also felt embarrassed to react to her stories with anything but dismay. At the same time, he found an intense urge to respond—to relieve her pain, to protect her—that went far beyond what he ordinarily felt toward his troubled counselees.

"I wish I could do something for you," he said, "but I don't know what that would be. Most people who come here want either counseling or, if they're Catholic, they want absolution. But the center provides counseling services only to students at the university—"

"I don't need counseling."

"—and as for absolution—"

"I'm not Catholic."

"You mentioned that earlier."

A sudden smile: beautiful, uneasy, at once generous and vulnerable. She said, "I'm not even sure *why* I'm here."

"Sometimes it's hard to know."

"And why *now?* I've been dealing with all this stuff for a long, long time."

Unbidden, an idea occurred to Frank. "Well, that's an interesting point. You've been dealing with this stuff for a long, long time. So you're right to ask why you'd feel what you're feeling—this reaction, this desperation—only now?"

"I honestly don't know."

He waited a while. Laurie sat before him looking not so much blank as *elsewhere.* She was mulling over something, or someone, far away. Frank followed a hunch and asked, "That woman at the accident—the woman who died. How old do you think she is?" He corrected himself: "Was."

Laurie turned her gaze to him. "Maybe thirty-five or so."

"And you are . . . ?"

"Thirty-seven." A pause. "Okay, I see what you're getting at."

"Just a thought."

Hardly a radical notion. Too obvious, even. Maybe that was the point. The old purloined letter trick, the missing item hidden precisely because it lay in plain view on the mantle.

"I'll think about that," she said flatly. Then at once, looking startled, she said, "What time is it?" She glanced at her watch. "Jeez, I'm wasting your whole day! I should leave you in peace."

Frank started to object. They'd found a key to the lock— Then he caught himself: the morning was half-gone already. "I'm glad you came by to visit."

"Me too, but I've taken so much of your time."

"Not at all."

"I ought to go."

"That's not what I meant." He felt terrible that she'd misunderstood. "Don't take my words wrong. I'm not asking you to leave. I just feel—helpless. You're doing so much. More than you know. All I can say is— Actually, I don't know what to say."

"I have to go." Now she stood, so Frank stood, too, and he saw her to the door.

"Thanks for talking with me."

"I should be thanking *you*."

"Bye."

"Goodbye."

She walked into the reception area, then out.

Frank returned to his desk, sat in the chair, and swiveled to look out the window. The view. For a while he stared at the mountains, then glanced at the clock.

Almost eleven. Laurie's visit had consumed a whole hour. Had he helped her? God only knew. He had tried, certainly. But now he felt off-kilter, exhausted despite the early hour. His next counselee would arrive at any moment.

All the more reason, then, to gaze out the window for a while longer.

2

Frank went about his business feeling haunted by the exchange with Laura—*Laurie,* he reminded himself—but his recollections of her visit soon diminished. He was too busy to think much about their conversation. She was neither a client at the Center nor a member of the campus community. Perhaps the discussion had let her vent some anxiety and, who knows, maybe think through her options. Beyond that, he couldn't afford to give Laurie much thought. Yet now and then shards of their discussion jabbed at his consciousness. The couple skinned alive beneath the skidding convertible . . . The baby suffocated under a pile of dead immigrants . . . The little girl dumped down the state park latrine . . . The drunk college student raped by EMTs . . . Tangled among these appalling incidents were Laurie's expressions of anguish over how much she had witnessed and how little she had eased the pain of other human beings. Frank admired this young woman and her earnest efforts. He worried about the toll these efforts had taken on her. He hoped she could find a less traumatic line of work. Time after time her tales of suffering bubbled up into his awareness.

Otherwise he kept doing what he always did. Helping to run the Center. Counseling students, faculty, and staff members at RMU. Performing his various sacerdotal duties—Mass, confession, baptisms, discussions at the Center, and all the rest. Of these duties, pastoral counseling was potentially the most interesting and the least tedious. The unpredictability of human experience offered the greatest options for surprise. Maybe not as much as he would have liked . . . Most of his counselees were affluent, coddled undergraduates between the ages of eighteen and twenty-two. A small percentage of the rest were similarly affluent, somewhat older graduate students. Another small population consisted of RMU faculty and staff members. They were human beings going through the usual gamut of experiences, challenges, and crises; they deserved respect and sympathy; and they merited whatever support, consolation, encouragement, and assistance he could provide. Frank had always felt ready, and he still felt ready, to do his part. The repetitiveness of his own experiences with them, however, chafed like a too-tight collar. Many of his interactions felt substantial and worthwhile, but others were annoying, pointless, risible, even empty. Too often he felt his attention stray even in the midst of counseling sessions. This impatience prompted annoyance toward himself, even self-contempt, but he felt impatient all the same.

What had he accomplished over the years? How much longer could he help these students through their late-adolescent crises before he started to feel like fare collector at a spiritual toll plaza? Pondering this question, Frank admonished himself: these crises mattered. To the students, certainly. Emancipation, self-definition, sexuality, career choice, yadda-yadda, were legitimate issues that caused genuine, often intense struggles. He had no right to dismiss or demean them. Even so, they grew tedious. Repetitive, anyway. At some point all the discussions of parent-child conflicts, of confusion over career paths, of sexual identity, of ambivalent relationships, blurred into a mass of young-adult angst. Worse, Frank couldn't feel confident that he made a difference helping his parishioners make sense of all this stuff. Yes, he spent time with them, offered solace, provided counsel. He offered reassurances. In many instances his words helped ease tension, anguish, or doubt. He did CPR on many young men's and women's faltering confidence in God or life or family, he jolted their fibrillating faith, he helped revive their pulses once again. And yet . . . And yet . . .

Perhaps these concerns explained his strong response to Laurie's tale of EMT burnout. Not that Frank deserved to feel anything as intense as what she felt . . . He had never coped with crises of the horrific kinds and the sheer number, that Laurie faced routinely. He had certainly spent many hours visiting parishioners at the hospital, among them young men and women who had suffered car accidents, faculty members who had developed dire illnesses, elders whose health had failed. Some of these people had died. Bedside conversations had often proved intense, even wrenching. Like any other member of the clergy, Frank struggled to offer solace. None of that was easy. Still, the sum total of his thirty years' work in the priesthood probably contained less anguish and stress than Laurie experienced in a single week. Why, then, should he resonate so fully to her expressions of physical, emotional, and spiritual fatigue? He had no right to feel anything of the sort. Yet he did.

For this reason Frank found it interesting to feel a sense of kinship with Laurie, a sense that her frustration resembled his own. He also felt a twinge of regret that their conversation had lasted so short a time and would never resume in a way that would allow them—as he often phrased the situation when speaking with his counselees—"to explore these issues further."

"Father, please—I'm counting on your help." With these words the caller, Zach, an RMU student in the business administration program, summarized his plea as they discussed a crisis over the phone.

"I'm afraid there's not much I can do," Frank told him.

"But in situations like this aren't you supposed to offer *counseling*? Isn't that your role before the wedding?"

Frank grew impatient. "Counseling, yes—for the bride and groom. I don't counsel the whole wedding party."

"That's not what I'm asking."

"It's all too close." He couldn't think of many situations he wanted more eagerly to avoid. Zach's fiancée, Mindy, had incited a rebellion among her bridesmaids. Mindy was a prime example of the so-called bridezilla. Her wedding plans would have put most coronations to shame. As if the preparations weren't *sufficiently* extravagant, there was the issue of the bridesmaids' appearances. Expecting them to wear perfectly matched designer gowns was only the start of what Mindy had ordained. The bride also wanted the women to present themselves in a state of perfect beauty. These young women were all—at least judging from photos—drop-dead gorgeous. Yet Mindy found fault with them; they weren't sufficiently gorgeous. She had told each of the six to lose weight, shape up at the gym, and undergo certain facial treatments. Microdermabrasion, chemical peels, Botox injections, eyelash extensions, airbrush tanning, the works. Four of the bridesmaids had agreed to Mindy's dictates, apparently with some enthusiasm. Two, however, had rebelled. Mindy was furious. Now Zach found himself caught in the crossfire.

"If you can't help me," the boy said, "this marriage will go up in flames before the ship ever leaves port."

Frank found the mixed metaphor more amusing than he should have: a smoldering cruise ship listing to starboard just a short distance off shore. "Let me clarify the situation," he told Zach. "I can counsel you and Mindy. In fact, I believe that the two of you should earnestly discuss certain aspects of your personal values. And, while you're at it, some of your communication issues. Consider me available to foster those discussions. However, I absolutely cannot mediate between Mindy and her girlfriends."

Silence.

Frank looked at his watch. "Call me if you and your fiancée want to talk."

"All right— All right. Thanks anyway," Zach said flatly.

"What was *that* all about?" Pete asked as Frank hung up, left the kitchen, and returned to the dining room.

"Pre-nuptial flapdoodle. The bride wants her bridesmaids to be a perfectly matched set of Barbie dolls." Frank sat in his chair at the table. By now Pete and Frank had almost finished the meal they shared each Sunday once the morning Masses were behind them. Just as well. "The maid of honor complained to the groom, so now he's caught between his fiancée and the bride's gal pals." Frank resumed eating his *panqueque de flor de calabaza,* a squash blossom-filled omelette, which by now had grown cold. He consoled himself with the *bolillo* he sliced, buttered, and spread with some of the creamy goats' milk *cajeta* he had purchased at a Mexican grocery store in west Denver.

Pete glanced at him now and then as Frank ate. Strictly a coffee-and-Danish guy, Pete had often expressed his puzzlement (or was it outright revulsion?) toward Frank's taste in breakfast foods. Frank's preparations of Mexican and other Latino cuisines had become a source of particular controversy. He didn't say anything blatant, since Pete understood that doing so would have insulted Frank's Mexican heritage. If nothing else, Pete now restrained himself from claiming that the mere sight and aroma of these spicy dishes ruined his appetite; he merely averted his gaze. "It's incredible what these young couples fight over," Pete said. "Dresses . . . Hair styles . . . Just incredible."

"This wasn't simply a question of dresses and hair," Frank told him. "The bride had a set up program for upgrading the bridesmaids' beauty. A whole spa regime."

Pete, reading his copy of *Golf Digest,* lowered the magazine. "I heard about a bride recently who wanted her bridesmaids to have breast augmentation surgery. All of them!"

"All of the breasts?" Frank asked, feeling mischievous. "Or all of the bridesmaids?"

Pete ignored these comments. "I don't know what amazed me more—that the bride offered to foot the bill for everyone's medical expenses, or that the women agreed to her request."

"These kids' values are way out of kilter," Pete said.

Frank found his attention wandering. He shared their dismay but didn't want to get in a drawn-out discussion of the topic. Before long the discussion would morph into an argument. Never mind that Frank and Pete basically agreed about the core issues; they would still find cause for conflict. Pete would resort less to Church doctrine than to all-purpose sacerdotal harrumphing. Pete was thirty-two, twenty-five years younger than Frank; yet to Frank, his conservatism made him seem much older. A Young Fogy, he called Pete in the privacy of his own mind. An old story, as he'd heard from friends in several orders: Pete was typical of the younger priests ordained since the late 1980's. It was typical, too, that young fogies often knocked heads with the more liberal priests, now in late middle age or early geezerhood, who had been ordained in the 1960's and 70's. More and more often nowadays, Frank simply kept his mouth shut.

"—and then check in with Brother Matthew about how to handle this sort of disagreement within a wedding party," Pete was saying.

Most recently there had been conflicts over homilies. Pete had complained that Frank's sermons were too brief. Frank in turn pointed out that Pete tended to run long, often very long indeed. Pete then countered that length wasn't the most important issue. Yes, his homilies went on at some length, but the congregation connected with them, found them comfortable, reassuring, and familiar; by contrast, more than a few parishioners had complained that the brevity of Frank's sermons confused them. Frank countered that he simply spoke for as long as made sense—neither too long nor too short a time. Perhaps his comment had made the point a little too strongly: "I'm not here to spoon-feed them an entire bowl of spiritual pabulum." Pete had taken offense at this phrasing. When Frank had attempted to do damage control, Pete started a long monologue about homiletic approaches that stressed the importance of guiding the congregation—"taking them by the hand, pastorally speaking, if necessary"—while Frank held his ground about trying to challenge what was, after all, a community of well-educated and generally thoughtful parishioners. Frank's using the phrase "I'll toss a grenade in their midst now and then" guaranteed that the discussion would be ongoing and contentious.

In reality, Pete was an accomplished, respected preacher in a contemporary, suburban, wanna-be-hip Catholic style. His sermons always started with a personal experience. Nothing wrong with that—Frank sometimes used the same approach himself. Connect with the congregation. Reveal a bit about your past. Admit to ordinary foibles. Show that you can relate to routine challenges, family life, and the workaday world. That's clearly what Pete was attempting at Mass that same morning. The story in question focused on his childhood in a predominantly German-American neighborhood of Chicago—where, as an Italian-American kid struggling for acceptance, he had cooked up a story in which he claimed to be a Sioux Indian. This got a big laugh from the congregation. Pete then elaborated on the consequences: teachers amused, parents outraged, school chums in quick succession impressed, infuriated, and inspired to seek retribution. Ultimately all parties saw the error of their ways, apologized, and offered mutual forgiveness. Pete extracted a radiant moral from the story and, like fissionable material refined from low-grade uranium, he cranked it up toward critical mass in the reactor of his sermon. Soon Frank grew weary. It wasn't a bad tale that Pete was telling—clever enough and amusing—but it went on too long, he tried too hard to generate energy, and soon enough the kids in the congregation began to fidget, the teenagers grew restless, and the grownups started glancing at their watches. Yet another instance of a shepherd flogging his sheep with a paternalistic crozier.

Usually, however, his sermons were altogether bland, relaxing, and utterly predictable. Only the most familiar texts from Scripture would suffice. The Prodigal Son . . . The Wise and Foolish Virgins . . . The Withered Fig Tree . . . The Way of Mary and the Way of Martha . . . If the text wasn't hoary enough to capitalize, he wouldn't use it. Worse yet, he couched everything in the most ordinary, least inspired, least interesting language. His sermons were the homiletic equivalent of elevator music.

Frank now became aware that Pete was speaking: "—and certainly reminds us to do a better job tracking how we promulgate Catholic values. How we're influencing this new generation."

Frank noted how much he looked and sounded like a business executive planning to launch a new product. Then again, he always did. He might as well be and accountant. The branch manager at a corporate office. The firm: The One Holy Catholic and Apostolic Church, LLC.

"Sorry," Frank said as he got up from the table. "I need to go water the garden."

The rectory, a nondescript little house built early in the 1960s, was small enough to be manageable but large enough for each priest to have his own bedroom plus access to three common areas—the living room, the kitchen, and shared office space for the Catholic ministry's day-to-day operations. There was a finished basement, too, outfitted as a chapel for the few parishioners who attended daily Mass. A comfortable residence, one that Frank found pleasant enough, if rather dull. The surrounding neighborhood seemed typical of the university area: post-World War II housing stock, one-story cracker boxes set in tiny yards. Roughly half of the properties belonged to young families or senior citizens; the other half were rentals that RMU students moved into each fall and generally ignored throughout the academic year, letting the lawns dry out, the gardens grow brambly, and the paint peel off the exterior walls. Frank felt more or less at peace with the setting. It remained fairly quiet—all that really mattered to him. He could go about his work undisturbed, walk to the campus in ten or twelve minutes, buy groceries at a supermarket right up the block, and exercise by working in the yard or by riding his bike in the area.

Two sets of neighbors flanked the rectory. One set was the Beaches, an elderly couple who had lived in their little house for longer than the Center had existed. Kermith Beach must have been around eighty-five—a lanky retired farmer from eastern Colorado who had moved to the big city in the 1950's. His wife, Margaret, was apparently younger than Kermith but looked much older. Together and separately, they puttered in their house and tended their lawn and garden with the precision typical of people who had come of age during the Depression. Kermith watered and fertilized the lawn as if raising a crop of wheat on which his family's survival depended. He mowed the grass at least twice a week. He obliterated any and all weeds with poison. Margaret's role, meanwhile, was to command an army of flowers: platoons of perfectly spaced marigolds, companies of phlox, regiments of roses, and, predictably, a few traitors among the ranks: zinnias lined up against the garage wall like prisoners awaiting execution by firing squad. Order must be maintained at all costs. A few months earlier, on a summer morning, Margaret had commented that the priests had allowed a few dandelions to sprout on their side of the fence, and, pointing as if to identify heretics to the Grand Inquisitor, she told Frank lugubriously: "I sure hope those dandelion puffs don't blow over here."

"Rest easy," Frank replied. "I'll take care of them."

"I work so hard on my lawn."

"I'll protect you, Margaret."

Maybe oldsters are so obsessed with gardening, he speculated, because all those tidy flowers present lush signs of life to people whose daily experiences are loss, decline, and decrepitude. Hard to say. He found both Kermith and Margaret a source of frustration, yet he tried to view them with compassion. They stood at the doorstep of eternity. They deserved his patience.

He had never really understood what the Beaches thought of him, but he could guess. Overhearing them comment to other neighbors about "illegals" and "all those foreigners invading our country," Frank assumed that they disliked Mexicans and, for good measure, Mexican-Americans as well. He assumed, too, that they suspected him to be one of the invaders . . . even though his family had emigrated to the United States over a hundred years ago. He also knew that the Beaches' upbringing had been raised in a small-town fundamentalist church, and he could tell that they didn't like Catholics. Kermith would often zing Frank with snide remarks, though always padded with the bubble wrap of male jocularity. "I bet you guys get a real earful at Confession."

"Sometimes we do," Frank responded.

Having opened that particular door, Kermit now walked through it: "But you know what, Frank? I never did see the point of Confession. At least not confession to a *priest*. In my view, sin is a matter best kept between the sinner and his God."

Frank nodded, not wanting to get pulled into an argument.

"I know that if I sin—or rather, *when* I sin, 'cause I know I'm a sinner—I turn to God and I say, 'O Lord, forgive me for that sin.' And I know God forgives me. Right then, at that very instant." Kermith snapped his fingers while gazing intently at Frank. "I don't need a priest to mediate between me and my God."

"I'm sure you hold your own in every negotiation."

Or else Kermith would start in on celibacy. "I just don't understand why you guys can't get married. Why, Jim Dale, the pastor at our church, has been married for oh, I'd guess forty years, he's a devoted husband, and he and his wife have raised a house full of kids, but even as a busy married man he sure as heck gives his all to the congregation."

"I bet he does."

"You can't tell me marriage is a problem for pastors. No, I just don't believe it. Marriage does a man a world of good. Marriage—" and now Kermith stared eye-to-eye with Frank—"marriage keeps a man out of trouble."

"What a coincidence to hear you phrase it that way!" Frank exclaimed. "Just the other day I used the same words in a conversation with the Pope. I said, 'Your Holiness, I think celibacy is a big mistake. Marriage isn't a problem. Marriage would do us priests a world of good. Your Holiness, marriage would keep us out of trouble.'"

Kermith's stare continued—that straight-shooter, man-of-the-soil gaze. "You're joshing me, aren't you, Frank? You told that to the Pope?"

"Sure. The Holy Father checks in with me every Wednesday afternoon."

A big smile now. "You're so full of it."

The other next-door neighbors were three RMU coeds. Off-campus rentals resembled tides at the seashore, students flooding into the neighborhood early in September, then flowing out again in late May. Frank and Pete never knew in advance who would wash up in the bungalow beside the rectory. Each year one or more students joined the prior year's tenants, or else one group moved out and a new one arrived. This year the tenants were three undergraduate women—Stacey, Tracy, and one whose name Frank could never recall. They were polite when he crossed paths with them in the front yard but routinely ribald, even foul-mouthed, whenever they believed he was out of earshot. "Goddammit, Tracy," shouted What's-Her-Name one afternoon, "if you keep using my coffee, I'm gonna tell Jed you're two-timing him."

"You better not."

"I'll do it. I swear I will."

"You won't."

"I will. And you know what? I'll tell him it's *Richard* you're screwing."

"If you do that, I'll kill you."

"No you won't, slutface, 'cause Jed is gonna kill you first."

"Fuck you, bitch."

"Fuck you, too. I'm gonna say it just one more time: *stop using my coffee.*"

All stated in the most jocular tones of voice.

Frank could generally ignore them. They left for classes and returned from the campus at various times of day, they played loud music during daylight hours but generally turned down the volume each evening, they carried on their raucous conversations, they partied on weekends with their svelte girlfriends and buff college guys, but otherwise they kept to themselves. They did live next door, however, so they weren't completely unavoidable. Most disconcerting was their predilection for sunbathing in their back yard. Stacey and What's-Her-Name, especially, spent an hour or more each afternoon during the warm months lying out there with their tops off and even their bikini bottoms loosened to allow the sun's rays full contact with all but a few square inches' surface area of their skin. Even more than her housemates, Stacey seemed to have undertaken a major R&D project to explore the limits of immodesty. After oiling down with suntan lotion, she would recline and soak up the Colorado sunshine, not to mention the gaze of any neighbors who happened to enter their adjacent back yards.

During the early weeks of this semester, Frank wondered how these young ladies could be so flagrant, especially with two priests next door. They certainly had a right to sunbathe, whether *deshabillée* or not, in their own yard. But didn't they feel any discomfort? Any awkwardness? Apparently not. Then at some point he understood what he should have grasped all along: these pretty lasses were taunting Frank and Pete; were amusing themselves at their expense.

What troubled Frank far more than the annoying but risible aspects of this situation was Stacey's resemblance to Erin. Like Stacey, Erin had been a dark-haired, full-figured beauty. Even his most cursory encounters with Stacey couldn't help but remind Frank of his senior year of college, the year of his cohabiting with Erin, which in turn reminded him of their breakup when he had decided to relocate to Mexico after graduation. Frank had attempted to convince Erin to come along. They would rent an apartment together in Oaxaca. They would continue what they agreed was a wonderful relationship. To Frank's dismay, Erin turned down the offer. Her explanation: a preference to go ahead with a longstanding plan and start graduate studies in psychology. She also expressed concern about living in provincial Mexico, a country whose culture was alien and a least a little threatening to an upper-middle-class daughter of Irish-American Bostonians. Frank had almost canceled his trip in favor of continuing the relationship. Not sure why but still compelled to follow his own plan, he had proceeded to Oaxaca. During whole year of that first stay, however, he had questioned his decision, had missed Erin, and had longed for the sustenance of her company, the richness of their time together, and the delights of their love life. How awkward, then, to find himself so vividly recalling his old flame every time he crossed paths with the more heavily tanned but otherwise physically similar Stacey.

Which, inevitably, he now found himself doing once again. Frank, having planted a vegetable garden that spring and tended it all summer, checked up on it daily as the Colorado autumn unfolded. The zucchini now lay on the ground in great abundance, tomatoes ripened on the vine almost daily, peppers swelled on their little bushes, and pumpkins grew yellow and fat among the vines and fan-like leaves. His work wasn't finished yet. The arid fall weather required constant vigilance. Though the Denver nights grew cool and snow had already fallen in the high country, the daytime temperatures could rise into the eighties. The air was so dry that even a few days' negligence could damage the vegetables' late growth. The melons needed almost daily irrigation. The tomatoes, too; otherwise they would toughen. The peppers, especially, would suffer damage—the sleek, pale green Anaheims; the squat *poblanos;* the bullet-shaped *serranos;* the bell-like *habaneros*—and, if damaged, these much-prized fruits of Frank's toil would jeopardize the quality of his cooking for many months. Better, then, to take care. Besides, Frank felt a special delight to be watering the plot at this time of year, when the flatter angle of the sun's rays in the late afternoon somehow created wider, deeper, broader rainbows, the aerosol of water smelled especially lush, and the plants took on nearly brilliant hues, the vast array of greens, especially, so intense as to make the vegetation appear illuminated as if from within. Frank felt great pleasure to tend his plants, and he saw no reason to neglect them just because a nearly naked Eve lay a few dozen feet away, taking a break from the many Adams who stopped by to visit her own garden.

To his surprise, though, he soon noticed that she had gotten up from the lawn and was now walking over to the fence.

"Hey."

"Hello, Stacey. How's it going?"

The towel barely covered her. "Just great, Frank. How about you?"

"Busy but fine." He couldn't help but observe yet again both how beautiful she was and how much her beauty invoked Erin's. How those clear blue eyes both contradicted her black hair and complemented it perfectly . . .

"I like your garden."

"Thanks. It's fun. It gets me outdoors."

"I love being outdoors."

What should he say? —*Yes, I've noticed.* "And of course having all these vegetables is great."

"I should eat more vegetables."

"True for all of us, I suppose."

They stood there for a long moment in silence. Frank grew aware that he had begun to fluster. "So—what's new?"

"Not much. Classes, parties, stuff like that."

The other disconcerting thought on Frank's mind was, of course, the jarring contrast between Erin's intellect and Stacey's. Erin had completed a double major in biology and psychology, then proceeded to complete a doctorate in clinical psychology. Stacey's interests were—well, Frank couldn't even guess. Perhaps she had declared a major in full-body tanning and a minor in getting laid. Or maybe her concentrations were the other way around.

He felt torn between wanting to be polite and just letting the conversation fizzle out. "What are you focusing on these days?" he asked. Then he quickly added: "At the University."

"Me? Fitness sciences."

"Fitness sciences. Which means—helping people get into shape?"

"Mmm-hmm. But not just that. Also sports psychology. Also training protocols. Stuff like that. 'Cause, you know, everyone needs to get healthy and fit. And I really like helping people get healthy and fit."

"A good choice, then."

She stood there and gazed at him, the upper reaches of her towel lightly held against her chest.

After an awkward pause, Frank decided to speak his mind: "I have a request for you."

"Oh? What's that?"

"Do you think you could cover up a bit?"

She smiled sweetly. "A bit?" she asked. "*Which* bit?"

"You could start almost anywhere."

"*Anywhere?*"

"Use your judgment."

"My parents say I lack good judgment."

"Here's your chance to exercise it."

"I get a lot of exercise, but I need to lose some weight."

"Don't say I didn't ask."

"I promise. It's our secret." Then: "Do you think I need to lose some weight?"

"You look fine."

"*Fine?*"

"Stacey, you know there's nothing I can say that would be—appropriate."

"Then say something *inappropriate!*" She guffawed. Her chest, a seismograph of remarkable sensitivity, registered the tremors of Stacey's mirth. She stifled her amusement. "Well, Frank—I have a request for you."

Could this really get any more awkward?

"Go ahead."

"I want you to buy one of those St. Francis statues? Since he's, like, you know, your *namesake?*"

He felt a wave of relief. "I was named after a different Francis. Francis Xavier."

"Never heard of him."

"Most people haven't."

"Well, I still think you should get a St. Francis. Then little birdies would come and roost on him, and you could come out and feed them."

"I'll keep that in mind."

"You do that."

Mercifully, she added, "Well, I better go. I've got some rays to catch." Turning to walk away, she revealed the lovely expanse of her bare back, her waist, her legs, and what minimal surface area of her buttocks the tiny bikini bottom obscured, her entire body *café au lait* in hue and unmarred by even a single mole, scar, or the faintest shadow of mortality.

* * *

Sometimes, feeling weary of the Center and impatient with Pete, Frank would leave the parish house, walk through the university neighborhood in the evening—late enough that people had switched on some lights but early enough that they'd left the curtains open—and he would glance in passing to spot members of the various households: at an old lady watching TV, a woman feeding her toddler in a high chair, a boy bouncing on the sofa, two schoolgirls doing homework in their kitchen, or any of the many college students typing away at their computers. During these walks Frank wondered what it would be like to have other people, specific other people, at the center of his life. The specificity itself was what he found remote, even mysterious. Not just people, but *these* people. *This* wife. *This* husband. *These* children. *This* roommate. *This* mother. *This* sister. What would it be like to have the commitment to others so clear in his mind? More than a few of his adult parishioners had told him over the years that despite all the demands of parenthood, they felt somehow freed by their role precisely because they knew exactly who depended on them for sustenance, safety, order, and love. The college students he counseled, free to graze in the vast pasture of their social scene, rarely mentioned that sense of freedom. They were so unconstrained that the lack of constraints had become a burden. No wonder they felt so stressed. Oddly, though, Frank found himself shouldering what felt like a still greater load. Without a bond to any one person, to any spouse or any child, he felt so free as to be—though he recoiled from using the word itself—trapped. He knew that many of his parishioners appreciated him and what he brought to their lives. He had a place at Rocky Mountain University, most of all within the Catholic campus community there. He knew that if he dropped dead that same night, many people would mourn him. Yet he couldn't help but see himself as peripheral, as a mere adjunct to their lives. Worse yet, he knew that on some level all of these people were peripheral to him as well.

Frank understood that in some respects he must have be sentimentalizing, or at least oversimplifying, what he glimpsed on his evening strolls. Family life emanated a golden radiance when glimpsed through a picture window, but the reality inside these houses might have been far different. If nothing else, his counseling work had revealed the strains of marriage, the complexities of parenthood, the stress of work, the uncertainties of day-to-day life. Some of the homes he passed on his walks belonged to parishioners. Frank understood what tough times some of these folks endured. What nightmares, even. He knew better than to accept at face value what he saw—to dumb it down into an early twenty-first century equivalent of a Norman Rockwell painting. In all too many houses what he observed on his walks wasn't convivial life but rather one family member to a room, each person staring at a separate TV or a separate computer monitor. Or else what he heard wasn't laughter or earnest conversation but accusations, derisive comments, marital bickering, or chilly silence.

Over the past months and years, he had noted an odd symptom of the wider situation: the personal ads that Frank read intermittently in the local alternative paper, *Front Range.*

> JAZZ DIVA, sparkling blue eyes, blonde, slender, hot-blooded head turner with great sense of humor. Lives in Front Range suburb. Loves hiking, biking, music, nature, movies, road trips, and spicy barbecue. My marriage has lost its spark. I'm looking for a smart, fun-loving, discrete man, 35–45, for friendship and romance.

My marriage has lost its spark . . . So why not seek to ignite the burner with another flame? Come on, Baby, light my fire!

> WARM, WITTY, ATTRACTIVE, SEXY NATURAL REDHEAD— sociable, loyal friend, well-traveled retired professional. Exploring theater and cultural life in metro area. Planning to spend next summer in Paris studying French and consuming fine cuisine. Looking for educated, fully employed, or retired man (doctor, executive, or independently wealth preferred), age 50-60, 5'10" or taller, athletic and in good health, who

appreciates the finer things in life and knows how to treat a woman like a lady.

What, no specifications for shoe size, hair color, or total net worth? Would this woman settle for *anything?*

BORED, MARRIED WHITE MALE, age 40 (six foot four inches, slim, 195 pounds, mid-fifties, athletic, entrepreneur) seeks petite, thin, bright, affectionate, sexy female, 25-35, for outings, elegant restaurant meals, high-voltage rolls in the hay, and long-term romance.

Frank felt no surprise to view the breadth and depth of longing evident from these ads; what surprised him was how openly these men and women revealed the landscapes of their desolation. One could hardly blame them for reaching out. *Ich und Du.*

Maybe, Frank mused, he should write his own ad:

OVERWEIGHT MEXICAN-AMERICAN PRIEST, 57, lonely and restless, awkwardly muddling through late-middle-age vocational/existential/psychological/interpersonal crisis, seeks female companionship for conversation, long walks, collaborative cooking, and glimpses of ordinary domestic life. Your age, height, weight, hair color, profession, hobbies, and ethnic background? All negotiable. Suggest your place, not mine. Ideal circumstances might include presence of well-behaved children and/or nieces and nephews to provide illusion of participation in family life.

Or maybe not.

3

"I n the name of the Father, and of the Son, and of the Holy Spirit."

"Amen."

"The Lord be with you."

"And with your spirit."

Frank spoke the words that priests speak. The congregation responded. Not a large group tonight, eighteen or twenty people: a handful of non-RMU folks from the neighborhood, a few faculty or staff members, maybe a dozen undergraduates. Later, during the winter months, a fair number of students would show up following their weekend ski trips, so Pete and Frank often scheduled the Sunday evening Mass here in the campus chapel rather than in the rectory basement; but now, in mid-October, only these few were attending, which made the turnout look almost pathetic in the roomy nave. Frank gazed out and saw just a scattering of people. Most of the pews were empty.

On the upside, sparse attendance allowed him full license to be brief. He wasn't "speed-dialing the liturgy"—Pete's recurrent criticism—but Frank wasn't going to rattle on, either.

He did what needed to be done. The entire congregation looked more than a little tired, and Frank was, too. He enjoyed celebrating Mass, still found it a source of solace . . . but surely everyone present, Frank included, wouldn't be eager for all the "fine print," as he sometimes described it, so he made his sermon even briefer than usual.

"When Jesus says, 'As the Father has sent me, I am sending you,' what is he telling us? Just this: get to work. You, me, everyone. The world is in flames. Let's help put out the fire."

A few members of the congregation stared at him expectantly, alert to whatever he would say next. He simply gestured; the congregation stood; and they proceeded to the Profession of Faith: "We believe in one God, the Father, the Almighty, maker of heaven and earth, of all that is seen and unseen. . . . "

Then, following the collection and the preparation of the gifts, the Eucharist. Of course Frank couldn't take any short cuts now, but dispensing bread to fewer than twenty communicants didn't take long, and everyone present probably felt as relieved as he did when they reached the concluding rite.

"The Lord be with you."

"And with your spirit."

"May Almighty God bless you, the Father, and the Son, and the Holy Spirit."

"Amen."

"The Mass is ended. Go in peace."

"Thanks be to God."

People started to stand, gather up their belongings, and leave. Within a few minutes the chapel was almost empty.

He felt surprised when someone waved to him from halfway across the nave.

He waved back cordially. "Thank you for joining us," he called out. "Have a good evening." He turned to enter the sacristy and change out of his vestments.

A woman's voice: *"Frank."*

He paused and looked at her again. The EMT from two weeks ago! "Laurie?"

She reached the aisle and walked toward him. "Hi there."

Wearing sleek jeans, cowboy boots, and a poncho-like garment that obscured her torso but accented her long hair, she looked even prettier than Frank recalled from her visit to the Center. "What a surprise."

"I wanted to see you in action."

"Action! So you pick what I call the Stragglers' Mass? There's not much action on Sunday nights."

"I enjoyed it."

"Blink and you'll miss the whole thing."

"Let's just say it was short but sweet."

They stood there till the silence grew uncomfortable.

"You have a moment?" she asked at last.

"I suppose I do."

"I hope you don't mind my just showing up like this."

"Everyone's welcome here."

"There's something I want to run past you."

Although Frank felt pleased to see her, the timing couldn't have been much more awkward. "The Student Union is closed on Sunday nights. Ditto most of the local restaurants." Reluctantly he added, "I suppose we could talk for a while at the Center."

"No problem."

"I need to change," he said, gesturing toward his vestments.

She smiled. "Guess we'd all do well to change."

Once Frank had retreated, put on his street clothes, and rejoined her in the nave,

They walked the short distance to the Center. Frank unlocked the door, then led Laurie up the staircase to the third floor. Another door, another key. They stepped inside and entered the waiting room, its comfy chairs and cheery décor so generic that the place could have been any corporate office or medical practice. He motioned toward his doorway on the right. "Please come in."

Laurie not only went in but immediately started sizing up the artwork arrayed on the bookshelves. The forthrightness of her interest struck him as both inappropriate and appealing. This woman's curiosity pushed past conventional decorum, yet he found it flattering. Was she merely interested in the pieces themselves . . . or in what they said about Frank? Hard to say. She stared at the little wooden retablos from Peru full of brightly painted clay figurines portraying Biblical stories—Adam and Eve in the Garden, Jonah and the Whale, the Nativity, Jesus and His Disciples. She considered the many non-Christian items: several Asian ink paintings, the bronze Hindu sculpture of a naked woman dancing, the seated Buddha. Then the photographs: a group shot of eight young priests wearing white robes; one of Frank, twenty-six years old, black-haired and black-bearded, stocky but not overweight at the time, dressed in hiking garb and posed with mountains in the background; one of Erin at twenty-two or -three; one of a large group of Mexican kids and teenagers amiably surrounding Frank, once again in his dark, muscular mid-twenties.

"Who are these people?" she asked, looking at the larger of the two group shots.

"Friends of mine a long time ago."

"This guy is *you?*"

"Guilty as charged."

"You look so happy."

"I was."

Now she turned to him.

"You have a nice office. Homey. Almost like a living room."

"I'm fond of it."

"Must be a great place to work."

"The setting is wonderful. The job itself— The usual mix of pros and cons."

"I'm sure it's satisfying to help your congregation. I can't imagine you don't make a big difference to them."

"I hope so."

"Back in the church I saw how much they respect you."

"I hope that too."

"Why wouldn't they?"

He found himself startled by his own discomfort. Taking a few steps toward the big windows that looked out over the campus and the expanse of city lights beyond, he said, "A good question, but it's hard not to wonder. When you came to visit me a few weeks ago—when we discussed your frustrations as an EMT—I really connected to what you said about emotional fatigue. Maybe I shouldn't say this, since it's not very professional— But when we spoke, I *resonated* with your frustrations. More so than I first thought. In some respects I'm in a similar situation."

"Frustrated with your work?"

"Emotionally fatigued, anyway."

"Fair enough. But you know what? I guess I'm surprised, just like you were surprised about me."

He turned to face her. "Perhaps each of us underestimates the stress in the other's profession. Or else we overestimate the satisfactions."

"Could be."

"Don't get me wrong," he said. "I respect and enjoy my parishioners. I have wonderful colleagues, clergy of many different backgrounds. This is meaningful work. I'm lucky to have it."

"You also have a right to feel burned out."

"Maybe so." He had never intended to open up so much. Of course he hadn't expected to cross paths with her at all, so he felt caught off guard. Still, it was awkward. He had switched roles with her, had put her in the position of playing therapist. He decided to disrupt whatever path they were traveling. "I shouldn't rattle on like this. You told me there's something you want to discuss, and here I am just yammering."

She smiled. "I don't mind, but yeah, there's something. And it's interesting that you've said you feel stressed by your work . . . So maybe what I'm going to suggest will appeal to you."

"I'm not sure what you're saying."

"How about if you join us?"

"Pardon me?"

"Join our squad."

He couldn't have felt more startled if she'd kissed him. "Are you serious?"

"Dead serious."

"But—why?"

"Because it'll be interesting. It'll be totally different from what you're doing." She grew animated as she explained her idea. "I've been thinking about this ever since we talked a couple of weeks ago. Our squad takes volunteers. We need the help. The payoff for us is your assistance. The payoff for you is the chance to do something different. Part time, of course. Just one shift a week."

He laughed out loud: not in mockery but in amazement. "I have no medical training," he told her. "I've never even taken as a first aid class. I don't know a damn thing about savings lives. I barely know how to put a band aid on a kid's knee." He pushed her suggestion away more and more energetically as he stated each of his objections.

"You don't need training—not at the start," Laurie told him. "All you need is a valid CPR card. You can ride with us as an adjunct member. You'll be an extra pair of hands."

"Probably all thumbs."

"If you like the work, and if we think you're doing okay, you can take the EMT course. One night a week for several months and you'll be certified."

"I'd be totally incompetent."

"Only at first, just like everyone else at the beginning."

"You have no idea." He couldn't restrain a laugh. Then, noticing a shadow in her expression, he said, "Don't get me wrong. You know how much I respect what you're doing. Your work fascinates me. You have a right to your doubts, but you make a huge difference in people's lives. This whole EMT thing . . . I can see how it's so important. But Laurie—I don't see how I could ever do it."

Surprising him, she lost her temper. "Damn it, that's such an easy out! You won't even try it. You'll just make excuses."

He couldn't respond.

She looked ready pull back, to apologize, but she didn't. She lit into him again. "You'll ignore the challenge. Great!"

"That's not it at all," he protested, feeling defensive but sounding vague, as if he couldn't take his own words seriously.

"No?"

"I just don't think I'm cut out for something so—I don't know, so practical."

Now she looked intensely annoyed. "Frank, I don't have time for this crap. If the work interests you, fine. If not, that's fine, too. If you're bored and frustrated with your job, there's stuff you can do to ease the boredom or vent your frustration. But don't tell me that EMT work is so fascinating, it must be wonderful, it's got a depth you've always craved—and then, when I point out how easily you could do it too, you avoid the whole thing by saying you'd be no good at something *practical.*"

He didn't fight back. He stood there and felt a confusing mix of emotions: curiosity about what her suggestion might involve, alarm at the implications, and pride that this attractive young woman would approach him to propose such a remarkable idea in the first place. "Pete . . . He'll have no idea why I'd do this."

"Who the heck is Pete?"

"The priest I work with here."

"What difference does it make what Pete thinks?"

"He'll certainly find out if I'm out riding around in an ambulance."

"Does he have to know?" she asked with a mischievous smile.

"We're a community," Frank said. "We make our decisions together. We share all our duties. Everything I do affects him, and everything he does—"

"So? Talk to Pete." Her anger welled up again. "Go make your decisions together. I mean, really! Is volunteering one night per week so terrible? Is it like joining a biker gang or a cross-dressers' club?"

"Of course not."

"Service to your fellow human beings, Frank. The world is in flames. Help put out the fire. *Hello?*"

"Point taken." He knew she'd got him. He said, "Well—" Then, abruptly coming to his senses, he told her, "No, I'm sorry—it's out of the question. I'm swamped with obligations. I have almost no free time. Taking on another commitment . . . " He stared at her feeling a sudden, deep sadness. "I can't."

She tried one last gambit. "Didn't there used to be monks who took care of sick people?"

Frank chuckled at this remark. "Certain medieval orders served as hospitalers. I suppose they were the medical personnel of the era. And of course there have been nursing sisters throughout the ages."

"All right, then," Laurie said. "Precedents. You can make a case for it. Go ask the Pope for permission."

He indulged her with a laugh.

"Phone the Vatican!"

He hesitated. "I'm sorry. Truly sorry."

They stood there a moment longer. Laurie said, "Okay, then. I understand. I figured it wouldn't hurt to ask."

"I'm sorry."

"I should go. I enjoyed the service."

"I'm glad you stopped by."

"I've never heard such a short sermon in my life."

"I hope that's a compliment."

"That's how I intend it."

"Please feel welcome here any time."

"I will. I do."

They walked downstairs, and he showed her out.

4

"I guess I'm kind of scared," the boy said, concluding his monologue.

For most of his session, Mark, an RMU freshman, had rambled about anxieties that focused on the so-called End Times. The kid's roommate was an evangelical Christian who had terrified Mark with descriptions of the imminent tribulation and global catastrophe. Mark had found his academic work disrupted and his whole life burdened by worries about the calamitous future. He needed to get his spiritual house in order. He needed either to choose business as usual or else, as the roommate insisted, to make drastic changes in his priorities. He was tense, exhausted, and upset.

Frank wasn't sure how to respond. As a priest he felt obliged to acknowledge these spiritual concerns. *Do not conform yourselves to this age . . .* Romans 2, was it? He should help to foster Mark's spiritual quest. At the same time, Frank felt leery about the source of these concerns. The boy's anxiety and depression probably had different roots, deeper roots, than those prompted by the conversations with his roommate. Family conflicts, perhaps? Adjustment issues? Substance abuse, even? The guy was intensely agitated. His millennial worries suggested something beyond what he stated—a volcano of angst on the verge of erupting, to be sure, but a volcano channeling red-hot magma from far below the surface.

The session had run its course. Had gone overtime, even. Another student would be waiting in the reception area. "Unfortunately," Frank said, "We need to wind down for today. But please schedule a session for next week, okay, so we can continue this discussion."

"Okay," the boy said obediently.

"I know you're worried, but I'm confident we can work through this situation together. Speak with Serena to make an appointment."

The boy nodded.

Interesting, Frank noted later, once the day's work had concluded. Mark's session wasn't the first time a student had come to him expressing apocalyptic anxieties. In fact, concerns about the end of the world had been cropping up with some regularity. The expressions weren't always couched in theological terms. Most students spoke of worries about the environment—pollution, global warming, depletion of resources. Others expressed fears about terrorist attacks. A few raised the same specter that had haunted Frank's own boyhood and adolescence: nuclear war. Only a few specifically made reference to the Second Advent. Two or three students, all manifesting high anxiety, were convinced that The End was nigh.

How, then, to respond? Frank wasn't sure. On a personal level, he felt that these concerns were off base. He wasn't convinced that the world was about to end. The overall outlook wasn't rosy; indeed, the planet was a mess. But he tended to believe that the human race would just keep bumbling along in its usual incompetent way. Life would go on. In the meantime, he and everyone else would have plenty of issues to figure out and problems to solve without spending time and energy on the Apocalypse. Fortunately, Catholic doctrine was consistent—for once, he noted with amusement—with Frank's personal beliefs. Coping with day-to-day tasks and the community's needs should be the focus of our efforts. *Attend to one another.* This was the message he could relate to his counselees and to the RMU congregation as a whole. His big task was always to keep people focused on the present.

Yet over the next few days, Frank found himself musing on the situation. He started to notice more and more references in the news to apocalyptic fears. Most appeared in supermarket tabloids. PSYCHIC PROVES WORLD WILL END SOON, blared The Sun a few weeks back. A recent cover story asked IS 2ND COMING IMMINENT? And in the local Safeway, where Frank waited in line to pay for his groceries, The National Enquirer shoved this warning in his face: EXPERTS WARN OF DOOMSDAY VIRUS. None of these articles surprised him. The tabloids would print anything. ELVIS SIGHTED AT LADY GAGA'S POOLSIDE BASH. JFK FOUND ALIVE IN SECRET HOSPITAL. DWARF WEDS 720 LB. WIFE. TOT SURVIVES 2-MILE FALL FROM PLANE. Armageddon was just another gimmick for peddling newspapers. At the same time, Frank couldn't write off everything he read. It was one thing to dismiss a Sun story about this or that psychic predicting the world's end next year; it was another to read about epidemiologists tracking the mutations of the Ebola virus, about arms control experts fearing that terrorists acquire "loose nukes," about environmental advocates raising concerns that lead, cadmium, chromium, and other heavy metals were polluting the entire world, about climate scientists noting the rapid shrinkage of the polar ice caps . . . The line between tabloid hysteria and mainstream journalism had blurred. Just a few months earlier, Frank had read that most astronomers now consider it plausible that an asteroid could strike the Earth in the intermediate future. Perhaps the tabloids weren't totally off the mark.

Frank felt skeptical. Humanity had an admirable knack for survival despite even the most appalling catastrophes. Somehow we would muddle through. We would cope. Even so, he couldn't resist raising the issue with Pete when they fixed sandwiches in the kitchen one afternoon: "What's our policy on the so-called End Times?"

"*Policy?*" Pete asked.

"The party line."

"I'm not sure what you mean by 'party line.'"

"A figure of speech. The official Church position."

"Why didn't you simply say that?"

"All right, I'll say it," Frank told him. "The official Church position. Surely the Vatican has a stance on this issue. Church teachings?"

"The Church teaches what she has always taught," Pete said, assembling a three-inch-thick Dagwood on his plate.

Frank began to regret raising the issue. Now he had no recourse but to hear him out.

Pete seemed happy to oblige. "Look. Jesus never specified when the end would occur, did he? In Matthew twenty-four, he says that only the Father knows the hour. There are certainly statements in the Epistles and in Revelation about the reign of the Antichrist, great calamities, disasters, and so forth. But the Church has always held that Christ will return 'like a thief in the night,' if you recall, and the end will take everyone by surprise. So the Church position is: yes, be ready. In the meantime, go about the business of loving thy neighbor as thyself, living the Gospel, and so forth."

Pretty much what Frank expected. He felt relieved. On impulse he asked, "Do you hear parishioners expressing anxiety about the End Times?"

"Now and then."

"More often than in the past?"

"Probably."

"And you?"

"I'd say somewhat more so nowadays than before," Pete told him.

"I'm hearing a lot of it," Frank said.

Pete shrugged as if to say, *What do you expect?* "Look, the world is a scary place. People want reassurance. They want consolation. That's what we're here for, isn't it?"

"That's what we're here for."

Both his earlier search and the conversation with Pete failed to answer how Frank should treat the issue theologically and psychologically, given the anxieties gnawing on some of his parishioners. Would the world come to an end according to the scenario presented in the Book of Revelation? The events described there seemed as likely as Elvis rising from the dead and leading the Chosen off to Rock 'n' Roll Heaven. How, then, should Frank cope with credulous, literal-minded members of the congregation? As Pete had implied, Catholic tradition got him off the hook. Let the fundamentalists squabble about this or that trumpet and scroll. Let the spiritual wackos cry *Repent!* from their rooftops. Frank would make calming pronouncements but otherwise attempt to focus everyone's attentions on less far-fetched matters than the Second Advent. Surely, he thought, we all have more urgent matters on our minds than the end of the world.

By comparison, a counseling session later that day nagged at his awareness long after it ended. Celeste, currently a junior at the university, had been estranged from her family for many years. Although Frank had counseled this young woman since the start of the academic year, he still couldn't clarify how her dilemma had taken shape. Her mother and father had apparently disowned her, though for reasons that Celeste couldn't (or wouldn't) explain. The parents' alcoholism was probably a factor. Some kind of mental illness among one or more family members might also have contributed to the overall situation. Beyond that, he wasn't sure. What seemed clear was that this lovely young woman— gentle, thoughtful, kind, and undemanding—had suffered through years of psychological cruelty at her parents' hands. Several years before entering college, she had either chosen to leave the family home or had been thrown out; she had moved in with a close friend; and, having acquired a scholarship on the strength of her own academic excellence, she had now spent over two years at Rocky Mountain University. Frank was doing whatever he could to bolster Celeste's shaky psychological state through regular sessions.

Just this past week, she had informed him of an attempt toward rapprochement during the previous Christmas season.

"They never send me presents, but I always give them real nice stuff," she had explained that afternoon. "I mailed something to each person in the family. And I did that again this year— lots of gifts, all wrapped really nice. And I thought: Well, maybe they'll send me something. Not like I care about the *gifts* . . . But I keep thinking they'll at least *acknowledge* me. So I wait and wait. Christmas comes and then it's over. No gifts. No thank-you notes for what I sent."

Frank listened to the words but also tried to detect any sign of hurt, anguish, outrage. He didn't hear even a hint of emotion in her voice. She might as well have been a businesswoman describing merchandise that had gone astray en route to a customer. Unsure what else to say, Frank told her, "I'm sorry."

"Then guess what happens? UPS leaves a huge box on the porch. Who it's from? My family!"

"That's wonderful."

"Yeah!" Celeste seemed to perk up now. "So I open it, and inside the cardboard shipping box is another box, a box that's beautifully wrapped. It's the biggest present anyone's ever given me." She held her hands as far apart as she could reach. "It's wrapped in beautiful shimmery green and red paper, and it has a golden bow. This is the first time I've ever got anything from them at all!"

Feeling deep relief, Frank said, "That's really great."

"So I open it," she continued. "I tear it open like a four year old. I open the present. And guess what's inside?"

He gestured eagerly, both hands palm upward.

"It's my gifts. They've taken my gifts—my gifts to them, still wrapped up exactly like I wrapped them—and they've sent them back to me."

Frank felt as if he'd been slapped. "Are you sure?" he asked. "The exact same gifts?"

"I open everything to check. Yup, the same gifts I sent. Same wrapping paper. Unopened. All of them."

What could he say? What words could he offer that wouldn't be the most banal, the most foolish, the most insulting therapeutic clichés? *So—how do you feel about that?*

They sat there for what must have been twenty seconds but felt like half an hour. Celeste looked altogether blank. Frank wanted to say something, to do something. He told himself to give her time and space. Even though the words had emerged from her own voice, she needed time to process the story she'd told him. Then, as the silence continued, he started to feel that Celeste was waiting for him to take the lead. But the lead to *what*?

"If you could tell your family how their actions left you feeling," he said at last, "what would you say?"

Celeste didn't speak for a long time. Then, quietly: "I'd say, Could you hug me?"

"That would be an understandable thing to ask."

"But you know what? They'd never do it. Ever. I'd wait for the rest of my life."

"I'm sure that's really hard on you."

Then, in a matter-of-fact tone, she asked, "Could *you* hug me, Father?"

Frank knew that he couldn't honor this request. Should not, must not. The Center's ethical and legal guidelines were explicit: other than a handshake, physical contact with a client was impermissible. Yet what could he do, really, given what Celeste had been through? To what degree would rebuffing her become yet another betrayal?

He stood. She stood. He opened his arms for her. They embraced, and he held her. She scarcely touched him—one hand on his left shoulder, the other on his right side—as if anything more than the lightest contact might burn her skin. Then she bowed her head against the side of his neck. He couldn't see the girl's expression, so he couldn't assess it. Celeste remained silent and motionless for a long time. He assumed she must be weeping.

Then, just as Frank started to worry again about the action he had taken, the line he had crossed, she pulled back from him, smiled a matter-of-fact smile, no tears at all evident on her face, and said, "Okay, thanks," in the same tone of voice she might have used if he had opened a door and let walk through the doorway ahead of him.

* * *

He couldn't help but wonder after that session what to do about this young woman's pain. Pain so abundant that she couldn't feel it. Pain so widely dispersed throughout her life that it was the air she breathed. How did she cope? What could Frank do, really, to make a difference?

He walked back to the rectory. Crossing Evans Avenue as he left the campus, he was so lost in thought that he almost walked into the path of an oncoming car.

What could *he* do, for that matter, to cope with all this pain? What was Laurie's word for the situation? *Pain-logged.*

5

More Millennial anxieties! Most of Frank's counseling sessions focused on the usual issues, yet no fewer than three students came to him that next week expressing worries about what they called the End Times. One was a young woman who, having read a series of potboiler novels about the so-called Tribulation, had worked herself into a tizzy. Another was a guy who had grown up in an evangelical family, had converted to Catholicism as a young teen, and had now started wrestling with the disparity between his childhood beliefs and those of the Catholic Church. The third was a graduate student with a complex psychiatric history whose troubled state of mind seemed to be using End Times scenarios to organize his frightful thoughts and chaotic emotions. Three very different people, of course. Three different sets of issues. What surprised and baffled Frank was why all three students had showed up during the same week—and on the heels of several other RMU students presenting similar concerns. Coincidence? Part of a pattern? He couldn't explain the situation. Neither could he simply let it drop. Unsure what else to do and dissatisfied by his brief exchange with Pete, he took the step that often eased his concerns: he sought the counsel of other pastors at the Center.

Marissa James, the Baptist chaplain, pondered the question Frank had posed to her. He felt content to wait for the answer. The words would be worth his patience; she was always thoughtful and open to his concerns. Another reason to wait: Marissa's serenity tended to be a source of calm and reassurance in the midst of Frank's own hectic life. He was always content to spend time with her; she was a great ally at the Center. So much the better that Marissa, forty-five or fifty years old, with curly, radiant blonde hair and a pale, almost creamy-smooth complexion, was so enjoyable to watch as she formulated her response. Her right hand, perfectly shaped, rose now and then as she slowly wound a curl around her index finger, a gesture that struck him as calm rather than fidgety.

"Well, the situation among evangelicals is much more varied than you might imagine," she began. "The End Timers get all the attention, of course. It's a much better sound bite on TV when you have someone shouting that God will smite us a week from Thursday. But as I say, the situation is complex." She paused for a moment. "Look—most evangelical Christians anticipate biblical prophecy to be fulfilled quite literally. At the same time, there's a growing movement in our corner of Christianity that emphasizes the importance of stewardship in the here-and-now rather than preparing for the end. To what degree do we have a responsibility to care for the world? To heal it?"

"Are these various trends evident in our students' attitudes and behavior?"

She gestured quizzically. "Yes, though in many different ways. There's a lot of anxiety on campus, to be sure. Some kids are looking inward as they see so much upheaval in the outside world. Others are rolling up their sleeves and getting down to work. A fair number of the 'green teens' we all hear about have a spiritual agenda that's not just some New Agey thing."

"I would imagine."

"I have to say, however, that others are rather worried."

"Buddhism has a long tradition of eschatology," said Janice Smith Roshi. As the part-time Buddhist pastor at the Interfaith Center, she taught meditation classes at RMU and at several other local universities. Frank had known her little more than a year but had felt close to her from the start. She was somewhat older than he, sixty-two or so, and was a licensed social worker in addition to being a Zen priest. Seated now in her simply decorated office—a few Japanese *sumi-e* paintings on the walls, a potted bamboo plant in the corner, two teak chairs near the desk—she elaborated on her first comment. "I forget which *sutra* it is, but there's one in which the Buddha says something like: 'A time will come when the great ocean dries up, evaporates, and is no more.' Pretty dire stuff. Wouldn't be out of place in the Book of Revelation. So, yeah, you can find prophecies, for lack of a better word, in the Buddhist scriptures."

"Prophecies of a sort that might alarm practicing Buddhists here at RMU?"

She laughed. The tiny wrinkles evident on her face grew more pronounced, especially about the eyes. Frank had often admired how she wore her aging without apology. Easy, he thought, when you have such a beautiful face, that waterfall of white hair, and those striking blue eyes. So many women would capitulate to social pressure—would dye the hair, would Botox those splendid laugh lines into oblivion. "That's hard to say," she said. "Overall, no. First, because most young American Buddhists don't read the *sutras* in the first place. Second—and I guess this is what's most important—the whole emphasis in Buddhism is always on fully inhabiting the present moment, rather than obsessing about the past or worrying about the future. The goals are mindfulness, clarity, and compassion. What's yet to come is secondary, whether we're talking about pie-in-the-sky or doom-and-gloom."

Rabbi Jenna Miller answered his question without hesitating even briefly. "No, the Jewish students here wouldn't really relate to what you're describing. Which isn't to say that they aren't concerned about the future—they most certainly are!—and for all the usual reasons. You name it, they worry about it. This is such a socially conscious, socially committed generation. Even here at RMU!" she added with a laugh. "I spend a lot of time working with them on outreach efforts of various sorts. Hunger. Social justice. Climate disruption. The students I interact with are generally far more concerned about solving problems than lamenting the future or getting ready for the end of days."

How bizarre, Frank thought as he listened, that the Church

would regard women as unsuitable for the clergy. In Jenna, as in Marissa and Janice, he saw the perfect rebuff to that policy. Maybe in Jenna most of all. He knew of no better pastor, and she functioned admirably not just as a woman in that role, but as a woman now six or eight years into married life, four years into parenthood, and over six months into her second pregnancy. Jenna was the perfect poster gal for the female clergy.

"Don't get me wrong," she continued. "There's an eschatological thread running through the history of Judaism. Central to it is the notion of the Moshiach arriving to usher in an era of peace and justice. Sound familiar?"

"I've heard rumors along these lines," Frank said "Far-fetched but interesting. No doubt someone could build a whole religion on that idea."

"That wouldn't surprise me."

"I wonder if they'll ever get it off the ground."

"You tell me," she said, raising her left eyebrow.

"I'll keep you posted. And among Jews?"

"Well, the concept varies from group to group. Some authorities in the Orthodox community, for example, believe that this era will lead to supernatural events and will culminate in the bodily resurrection of the dead. Conservative Jews debate whether the Messiah will be an actual, living charismatic human figure . . . or whether *Moshiach* is perhaps more of a symbol for the redemption of mankind. Reform Jews would generally concur with the more liberal Conservative perspective of a future messianic era rather than a personal messiah. Generally, though, I'd say that Judaism concentrates on the importance of the earthly world in the here-and-now over something more abstract, ideal, and future-oriented."

Earthly world indeed, Frank noted. To have such people in it as this one now seated before him. He had admired Jenna ever since she arrived on campus five years ago. She and her husband, Jake, a thoracic surgeon, had welcomed Frank into their home and had quickly become two of his favorite people in the RMU community. Throughout the years of their friendship, he had grown to respect Jenna for her thoughtfulness, her supportiveness as a colleague, her warmth toward students and her acuity as a pastoral counselor, and her openness to Frank as a colleague and friend. He had also harbored a secret crush on her from the start. On such occasions as people asked him What's she like? he always thought (but never said), "Jenna? She is the mind of Abraham Joshua Heschel in the body of Ingrid Bergman." But the comparison wasn't accurate. Her mind was Heschel-like in its acuity, but Jenna was much prettier than Bergman even in her Casablanca prime. The Semitic cast to her features also made her face far more interesting. The mane of curly black hair was so ample and lustrous that Frank found it difficult to resist reaching out and gathering it up, feeling its texture like a skein of fine wool, hefting it just to revel in its sheer substance. Her nose, perfectly sculpted, had an aquiline ridge so lovely that whenever he gazed at her, he wanted to trace its line with the tip of his index finger.

Aware just then of her somewhat puzzled expression, Frank realized that he'd lost track of what she was telling him. Ah, yes: Jewish eschatology. "That's what I've understood," he said, hoping to hide his distraction.

"So, as you can imagine," Jenna went on, "most Jewish students wouldn't spend much time worrying about the sky falling—at least not in any cosmic sense. Given what's going on these days— As you can imagine, there are plenty of concerns about more immediate, more tangible problems."

"True."

"It's enough to make me worry, too. Whether it's such a great idea to bring another child into the world . . . "

Lovely, how she stroked her abdomen almost absentmindedly as they talked.

He found it difficult not to stare. How she shifted now and then to get comfortable. How she rested both hands on her belly as if to calm the child inside. "What does it feel like?" he asked before he could catch himself.

"Feel like?" She looked uncertain but not offended.

"The baby moving."

"Oh, that. It's different things at different times." A faraway smile. "When I first became aware of her, the sensations were so light I thought I must've imagined them. Wispy. Feathery. Then the baby grew and what I felt got stronger. Now she's so big and so active I sometimes feel she's beating me up from the inside out! At other times it's just—I don't know, a *shift*. A wiggle or a slippy-slidy feeling. When I think about what I'm feeling, I realize it's the tactile equivalent of what you'd see if you watched a baby turning over in her sleep."

"It sounds wonderful."

She smiled. "Usually it *is* wonderful. Not always, though—especially when she wakes me up at night. Which she's starting to do rather often now. To be honest, I'm entering that phase where it'll starts to get a little tougher. But I wouldn't miss this experience for anything."

For a moment she just stared at her hands where they rested on her abdomen. Then, startling Frank, she smiled, reached out, grasped his right arm by the wrist, and placed his stout fingers on the dome of her belly. They were sitting close enough to each other, almost side-by-side, that she could do so without tugging at him. Her motions were so confident and so matter-of-fact that he didn't have time to feel embarrassed. She moved his heavy palm this way and that. He couldn't tell what he was feeling—other than the warm, remarkably taut surface of her silk dress, of course, which in itself provided such a lovely sensation that the back of his neck tingled.

"There," she said. "A foot or a knee or something."

He wasn't sure what she meant. Then, at once soft and forceful, like a dog's nose nuzzling his palm: a nudge. Frank exhaled suddenly. He couldn't keep from smiling.

"You feel it?"

"I do! I do indeed!"

The knee or foot moved laterally against her belly. When Frank's hand moved as if to follow it, whatever was pushing now pushed back as if offering an answer to a question. He was so stunned that he didn't know what to say. Tears rimmed his eyes. A phone rang somewhere else in the Center, and for a moment Frank snapped back into ordinary awareness. If someone were to walk into this room right now . . . Even Serena would have been appalled. Pete? Apoplectic. Then he eased back into whatever realm of awareness he had left. He didn't care how it looked, it didn't matter, and within moments he had settled back into this strange, serene state, where all that concerned him was the palm of his hand against his friend's belly and the gentle but earnest pressure exerted against it.

Returning to his office after this colloquy had ended, Frank found his concentration shot. As if Jenna weren't sufficient distraction, he found thoughts of Erin suddenly troubling him again. He walked to his desk and sat.

Erin . . . What had become of her? What would have become of them as a couple if they'd stayed together? Surely they would have married. What would the marriage have been like? Would they have had children . . . and if so, how many? What would being a parent have been like—being a father in the most literal, most tangible, most quotidian way? Frank couldn't help but wonder, and he felt no shame about his curiosity. Yet his conjecture felt like outrageous, pointless speculation, akin to wondering what forms life might take on other planets. And yet . . . How astonishing it would have been to take a journey such as what Jenna and Jake were taking together, to marvel at his wife in so many ways, to share in the creation of another life.

Frank and Erin had stayed close friends after the affair ended; they had corresponded throughout the years of her grad school training and his time at the seminary; and they had sent occasional messages, mostly Christmas cards, once he had settled into the priesthood and she into her career, her marriage, and parenthood. Then, gradually, their far different obligations had distracted them. They had fallen out of touch. Frank hadn't received so much as a postcard from her since the late 1990s. He had no idea where she was or what she was doing.

Of course in years past, finding out would have required a lot of phone calls—not a great situation when the caller was a priest pushing sixty and the recipient his now long-married ex-girlfriend. Thanks be to God for the Internet—or to Bill Gates, rather, or to whatever omnipotent force presided over cyberspace. A few keystrokes and he would surely track her down. Frank roused his computer from its slumber and started what would be a quick and simple process.

Except that it wasn't. Typing "Erin Fitzgerald" into the search engine cast a net into a sea teeming with fish. Even his first try pulled up several dozen Erin Fitzgeralds: a soccer coach, a dermatologist, a chef, an exotic dancer, two musicians, a social worker, an author of romance novels, six recent brides, and a more or less limitless number of college and high school students. Narrowing the search to "Erin Fitzgerald, Ph.D." helped, but less so than Frank had expected, since that yielded a hydrologist, a museum conservator, and a bevvy of professors. When he recalled that her degree was a Psy.D., not a Ph.D., the Web produced another embarrassment of riches: four Erin Fitzgeralds, each with the same initials tacked onto the name, but their ages and other attributes ruled out every one.

He grew exasperated and gave up.

Later, after Frank coped with a few minor crises at the Center, returning to the rectory, and eating a quick supper, he started rummaging through the clutter on his rolltop desk, and, right there in one of the pigeonholes, he found a Christmas card from Erin. The envelope clarified the problem. Although she had retained her own last name initially, she had swapped it for her husband's when their kids were born. Frank had never broken the habit remembering her as Erin Fitzgerald. But her last name was Sutter. Noting that surname and her city of residence, he needed only a minute to obtain her phone number from directory assistance.

The phone rang for a long time. Just as Frank decided to hang up, someone answered. "Sutter residence." A deep male voice.

"Oh—good evening," Frank said, flustering. "I'm so sorry to bother you. My name is Frank Ochoa, and I'm an old friend of Erin's."

After a brief pause, the man's voice said, "Yes?"

Great. Not only had the husband answered: the guy clearly had his guard up. "I'm a priest in Colorado. Erin and I knew each other back in college."

"I recall that."

That could mean anything. The husband—Nat, was it, or Nate?—left this comment floating face-down and motionless, drowned in a pool of digital silence. Frank knew he had maybe one more chance to get things right. "I'm just calling to say hello. I've wondered now and then how y'all are doing," he said, trying to sound folksy, "so I thought I'd just—"

"You don't know, do you?"

"Excuse me?"

The man's tone changed. "Erin passed away just a little more than a year ago."

Frank felt as if the room temperature had suddenly spiked. His back and shoulders prickled. Sitting there at his desk, he heard the sound of a ballgame on the living room TV. His office felt tight, claustrophobic. An image of Erin materialized: not the stocky, short-haired matron she had revealed herself to be in recent family photos, but the curvy lass, black-haired and fair-skinned, of decades earlier. This image then transformed itself into another, even more vivid memory, all the more intense for being rooted in his last evening with her.

They had made a post-graduation visit to her uncle in the Midwest—Uncle Liam, as Frank recalled. That stay had allowed them three more days together before Erin caught a plane back to Boston and Frank proceeded to Mexico. The uncle, rich from selling agricultural equipment, owned a huge property west of Milwaukee. Notable on the premises was indoor swimming pool. On the second day of visiting this family, as Liam and his wife put their young children to bed, Frank and Erin had disengaged from the family and had gone for a swim in the pool. They had the whole place to themselves. Glass walled, the facility didn't afford enough privacy for them to act fully on their pent-up lust, but while cavorting they could at least kiss and fondle each other to the degree that submersion in the water and a distance of fifteen or twenty yards from the house would make inconspicuous. Frank now recalled with pained delight the warmth of Erin's body as they embraced, the bulk of her breasts against his chest, the perfect smoothness of her skin when he slid his hand through the leg hole of her silvery green one-piece swimsuit until his fingers found their way past the hair to her slick labia. Fooling around like this soon ceased to be sufficient. They couldn't stay in the water much longer, but they couldn't bear the tension, either. Yet simply returning to Uncle Liam's house was unthinkable: no privacy. So, as they emerged streaming from the pool and walked to the his-'n'-hers changing rooms, both of them realized that this stark place—hardly a love nest with all its varnished wood, painted concrete, fluorescent lights, and reek of chlorine—would be the only option available. They held each other and kissed. He said, *I want you.* She said, *Yeah, but where?* He said, *Anywhere. Right here.* Her expression showed a mix of longing and exasperation. *The floor's too hard—it'll be uncomfortable. There's no good place to lie down.* Frank couldn't tolerate the thought of parting without one last chance to make love. They stood staring at each other. Maybe this wouldn't work out after all . . . Then Frank reached out to her, hooked his thumbs around the straps of her swimsuit, and in a single motion smoothly peeled the wet Spandex off her body and down to the floor. He led her to a wooden changing bench on the right. She understood and sat. *Scoot forward so I can get at you,* he said. She eased toward him. For this last time together, Frank made love with her on his knees. Throughout the rest of his life, every occasion of assuming that ordinary Catholic posture of prayer reminded him vividly and richly of their stolen time together in the changing room. *Ich und du* indeed.

"Hello?"

The rectory. The phone.

Frank jolted back to the present. "I'm so, so sorry," he said, struggling to regain his composure. He couldn't speak at first, then forced himself to say, "This is a terrible shock."

"I tried to contact everyone in her address book," said Erin's husband. "Somehow I must've missed your name."

"I understand."

"As you can imagine, I've had a lot to deal with."

Frank couldn't decide what to do—simply to say goodnight and hang up or to press ahead. "I want to apologize for intruding," he said. "I just had no idea."

"It was quite sudden."

"Do you mind my asking—?"

"Pancreatic cancer. She was sick only three months."

"My God."

"There wasn't much the doctors could do for her."

"Look, I should leave you in peace. I was calling just to say hi and catch up. I deeply regret bothering you."

Another long silence. For a moment, Frank felt that the only decent thing to do would be to say, "Thanks for talking with me," and wind down the call.

Then, calmly, the husband's voice once more: "Tell me your name again?"

"Francisco Ochoa. Frank."

"Right. You're the campus chaplain . . . Her college boyfriend?"

"That's correct."

"Erin sometimes talked about you. She spoke of you with great fondness and respect."

Frank felt so moved that he couldn't respond. Great fondness and respect . . . What did it mean, exactly, that Erin was dead? How was it possible that Erin was dead? At last he managed to say, "The fondness and respect were mutual."

"If you'll give me your address," said the husband, "I'll send you a copy of the program we printed for Erin's memorial service."

Frank gave him the address. "Thanks for talking with me."

He faltered. Struggled to talk.

At last he got some words out—"God bless you"—before hanging up.

11

SHIFTS

6

"U nknown medical." Laurie slammed the driver's-side door and started the engine.

Frank settled into the passenger seat beside her. Fastening his seatbelt, he heard Tyler's belt click somewhere behind him in the patient compartment. "Which means?"

"Just about anything."

After the squad's garage door finished rising, Laurie drove the ambulance out of the bay and onto the street.

He fought the temptation to ask more questions. Why did the dispatcher provide so little information? How would they know what to do? He felt his neck prickle and his palms grow damp.

A short ride followed—a right turn, a mile straight down a four-lane boulevard, then a left and a brief stretch up a residential street. Their destination was a stark-looking condo development, blocky units lacking shrubbery or trees.

Laurie parked the ambulance. Everyone got out. Tyler and Laurie grabbed two medical kits. Once inside the condo, Tyler started interviewing the patient's wife while Frank and Laurie headed upstairs to see the patient. "He's just not acting normal," the anxious woman was telling Tyler. The staircase, like the rest of the house, was a mess, so many stacks of magazines cluttering the steps that Frank could scarcely find his way up. The upstairs landing was even worse: cardboard boxes, piles of dirty clothes, and broken furniture blocking Laurie and Frank's passage to the bedroom. Somehow they eased their way through.

"I'm so glad you're here."

The speaker was an elderly man—mid-seventies, pink-faced, plump, with sweaty gray hair at the fringes of his otherwise bald head—who stared at the EMTs from a mussed-up bed. He smelled as sour as a moldy basement.

"What can we do for you?" Laurie asked.

"I don't feel good." The man's hands moved about, agitated, touching his face, flopping onto his lap, fidgeting with the bedcovers, clinging to one another for comfort. "I had this operation."

"What kind of operation?"

"Hernia."

"When was that?"

"A week ago."

"You're under a doctor's care?"

"I was supposed to go back for a checkup."

"Did you?" Laurie asked, nodding to Frank as she spoke and tapping the big blue kit he had carried up with them.

He snapped out of his anxious reverie. Frank should do things, he told himself, not just watch and listen. He set down the bag, opened it, and took out several items: the oxygen tank, a clear plastic mask, a blood pressure cuff, a stethoscope . . . Grabbing the cuff and scope, he started to take the man's blood pressure— assuming, he noted, that he could recall what Laurie had showed him. Blood pressure, indeed! He could feel his own pulse pounding inside his temples.

"I didn't go to the appointment," the man said, "because I didn't feel so good."

"One fifty over a hundred," Frank told Laurie. He felt a twinge of pride about successfully performing this task.

"You have a history of high blood pressure?" Laurie asked the patient.

He nodded.

"Are you taking any medications?"

Again he nodded, looking at once dazed and frantic. His hands twitched on his lap like dying birds.

"You been taking your medicine?"

"I was feeling okay for a while, so I stopped."

Frank started to guess where Laurie was heading. This man,

Bernie Jensen by name, turned out to have multiple health problems. Diabetes, hypertension, kidney failure, heart issues . . . Recent surgery to correct a hernia would have been a minor matter in a healthy man, but Bernie wasn't healthy, and he had ignored most of his doctor's post-op instructions.

By now Tyler had come upstairs. He gestured tersely: a single nod in Bernie's direction. She raised her left eyebrow. That was it. Frank felt impressed by the precision of whatever message they had exchanged.

Examining the patient, the EMTs had their worst surprise. Laurie and Tyler pulled back the covers and eased down Bernie's pajama bottoms to find his abdomen bright pink and puffy. Worse yet, the surgical incision running along the left side of his groin had split open. It looked raw and torn—a vast gaping mouth. Deep inside the cut Frank could see some shiny gray stuff. The sight hit him like a slap and left him dizzy.

Laurie said nothing at first. She eased Bernie's pajama pants up again, then turned, putting herself between Tyler and the patient. "Okay, let's hustle," she told Tyler and Frank.

Frank left to bring the stair chair; he carried it up to Bernie's bedroom; he helped Tyler clear stuff cluttering the steps; and, working with Laurie, they secured Bernie in the chair and carried him downstairs. They transferred Bernie onto the ambulance stretcher and settled him into the patient compartment. Within a few minutes they would be leaving.

"Did you see that incision?" Laurie asked Frank when they stood together beside the ambulance, well out of Bernie's earshot.

"That was disgusting." Even recalling the sight made him feel faint.

"Darn right. Totally dehisced."

"De-what?"

"Dehisced. The wound came unstitched."

"So that gray stuff down there was—"

"Guts."

Frank felt a wave of nausea wash through him.

"I don't know what the guy was thinking," Laurie said, "but he's got multiple chronic health problems *plus* a busted-open belly *plus* what looks like a badly infected wound site."

"What's the outlook?"

"Hard to say, but at least his wife called us." She went around to the driver's side and climbed into the ambulance. Frank eased onto the passenger seat; Tyler stayed in back with the patient. "Assuming," she said, "there's no traffic between here and Jeffco Med Center."

"How could that guy not know he'd split open?" Frank asked later, once they finished dropping off the patient and returned to the squad house.

"Good question," Laurie said.

"Was he waiting for his insides to fall out?"

Tyler chuckled derisively. "Even then he might not've noticed till he tripped on 'em."

Frank flinched in disgust.

"You wouldn't believe what people don't notice."

"But to split right open—"

Laurie said, "I stopped feeling surprised years ago about what people notice or don't notice." She popped open a soda and took a long drink. "One evening we answered a call for a woman complaining of abdominal pain. Tyler and I responded. She was a twenty-five-year-old who must've weighed three hundred, three-fifty. Huge. She said she might've caught the flu that was going around at the time. When I examined her, though, guess what I found?"

"Appendicitis?" Frank asked.

"Nope. She was crowning."

"Which means—"

"A baby's head was starting to pop out between her legs. We delivered the kid five minutes later."

"She didn't know she was pregnant?"

"Said she had no idea."

"The baby must've got there *somehow*," Frank told them.

"She denied it all the way to the hospital," Tyler said. "Simply couldn't believe it. Who are we to argue? I guess she just gave birth to a seven-pound, five-ounce bellyache."

They sat there in silence as Laurie drank her soda and Tyler filled out some paperwork.

Frank couldn't help asking the question nagging at him. "How do you deal with this stuff? The—*strangeness* of it?"

"Here's how I see it," Laurie said. "Each call is a puzzle to solve. That's one of the things I still like about this work—not just helping people, but solving the puzzle. It makes the work stressful but also makes it interesting. It's what keeps me coming back."

$$7$$

Frank lay awake all night replaying and reviewing that first shift. The slow, chatty initial hours. Discussions of equipment and procedures. A guided tour of the ambulance. Then two minor calls: a restaurant worker with a cut finger, a police officer with a twisted ankle. An hour or two back at the squad house. Then, without warning, the interaction with that post-op patient, Bernie. Frank couldn't shake the memory of seeing the man's ruptured belly. The smell, too: rank, damp, mossy. At least they had successfully transported the guy to the hospital. Had they saved his life? Maybe so. What an amazing experience—to parachute into Bernie's life, to intervene, to make a difference. So tangible, so straightforward. So different from Frank's often ambiguous efforts to help his parishioners. Unnerving, yes, but exhilarating too. He felt thrilled to have participated in this little drama. Now he lay in bed feeling both jangled and pleased.

One other aspect of the shift lingered in his mind all night: recollections of Laurie and Tyler. Such different personalities, yet somehow two people in tune with each other and effective as a team. Yin and yang? Oil and vinegar? Laurie's matter-of-fact warmth balanced nicely with Tyler's emphatic, almost astringent sense of authority. She didn't defer to him, exactly; she just made her opinions known by less direct means. An interesting pas de deux all evening, most notably during the call with Bernie. Frank could tell that Laurie and Tyler had worked together for a long time, long enough that they could communicate by the subtlest means—a glance, a nod, a raised eyebrow. Impressive. He felt reassured to have their guidance.

Then there was the pleasure of their company. The no-nonsense way they went about their work. The playfully abrasive banter between them. The lack of intellectual grandstanding. What a relief to spend time with these working-class folks after so many years in the academic hothouse and its exotic, sometimes delicate blooms. Frank felt recharged even by twelve hours in what the RMU students called the Real World.

Something else, too, gave him a boost: the energy he felt in Laurie's presence. Whatever trauma she had suffered, whatever depletion her suffering had caused, she somehow retained a remarkable forthrightness, an ability to take action, that he found at once reassuring and attractive. Some sort of life force? Perhaps a specifically female energy? Hard to say. In any case, Frank found himself aware of it, drawn to it, and stimulated by it. How thoughtfully she interacted with the patients even while making quick decisions on their behalf. How carefully she chose her words. How calmly she spoke even while tracking the medical aspects of the issues at hand. All the while she seemed oblivious to her own loveliness. That plain EMT uniform—the dark blue slacks, the white short-sleeved polyester shirt—couldn't obscure Laurie's womanly curves. The various official-looking patches and insignias on the uniform couldn't contradict her innate elegance. That amazing hair, too: even braided it was impressive, a golden rope dangling almost to her waist.

This image finally eased Frank toward sleep: Laurie, resting her hand on Bernie's chest once the patient lay safe inside the ambulance. "Don't worry, sweetheart," she told him in the warm, matter-of-fact voice of a mother calming a frightened six-year-old. "We'll take good care of you."

8

He reached his decision. He would volunteer as an adjunct member of the Foothills EMS Squad, sign up for the state-sponsored EMT course, and spend a shift on duty from seven each Thursday night till seven on Friday morning. Beyond that, he would simply see what came of this provisional arrangement. If the first few shifts worked out all right—"all right" meaning that he handled the stress, didn't make a nuisance of himself, and didn't screw up in any of a thousand ways—then maybe Frank would make it through the course and get certified. Classes met once a week for three months . . . or was it four? Whatever. Frank would attend the course, then take a qualifying exam to prove his mastery of the material. Six months' successful work as a probationary EMT would complete his formal training. Beyond that, it was all OJT—which, as everyone assured him, was what mattered most anyway. Laurie, Tyler, and other squad members would show him the ropes. He would gain skills and confidence. Who knows, maybe he could make himself useful.

Surely this situation would be manageable. Frank felt a surge of excitement of a kind he could recall only from the distant past, excitement all the better for being so unfamiliar.

Of course he would have to resolve a few other issues first.

"What I'd like to know," Pete said, "is how in heaven's name you'll fit all this stuff into your schedule."

"Same way I fit in everything else," Frank told him. "Same we both do. I'll shuffle things around, bust my butt, and work like a dog. Same old story, just a different lineup of activities."

Seated at the kitchen table, Pete nursed a cup of coffee and gazed out the window. "I just don't get it," he said. "You want to be a *medic?*"

"An EMT."

"Same thing, isn't it?"

Frank forced himself to stay patient. "There's a big difference. Medics are much more intensively trained, and they do a lot more procedures in the field. EMT's—or at least EMT-B's, which is what I'd become—do basic life support. First aid, essentially. In the particular squad I'll be joining, I'd play second fiddle to the more experienced EMT's on board."

"On *board?*"

"The ambulance."

No response. Pete turned briefly, stared at Frank for a moment, then returned his attention to whatever he was watching, or was pretending to watch, beyond the window.

Frank fought the temptation to get up and leave. Since you're not really interested, he almost blurted, *Maybe there's nothing more to discuss.* Or else he would leave without even bothering to comment. Instead, he forced himself to stay seated, to interact with Pete, to do what were they always urging parishioners to do in their relationships: *to practice good listening skills and to foster open, nonjudgmental dialogue.* After what felt like a long time, Frank said, "Let me assure you—nothing I'm about to do will put any pressure on you."

Pete took a slow sip from his coffee. Frank noted that if anyone he knew could make sipping coffee seem hostile, Pete would be that person. "How so?"

"The same way my other personal activities don't pressure you. I'll schedule the squad shifts on my days off. Not just the shifts, but the EMT class as well."

"The EMT class?"

"I have to get certified," Frank said. He decided to loosen things up with a little joke: "Consider it the EMT equivalent of ordination."

Pete chuckled derisively. "Ordination? Please."

"In a matter of speaking."

"How frequent are the classes?"

"Once a week."

"For how long?"

"What difference does it make!" Frank said, raising his voice enough to startle both of them. He backed off at once: "What I mean is—since all this stuff will happen on my own time, you needn't be concerned. I won't inconvenience you. I'll be fully available here in all the usual ways. The EMT commitment won't be any different from my taking a psychology class or volunteering at a soup kitchen. Please don't worry."

"I'm not worried," Pete said. "I'm just asking the same questions you would ask if I made a new commitment that might affect us collectively."

A long silence followed. Frank felt tempted to manage the conversation, to shape it, but he restrained himself. It's like doing therapy, he noted: you don't intervene too quickly; you provide ample opportunity for people to reach insights on their own. Who knows, maybe Pete was starting to understand.

Pete said, "Something else. Not to be nosy, but—why, exactly, are you doing this?"

Ah, Frank thought. The question he most welcomed and most dreaded. "It simply feels like something I need to do. It's so—specific. So tangible. There's nothing abstract about it. From what I've heard, it's totally here-and-now."

He could see Pete twitch almost imperceptibly in his chair, as if stifling a chuckle or a snort.

Frank decided to gamble. "I'm doing it because it'll be interesting. Because it seems important. Because," he said, hesitating, "there's so much pain out there."

"There's not enough pain here on campus?" Pete asked abruptly. "Not enough to keep you busy? Not enough grief, loneliness, and despair? Not enough to keep us both busy more or less twenty-four seven?"

"Don't get me wrong. Of course there's enough—too much."

"So you need more?"

"Easing one kind of pain doesn't rule out easing another."

"No, of course not," Pete said. "Not if you've got the time and the energy."

"It'll be a total change of pace from everything else in my life."

"That's for sure."

"If this is what you want," Pete said, "fine. You can have it. To each his own."

Frank waited, forcing himself to keep quiet. When Pete made no further comment, Frank decided he had given him as good a response as could be expected. "Fair enough."

One other person's opinion mattered to him.

"All right, let's have a listen." Dr. Bedarian removed the stethoscope from where it had draped around her neck throughout the earlier phases of Frank's annual exam; she warmed the business end of the scope for a few moments in the palm of her left hand; then she placed it against the left side of his chest.

How lovely to be touched, Frank noted. How lovely to be touched by Marci Bedarian, M.D., in her off-white skirt, floral blouse, and white lab jacket. Standing next to the examination bench where he sat, she rested her left hand on his shoulder as she moved the stethoscope here and there across his skin. Frank noted with dismay that other than perfunctory hugs from parishioners and colleagues, this moment was the first instance of a woman touching him in—how long? Probably since his last physical over a year ago. So much the better, then. Her scent was warm and slightly herbal, the aroma of a healthy forty-something female tinged with notes of Dove soap and of whatever shampoo she used on her lush mahogany hair. He could hear the faint susurrus of her breath as she inhaled and exhaled. How delightful to be sitting here as she assessed his cardiac function . . . and how ironic, how silly, how totally ridiculous to be so passive, so naked except for what little modesty the folds of this skimpy paper gown—this overgrown napkin!—provided.

Did she notice, Frank wondered, that his heart was beating faster as the examination ensued?

Now she checked his lungs. "Take a deep breath," she said, "and exhale."

He obeyed.

"Again."

Once more he obeyed. I will take all the deep breaths you want, Frank told her in the silence of his mind. Your aroma is Prozac for my heavy soul.

Dr. Bedarian shifted slightly, moved the stethoscope to his back, and proceeded from one area to another. Frank would have been happy to sit there all day. Examine anything you want, he would tell her.

Finishing, she stepped over to a small desk, sat, and typed notes into the laptop resting there. Frank watched in silence, admiring the fullness of her ponytail and its luster where it dangled against her back. Then Dr. Bedarian pushed the chair away from the desk, swiveled around in the seat, and crossed her legs. "Okay. Overall you're in good health. Heart is strong, lungs are clear, digestion seems good, and so forth. You mentioned having to get up several times each night to urinate, which may indicate some hyperplasia of the prostate—not atypical in a man your age, nothing worry about at this point. Let's have the urologist check you at some point fairly soon, though. Your blood work has been good in the past except for LDL and triglycerides, which are moderately elevated, so we'll do a lipid panel along with the other routine blood work. I guess my main concern is still your weight."

"I knew you'd say that."

"Sorry, but I'm duty-bound to press the point."

"I know, I know. I'm working on it."

Perusing the chart, she said, "The pounds keep creeping upward."

"They do, don't they? Believe me, it's not from lack of effort. I monitor what I eat. I'm trying to exercise. But still— As you can imagine, it's tough in such a sedentary line of work."

"I understand. Don't get me wrong, Frank. I'm totally sympathetic."

"I'm trying to get it under control."

"I'm sure you are."

After a moment's hesitation, he chose to spring his news. "There's something else I want to tell you. I've decided to join an EMT squad."

She looked as startled as if Frank had announced an intention to become a rabbi. "Really!"

"It's a volunteer position one night a week."

Her face showed both amazement and amusement.

"Seems like time for a change," he went on. "It'll get me out of the office and out of my head."

"That's for sure."

Frank couldn't tell if her tone of voice showed concern or merely surprise. "Is there any reason I shouldn't do this?"

"Not really. No, it sounds great. More power to you. But because you're overweight—significantly overweight—I want you to be careful. Overexertion could be a problem. Joint issues, back issues. Lifting patients— You could easily pull a muscle or slip a disc. I assume your EMT mentors will teach you good body mechanics? Proper lifting techniques?"

"I'll be taking the state EMS course."

"Good. So—yeah, that could be interesting." A pause. "Who knows, maybe it'll inspire you to lose those extra pounds."

"I'll work on it."

"Very well, then. Go ahead and get dressed."

When Dr. Bedarian stood, picked up the medical chart, and stepped toward the door, Frank asked, "You think this is okay to do? Joining the squad?"

"Sure. Just be careful."

9

Frank felt tense, almost panicky, as he sensed Laurie's and Tyler's alarm. "Pediatric respiratory distress," Laurie said as they sprinted for the ambulance. A child had stopped breathing . . . This emergency had prompted the most abrupt departure Frank had experienced so far. Tyler drove the ambulance through town faster than on any prior call. The siren seemed louder, the rig's swaying more severe.

He glanced over at Tyler, who drove with a surprising sense of confidence despite the speed. "Could be anything," Tyler said. "Could be asthma, flu, obstructed airway. Amazing, what kids'll put in their mouths."

"So I hear."

"When my son was a toddler, he must've swallowed half a dozen small objects by the time he turned three. Coins, buttons, stuff like that. Luckily he never choked to death—no thanks to my ex-wife, I might add, who thinks she's Ms. Guardian Angel but didn't even clock these emergencies half the time. I was living with 'em back in those days, so not much excaped my notice." This monologue continued even as Tyler wrenched the ambulance through the late-evening traffic.

"Any suggestions?" Frank tried to sound calmer than he felt.

Tyler chuckled in amusement. *"Suggestions.* Yeah: pay attention, do what we tell you, and don't get in the way."

The house was a mile or so from the squad house. Tyler pulled the rig over; Frank, Laurie, and Tyler climbed out. Frank noticed a police car in front.

"Either we'll have the smiling parents meet us at the door," Laurie said as they grabbed two of the medical bags and headed up the walkway, "or we'll have big, big trouble."

No smiling parents met them at the door. Instead, the crew entered the house to find a frantic scene in the family's living room. A cop was holding a baby face-down on his left forearm while thumping the child on the back with the palm of his other hand. The mom, a lean woman dressed in sweatpants and sweater, watched red-eyed from nearby, her hands forming a little tent over her nose and mouth. A five- or six-year-old girl clung, weeping, to her mother.

Frank took in this scene with growing dismay and fear. It wasn't just the desperate efforts or the emotions they inspired that shocked him. It was the sight of that baby. Clad only in a diaper, he looked almost as gray as the mom's sweatshirt.

"Give me the kid," Tyler said in a matter-of-fact tone.

The officer obeyed.

Holding the limp child against his left arm, the head cradled in the palm of his hand, Tyler tilted the baby's head back, opened his mouth, and looked inside. At once he used the heel of his right hand to shove repeatedly into the child's belly. No good. Then Tyler eased the kid onto his right hand to try the same kind of back blows that the officer had been doing earlier.

Frank heard Laurie asking the mother some questions.

"—been sick lately?"

"No, not at all."

"Any history of asthma?"

"No."

"Could he have choked on something—?"

"I just don't know."

"A coin? A little toy?"

"Please *do* something!" she pleaded.

Frank glanced toward Laurie, who returned his gaze. Her expression showed an alarming sense of helplessness.

"Verify ALS arrival," Laurie stated into her radio.

Frank couldn't follow the whole message, but he caught a few of the dispatcher's words: "—ten to fifteen minutes—"

He noticed Tyler glancing around. The house was a mess— toys, kids' books, and stuff cluttering the floor. One of the items visible was a vacuum cleaner, the tank type, not an upright, with a hose and steel wand attached. Tyler nodded toward it. Laurie shook her head. Frank couldn't make sense of their signals at first; then, as Tyler reached down with his right hand to grab the steel wand while keeping his hold on the limp baby with the other hand, he started to understand.

A flurry of half-shouted words flared up between Laurie and Tyler.

"—to dislodge what's there—"

"But there's no protocol—"

"What's the alternative?"

Within moments Tyler handed the child to Laurie; he inserted the tube into the child's mouth; and he turned on the vacuum cleaner. A moment passed. Frank saw Tyler's intention but couldn't tell if this desperate move had helped or not. Then, startling everyone, the baby gasped.

The kid wasn't the only one. Frank realized just then that he himself had been holding his breath. He exhaled loudly. Everyone else was hollering and crying. The mother and the cop hugged each other.

"Now wait just a darn minute," Laurie scolded them. "We're not finished. Don't anybody get too relaxed."

There was a further scramble as she directed the crew to mobilize. Tyler pulled a tiny ambu-bag from the respiratory kit while Laurie prepared the O_2 tank and connected a length of tubing to the bag. While Laurie started squeezing air into the child, forcing oxygen into his mouth and nose through a little face mask, Frank stooped, grabbed a pediatric blood pressure cuff, and took the baby's blood pressure and pulse. Tyler got on the radio to double-check on the medics' whereabouts. Frank could guess his concern: although they had pulled this child back from the brink, the kid had been without oxygen long enough for Tyler to worry about lingering consequences. Brain damage? It didn't surprise Frank when the whole crew carried the baby to the rig and, accompanied by the mother, headed off to the Jefferson County Medical Center.

* * *

They retreated afterward to a pancake house for coffee and food.

"That was brilliant," Frank said.

"Damn right," Tyler said, clearly annoyed that anyone would have to state the obvious.

"Never would've occurred to me."

Tyler sat there smirking.

Laurie, eating pancakes and sausage, ignored the men for a few minutes. Then, after letting Tyler gloat for a while, she told Frank, "Don't get any funny ideas."

"Funny ideas . . . ?"

"That was a tough call. If Tyler hadn't used his clever vacuum trick, we'd've probably had a dead baby on our hands. But let me say in no uncertain terms: using the handy-dandy Electrolux isn't an approved protocol. First of all, cowboy stuff like that rarely works. Second, if the Department of Health finds out that we stuck a vacuum down a child's throat, we could lose our state accreditation."

"I don't get it," Frank said.

Tyler leaned back as if to say: *I dare you.* "Here's the only thing worth getting: what I did saved the kid's life."

"That's not the whole story," Laurie went on. "Yeah, you saved the kid's life. This time. But maybe not next time. Or maybe even this time around the kid survives but ends up with the I.Q. of a turnip. So, yeah, you saved the kid's life."

"Have I missed something?" Frank asked, feeling bewildered. "Isn't that indeed the point? Saving the kid's life?"

"Sure—saving the kid's life," Laurie said, echoing Frank's tone of voice as well as his words. "But we don't make the rules. True, we're supposed to use our judgment. We have to. Every call is different. In this business, you never know what's coming at you. But believe-you-me, we have to follow standard guide-lines, and sometimes those guidelines are very, very narrow."

Frank asked, "Is it better if the patient dies?"

"Of course not. All I'm saying is: you're supposed to do what you're supposed to do. Sometimes you're gonna push the envelope. And sometimes if you do that, you're gonna get screwed even if you save the patient's life."

"Typical bureaucracy," Tyler said. "Forget about doing what makes sense. Just follow the effin' rules. When you're done, make sure to fill out all the required paperwork. Including the incident report about why your patient arrived DOA at the hospital."

Laurie skewered a piece of sausage on her fork. "Case in point. A guy named Josh rode with us for maybe eight or ten years. First-rate EMT. Great skills, great judgment. I'd've trusted him with my life. He saved many patients. Then one day he responded to a respiratory distress call at a restaurant. Classic scenario: drunk dude with a piece of meat stuck in his trachea. Hard as he tried, Josh couldn't clear the guy's airway doing Heimlichs. Patient turned gray as a sidewalk. Josh wasn't the kind of EMT who stood on ceremony—or who'd let a man suffocate just because some know-nothing health department bureaucrat set the guidelines while seated at his comfy desk in downtown Lakewood—so he decided to improvise a tracheostomy."

"Meaning . . . he opened up his throat?" Frank asked.

"You got it."

"But at the EMT class they said we weren't authorized—"

"My point exactly. Damn right we aren't. We aren't trained to do it. We don't carry the proper instruments. Josh went ahead anyway. He improvised. Sorta like Tyler grabbing the vacuum cleaner. Except this time the tool in question was a steak knife."

Frank flinched at the thought. "He opened his throat with a *steak knife?*"

"What's he gonna use?" Tyler asked in mock outrage. "A teaspoon?"

"He trached the guy with a steak knife," Laurie said. "Did a great job, too."

"The man survived?"

"He survived—"

"Thank God."

"—for a while." Laurie fell silent, waiting, watching Tyler and Frank. "But the patient had suffered severe hypoxia by then, so he went into a coma, stayed there for months, and eventually died. The man's family slapped everyone with lawsuits. The restaurant. The hospital. The squad. Everyone. Even Josh."

Frank said, "That's ridiculous. Josh almost saved the man's life. If he hadn't trached him, he would've died anyway."

"Of course."

"I can't believe the family would do that."

"You have no *idea* what folks will do."

"So what happened?"

"Josh lost his shirt. If he'd held off doing the tracheostomy, the patient would've died right off, but his family would've had no grounds for complaint, since Josh would've been following all the protocols. The catch: EMTs in Colorado can't trach patients, so Josh set himself up real good. The patient's family cleaned him out—house, car, bank account, the works."

They were all silent for a while. Frank couldn't tell what Tyler was thinking—it seemed unusual for him to hold back for so long. "The moral of the story?" he asked at last.

"The moral of the story," Laurie said, "is keep watching Tyler, who's the best damn EMT in the county—"

Tyler smiled cagily before interrupting her: "Here comes the fine print."

"—but don't get any ideas about doing exactly what Tyler does. Not unless you want to get your ass in a sling, too."

10

Indian summer faded. The leaves turned and fell. There was little rain. Frost silvered the lawns once or twice; otherwise the weather stayed surprisingly warm. In late October the light shifted and became powdery, almost a substance suffusing the air. Was it simply the lack of leaves, Frank wondered, or something more fundamental, a real difference in what the sun and the air conspired to create? He couldn't tell. All he knew was that the light seemed a revelation, though he couldn't decide or even guess what had been revealed.

As the weather cooled, Frank noticed that Stacey, Tracy, and What's-her-name spent much less time outdoors. He missed their presence on the lawn; he felt embarrassed about longing for the sight of them; and he could scarcely stifle his delight on the rare occasions when the next-door coeds took advantage of the autumn's last, unpredictable days of warmth, emerged from their bungalow, and rewarded his patience by lying out there in the sun. Stacey and What's-Her-Name happened to be sunbathing one afternoon while Frank watered what remained of his vegetables. Pumpkins, mostly, as well as the final crop of peppers and tomatoes. Soon the frost would hit hard enough to ravage these late arrivals. Amazing, he thought, that none of the Front Range area's famous early snowstorms had struck yet. A providential stay of execution? Or just a consequence of climate change? Either way, it would be a relief in some ways, he noted, when this endless Indian Summer came to a close and cold weather finally arrived. In the meantime, he had a right to putter in the garden. If Stacey and her housemates wanted to lie outside half-naked for the entire world to see, that was their choice. It wasn't Frank's responsibility to take protective measures against the sight they presented. Neither was he responsible for shielding Mrs. Beach, who happened to be patrolling her own yard that same afternoon on a search-and-destroy mission against the scourge of autumn weeds.

"What those hussies are doing," she cluck-clucked, addressing Frank from across the fence—"it's just *turrible.*" She motioned toward the coeds with her long, dirt-encrusted dandelion fork.

"Margaret, they're not hurting anyone."

"There oughtta be a law."

"Write to your congressman."

"The kids these days don't have the least bit of decency. You should talk to them. Maybe they'll listen to you."

"Sorry, it's not my problem."

"You don't seem very concerned," she noted grimly. "I'd have thought that you, of all people, would be concerned."

"Let's just say this particular item isn't way up there on my list. I have almost six hundred parishioners in my church. Some are sick, many are depressed, and a few are suicidal. The Center has money problems. The Order wants a report on just about every last little thing Pete and I do here."

"You should also pay attention to what's going on in your own backyard."

"It's worth noting that the girls are actually in their backyard."

"You should make them stop."

"Margaret, I read somewhere that a hundred and eight armed conflicts are in progress worldwide at this very moment. More than a billion people go to bed hungry every night. The global environment is rapidly deteriorating. Am I concerned about two young women lying over there in the sun? Is that the issue I'm going to worry about?"

Staring at him, Mrs. Beach shook her head.

"Besides," he told her, "there's a verse in the Bible: 'Verily, I say unto you: mind thee well thine own business.' Second Thessalonians, I believe."

She pondered his words for a long moment. "I don't recall any book of the Bible called Second Thessalonians."

"I'll double-check it. Maybe it was Third Corinthians."

Mrs. Beach continued to stare at him and, without a flicker of a smile on her face, she said, "I'll tell you this: they should be ashamed. And you should be ashamed."

Throughout this conversation, Stacey's voice, husky and low, reached Frank from across the yard as she and What's-Her-Name reviewed who had hooked up with whom, who had done what to whom, and which guys had proved especially adept or especially inept in guiding Stacey and What's-Her-Name through the wilderness of sexual frustration into the Promised Land of orgasm. "I don't think there's any guy on the planet who comes quicker than Ben," Stacey stated emphatically. "It's like when I was a kid and we played with firecrackers on the Fourth of July. Those little bitty ones? About an inch long? We'd light 'em and flick 'em into the air. Did you do that, too? We sure did! And you really worried about the ones with a short fuse because you lit 'em and then immediately: *kaboom!* Except with Ben there's not much of a bang."

Mrs. Beach gave one last admonitory glance at Frank, then turned and walked away, the dandelion fork clutched like a dagger in her right hand.

"I know what you mean," said What's-Her-Name. "It's like that guy we're reading in my English class? That, you know, poet? I forget his name. He's one of those guys who's got only initials instead of a first name? But he wrote this poem that ends: 'Not with a bang but a whimper.'"

Stacey guffawed. "Right! A whimper!"

Good God, they're beautiful, Frank told himself as he soaked the garden. Beautiful and preposterous.

"Hey, Frank!"

Stacey's voice. He looked over to see her waving to him.

"Come here a sec."

"I'm a little busy." Would they really have him walk over now?

"Frank! Come and visit us!" Stacey shouted. "We're *lonely!*"

"Very lonely!" called out What's-her-name.

"We won't bite—I promise!" A cascade of giggles.

He really had no recourse. They were intent on torturing him; there would be no escape. Besides, going over to chat with them would give Mrs. Beach something to fret about for at least a week.

Frank walked the ten or twelve paces to the fence. "Hello, ladies."

"How ya doin'?" Stacey asked, propping herself up on her elbows.

"Just fine."

"I don't see you around much any more."

"I've been busy."

"Frank, you work too hard."

"Story of my life."

"I worry about you. You need some R&R. Some TLC."

"Don't I wish."

"Why don't you come outside any more? Your poor veggies are gonna die!"

"I've joined a first aid squad."

A moment of stunned silence. "No shit!" Stacey snorted, then covered her mouth suddenly with both hands. Her expression showed a mix of incredulity and delight. "You mean you, like, ride around in an ambulance?"

He nodded, suddenly embarrassed by the swell of pride he felt.

"That's awesome! A priest in an *ambulance!"*

"It does sound strange, doesn't it?"

"No, it's *fantastic.* Frank, that's just *so cool!* Your patients are *so lucky!* I mean, think of it: a priest in an *ambulance."*

"I'm not sure they're so lucky."

"Frank, that's *fabulous!* I'm so, so proud of you!"

"Thanks, Stacey."

"If I ever have a heart attack," she said, "I want *you* to come over to do CPR on me."

"I'll keep that in mind."

"Mouth to mouth."
"I promise."

11

The EMT course started just before Halloween: a three-hour class each Tuesday evening plus a full-day session one Saturday per month. Fitting these sessions onto the calendar took more effort than Frank had expected. He twisted his own schedule to accommodate so much time away from the Center, and Pete needed to be even more flexible about the situation than Frank would have liked. To his surprise, Pete agreed to Frank's requests and held back most of the complaints he had anticipated. Perhaps the temporary nature of the course eased his annoyance. Frank half-suspected, too, that Pete thought the heavy demands on his time would dampen his enthusiasm for what Pete called The EMT Thing. Surely Frank would see his mistake and drop the whole business. That didn't happen. True, the EMT course tested Frank's patience. Each class session involved mastering huge masses of material—anatomy and physiology, biomedical equipment, basic pharmacology, procedures and protocols—and the instructors drilled their students with boot-camp rigor. Frank quickly found his brain swamped and his body fatigued beyond anything he'd experienced since his early years as a priest. Could he keep up the pace? Maybe The EMT Thing *was* a mistake. Maybe he should just admit it, bail out, and move on. Yet the very thought of retreat emboldened him. He would master this body of knowledge! He would acquire these skills! He would manage the crazy schedule facing him over the next several months. Not just because he wanted to make a difference to other people—he also wanted to disappoint Pete. Abandon The EMT Thing? Never. Confirm Pete's suspicions that Frank couldn't handle it? Not a chance. Allow Pete the delight of seeing him overreach and fail? *¡Ni modo!*

What dissuaded Frank from quitting was the shift each week. The welter of information he found overwhelming and tedious in the classroom became overwhelming but *exciting* in the field. Calls lingered in his mind for days. It was true that he needed a long time to purge himself of the sights, sounds, and smells of sick and injured patients. The shrieks of a five-year-old who had slammed his hand in a car door. The look of panic on a woman's face during her asthma attack. The dark, gritty appearance of an ulcer patient's vomit. The sour smell of a car accident victim as he went into shock. The sandpaper sound of a carpenter's broken femur when the EMTs put his leg in traction. These sights, sounds, and smells chewed on his guts for days like a hungry tapeworm. Yet the sheer intensity of experiences in the field were so powerful that they drew him forth and convinced him to keep going.

The bad calls left him at once jumpy and exhausted. Once, having helped care for a teenager who'd been hit by a car, Frank didn't sleep well for almost a week. It wasn't just that the girl had suffered many broken bones and probably a serious head injury as well. It was her mother's response to the accident that brought the crisis home to Frank. "She'll be all right, won't she?" the woman asked as the EMTs loaded her daughter into the ambulance. "She'll be okay, right?" When Laurie said only "We'll do everything we can for her"—the mother moaned like a wounded animal. Frank wouldn't forget that sound for a long, long time.

There was a twelve-year-old boy, too, who had burned his face while messing around with chemicals, and the smell of his seared flesh somehow clung to Frank's nostrils and left him nauseated for hours.

There was a man who had ignored several hours of chest pains, finally called 911, and then went into cardiac arrest just after the squad arrived, so that his last utterance—*"Sorry"*—lingered like a foul aftertaste.

Frank and the crew arrived at the scene of a two-car auto accident in which no one appeared to have been hurt. Two men and a woman stood around discussing the damage to their vehicles. Laurie and Tyler checked them out. The men refused treatment and transport. The woman did, too, but Laurie had a funny feeling about her and, after a little persuasion, convinced her to get checked out at the E.R. She began to act disoriented on the way to the hospital; then she passed out. By the time the rig reached Jeffco Medical Center, she was clearly going into shock. Her pulse shot upward; her blood pressure plummeted. Even the IV that Tyler started didn't do much to help. Fortunately, the crew reached the hospital before the patient went into cardiac arrest. Laurie found out later that this woman had ruptured her spleen and had begun to bleed internally; if the crew hadn't gotten her to the E.R. so quickly, she probably would have died.

The crew also arrived in time at an athletic field where a young football player was having difficulty breathing. Laurie sized up the situation, realized that the kid was choking, and did the Heimlich maneuver on him, expelling a wad of chewing gum.

There were calls for people with emphysema, asthma, chest pain . . . Frank couldn't even recall how many folks they transported who seemed on the verge of respiratory or cardiac arrest. Often as not he couldn't remember their names. Sometimes he couldn't remember the specifics of their emergencies. All he could recall was that somehow things had worked out.

Sometimes nothing much happened, or at least nothing that struck him as medically dramatic, yet the calls left him reeling. One evening Frank, Laurie, and Tyler reached a little bungalow with instructions from the dispatcher to assess the elderly woman living there. Police had already arrived on scene. On entering the house Laurie, Tyler, and Frank found a bizarre sight inside: two or three dozen birds among the overstuffed chairs and floral décor. Parrots, parakeets, cockatiels, mynah birds. Green, yellow, red-yellow-blue, pure black, white-as-snow, and pale blue birds. Birds dancing back and forth on their perches. Birds glaring from behind the bars of their cages. Birds roosting on the curtain rods. Birds flying back and forth in the living room. Birds dive-bombing the EMTs as they entered. The entire house was squalid;

weeks or months had surely passed since anyone had cleaned the place. Little stalagmites of shit rose from the floor under each of several pole-like perches. Entire rooms had been shat all over by the free-flying members of the flock. The stench was so awful that Frank felt as if splinters of glass had lodged in his sinuses. He could barely restrain the urge to vomit. What he found even more unsettling than the stench was the noise. Birds squawked, shrieked, chirped. Worse than that, they talked. They shouted. They hollered—all of them at once.

"Annie get your gun!"
"Come here, sweetie pie!"
"Who's the best little birdie?"
"Who are *you*? Who are *you*?"
"Don't split your tongue!"
"Come here, sweetie pie!"
"I *want* one! I *want* one! I *want* one! I *want* one!"
"My name is Sam!"
"You're a good little boy!"
"Don't split your tongue!"
"Who are *you*?"

These and other exclamations filled the air, each jabbing at Frank's ears as painfully as the odors stabbing up his nose. He could scarcely hold back from fleeing the place in revulsion. As Tyler, Laurie, and Frank followed the police through the house, he realized he would have no escape.

An old woman lay on a bed in the bedroom. Tiny, pale, and as wrinkled as much-reused tissue paper, she stared in agitated puzzlement—first at the two officers standing nearby, then at the EMTs entering the room. "Tell me what you want," she said. "What have I done that is wrong?"

A parrot shot past as Frank followed Laurie over to the bed.

"One two three!" cried a mynah roosting on a bedside lamp. "Four five six!"

The squalor of this place and the pathetic state of this ancient woman quickly agitated Frank. How could anyone live like this? Not just because of the sheer fecal mess of it all: the sense of isolation chilled him even worse. How lonely would you have to be to find solace in the companionship of three dozen raving birds?

Laurie leaned over, resting a hand on the old lady's shoulder. "You haven't done anything wrong. Nothing at all. We're here to help you."

Tyler told Frank: "Get her vital signs."

Frank snapped out of his trance. Vital signs . . . He opened the medical bag, took out the blood pressure cuff and a stethoscope, and set to work. The old lady's arm felt like a wooden stick inside a sheath of worn-out cloth.

As Tyler discussed the situation with the cops, Laurie tried to assess the woman's medical condition.

"Who are *you?*" asked the old lady.

"Who are *you!*" asked a parrot on the bedstead.

"My name's Laurie—"

"Laurie! Laurie! Laurie!"

"—and we're here to help you."

"Help you, help you!"

Ten or twelve minutes passed. Laurie, Tyler and Frank sized up the patient, attempted to make sense of her jumbled answers, and readied her for transport to the hospital. She was clearly dehydrated and undernourished. She was probably demented. The wretched state of hygiene in the house, if nothing else, was a threat to the woman's health. Without any way of contacting her next of kin—if, indeed, any kin existed—the EMTs had no recourse but transport the old lady to Jeffco Med Center for observation and revaluation.

Witnessing this process, Frank felt impressed once again by Tyler and Laurie's teamwork and, especially, by Laurie's gentleness. She treated this loopy old woman with daughterly sweetness yet without condescension. "Honey, you're gonna be fine," Laurie said as they bundled her, carried her outside on the stair chair, and transferred her to the gurney.

Then, just as they loaded the bed onto the ambulance, closed the doors, and prepared to leave, the old lady panicked and began to shout. "I can't leave! I can't leave!" she cried out. "Who will take care of my babies?"

<h1 style="text-align:center">12</h1>

Something else intrigued and baffled Frank during his squad shifts: Laurie and Tyler. How to grasp the odd situation of spending time with them each week. What to make of them. What to do with them. What he faced during calls, the emergencies themselves, wasn't really the issue. He observed them, noted what they did, learned from them, followed their directives, and tried to make himself useful. Fair enough. Both Laurie and Tyler were often demanding but always informative. At every turn Frank found himself challenged but inspired by watching how adroitly they addressed the crises, how cleverly they solved problems, how calmly they behaved with the patients even when alarmed about their injuries or illnesses. Somehow their different styles complemented each other, too, augmenting rather than limiting their respective skills. At the same time, Frank found Laurie and Tyler an odd pair, dissimilar to such a degree that he couldn't figure out how they even got along, much less worked so well together.

Spending time with each of them separately, which happened now and then at the squad house, gave him a somewhat better sense of them.

"What's it like living with the other priest?" Laurie asked abruptly during a lull one night. She seemed curious, cordial, and open-minded about his work, his roles as a priest, and, for that matter, about the nature of his life.

Frank couldn't help but chuckle at the question. "Ah, yes—the other priest. Let me put it this way. Part of being in a religious order is community life. It's one reason the orders developed in the first place. In theory, that's wonderful. Selfless service, shared spiritual practice, and so forth. In reality, at least for me at the moment, it's basically just another way to have a boring roommate."

"You don't get along?"

"We get along. To be honest, we actually work pretty well together. But it's—difficult. It can be tedious. We squabble over who did the dishes last time around, who left socks on the bathroom floor, who used groceries without replacing them."

"Could be worse," she said. "Especially when guys are living together. At least from what I've heard."

"True. I just wish it had more emotional substance."

"Living alone isn't so great, either."

He noted this comment and decided to gamble on getting more personal. "Don't take this wrong, but I'm inclined to think you'd have your pick of male companions."

"Don't I wish." She smiled at the compliment. "There's been no shortage of guys, and I've been engaged a couple of times. Each time the fiancé in question got cold feet."

"Commitment phobia?"

"Laurie phobia."

"I can't imagine that's *your* fault," Frank said. "Or even your doing."

"I'm pretty high maintenance."

Interesting, how she wouldn't meet his gaze as she spoke those words. Frank said, "You're clearly bright, capable, and full of energy. If that means you're high maintenance, more power to you. Even if guys find that scary."

"Even if they hang out for a few months, then head for the nearest exit?"

"Sooner or later you'll find someone who sticks around."

"Actually, there is one—but that's another story. A bit of a problem." Then abruptly she said, "Let's talk about you."

"Nothing's so interesting about me."

"I've never known a priest before."

"I'm sure you'll find me quite boring."

"I don't! Partly because I've never known a priest. But also: you're not exactly what I've expected."

"There are all kinds of priests."

"I'm sure. Still— You just don't seem like the kind of person who would've become a priest."

"I planned to be a professor. Comparative lit. But I found academia rather—empty. Not enough action. Not enough *fire*. So I cast about to see what else I might consider."

"And you were religious, so you became a priest?"

"Catholicism is simply part of being Mexican-American. I went to Mass on Sundays, I went to Confession, and I prayed in the usual ways, but so do most Chicanos, even teenagers, regardless of their piety. So—no, I wasn't particularly religious, though I guess I was religious enough to get type-cast as a Jesus freak during the Sixties."

"Enough to miss all the free love and weed?"

"I wasn't that much of a Jesus freak."

"So—if you don't mind my asking—why *did* you become a priest?

"Why would I make such a ridiculous decision?"

"I didn't mean it that way. Sorry."

"No offense taken. It's a good question. I've asked myself the same thing many times. The truth is, I've enjoyed being a priest. I enjoyed it more in the past than I do now, but it's what I chose to do. For me it's been mostly a means to an end. I wanted to help people, and the priesthood gave me a way to do that."

"That's it?"

He couldn't help but chuckle. "I know that sounds rather thin."

"I mean, you could've become a social worker, a nurse, a teacher . . . Damn—if you were desperate enough, you could've become an EMT."

"All quite true. So, yes, that's not the whole story."

She smiled at him. "Then tell me the whole story."

"Too difficult," he said. "Not because it's painful. People often assume there's a terrible secret in a priest's past, some source of guilt that prompted a decision to wear the collar. But that's not so common, actually, and certainly hasn't been true for me."

"So then why would you— Not to get personal or anything."

"It's hard to explain. Some things happened, but they were positive. So positive that I can't really describe them."

She gazed at him and waited.

"I'd tell you if I could."

She smiled. "All very mysterious."

"To me as well."

"What was positive back then isn't positive now? "

After hesitating for a long time he said, "Maybe it's like falling out of love. Maybe my relationship with the Church is like the marriages of many people I counsel. They've been together for a long time, they still get along, but they're not in love any more and, to be honest, they can't quite remember why they got hitched in the first place. Same with me and the Church."

"You could leave, right?" she said perkily. "I've heard some priests do that."

"It happens."

"You could leave too."

"I made a commitment," Frank said. "It has some drawbacks, and I'm not thrilled with the situation. I have reservations about the Church—lots of them. But overall it seems best to keep my commitment."

She fell silent. "Still—"

"Still what?"

"Never mind," she said.

And Tyler? Frank found him intriguing and baffling too, though in completely different ways. Pushy but interactive during calls, this tense young man withdrew into a cocoon of silence whenever he and Frank were alone together. Sitting around in the squad house ready room was a particularly brittle experience if Laurie happened to be somewhere else. Tyler watched TV, flipped through magazines, or scarfed the fast food he brought along for his shift. If Frank asked a question about some aspect of the work—"How often do we order supplies?"—Tyler would answer abruptly—"Whenever we need them"—and then fall silent. Frank's efforts to make small talk invariably fell flat. Comments about TV programs or recent news events drew a dismissive glance, a shrug, or no response at all.

"How many people do you think you've saved?" Frank asked Tyler during a slow shift—a question prompted more by sudden, irresistible curiosity than by an urge to make small talk.

Tyler's face showed an odd mix of boredom, amusement, and contempt. "Saved? Meaning, saved outright? They woulda died otherwise?"

"Right. You saved their lives."

Stretching, shoving his fists against his ears and angling his elbows outward until his biceps bulged, he yawned widely. "Shit, I have no idea."

"Just a guess."

"Several hundred—three, four, maybe more. It's hard to know. We drop 'em off but don't usually hear the final outcome."

"You figure a few hundred people."

"The CPR calls alone would be at least a hundred. Then of course you have your MVA's, all the folks we've extricated from cars who woulda bled out or gone into irreversible shock, eck cetera, plus now and then—mind you, this doesn't happen very often—we pull the victim out and then *foom!* the vehicle burst into flames. You have your pediatric respiratory distress cases, toddlers choking on a coin or half-drowned after falling head-first into the toilet. You have your other kid emergencies— burns, dog attacks, ingestion of household cleaners, falls down staircases, damn, all the crazy things that happen to kids. You have your handy-dandy husbands who slip off ladders or lop their hands off with snow blowers. You get the idea."

"I get the idea."

"So, how many? I stopped counting years ago."

"Hundreds, though."

Tyler stared at him with strained patience. "You want me to get a calculator and do the math?"

"An estimate would be sufficient."

No shift went by without the challenge of Tyler's snappy remarks and half-visible smirks . . . not to mention the constant background static of his irritable moods. These interactions quickly led Frank to realize how challenging this guy would be. Both knowledgeable and exasperating, Tyler would be at once worthy of attention and—difficult. *Dyne-o-Mite!*

Worse yet, Frank had to figure out the mystery of Tyler's relationship with Laurie. He quickly realized that these two were a couple. But why? What in God's name was Laurie doing with this abrasive guy? She was a tough cookie in her own way, so it wasn't altogether a surprise that she would pick a macho, rough-hewn boyfriend. That said, she was also bright, thoughtful, and sensitive in ways that made her romance with Tyler—if "romance" was the right word!—seem like a bad joke. There was no accounting for taste . . . If Frank had learned just one thing from his years of counseling couples at RMU, it was the unpredictability of the human heart.

Still: Laurie and *Tyler?*

13

The Center felt drab and tedious compared to the squad. Meetings and paperwork provided a dull bass line to the melody Frank sang all week, the tune itself being the liturgy and his sessions with RMU students. The liturgy was pleasant enough: Frank enjoyed celebrating Mass, especially at the weekday services that allowed him to indulge himself in his sixty-second sermons. One by one the counseling sessions weren't a problem, as he valued his time with students and wanted to help them, but their repetitive nature gnawed at him like chronic indigestion. So much late-adolescent anxiety! So many conflicts with parents! Such confusion over identity! So much distress over sex! All of these issues were important, all deeply felt, but . . . but . . . but Frank grew tired of hearing the same stories, of asking the same questions, of hearing the same responses. He could walk into the Center on any given day and generally know what his counselees would have to say.

Less common but still frustrating were the students who had begun to bestow on him the odd, dark bouquet of apocalyptic fears—among them Mark, the earnest first-year student whose Bible-thumping evangelical roommate inspired the boy's deepening sense of anxiety.

"Father, things are so terrible. The world is such a mess," the boy said during that week's session.

"Altogether true."

"You're not worried?"

"Of course I'm worried," Frank told him. "There's ample reason to be worried."

Mark's face showed a mix of relief to have his fears acknowledged and discomfort to hear the priest admit his own concerns.

"So . . . do you think the world is coming to an end?"

"The world comes to an end a million times a day. As Jewish sages have noted, every time a human being dies, the world ends."

"That's not what I mean."

"You mean, Is the whole world ending?"

"Right."

"I have no idea."

"What about climate change?"

"It's a huge problem."

"And the risk of nuclear war?"

"Still a terrible threat."

"Father, I guess what I'm asking is— Do you think God is just gonna, you know, *smack* us?"

"Look," Frank said, trying to stay patient. "If I were God, I'd be in a mood to do some serious smacking. But, number one, I have no idea what God is going to do. Number two, I'm not convinced that God finds it worth His trouble to go around smacking us thick-headed human beings. However, I'll tell you this: when I look at what's happening these days, the situation really does look dire . . . yet when I try to figure it out—and especially when I try to decide if our troubles are the result of divine retribution or just normal human stupidity—I always put my money on human stupidity."

"So what should we do?"

"Don't contribute to the overall stupidity. Do something worthwhile. Care for other people."

"But Father— That doesn't seem like very much."

"It's all any of us can do."

14

Frank, sitting with the Reverend Marissa James in RMU's main auditorium, listened to the candidate rattle on. He was handsome in a Central Casting way—the quintessential tall, fit, broad-chested male politico—and he now worked his way through his talking points with great confidence. Although running for the Senate in Colorado, he spoke with enough of a twang that Frank suspected him of being a transplanted Southerner or Texan, or, who knows, perhaps just a city slicker who affected the country-boy accent. Frank had found the guy gimmicky from the start. Now Joe True Conservative was doing Q-and-A with the several hundred students, faculty members, and outsiders present in the auditorium to hear his speech.

An earnest young man dressed in jeans and T-shirt was pressing the candidate on environmental issues: " . . . but given all the evidence, how can you justify your many statements that climate change isn't happening?"

The candidate smiled wearily. "Well, now, you're making quite a few assumptions," he said. "Evidence, you say. It's true that some weather events have taken place—hurricanes, tornadoes, heat waves, and the like. But tell me, please, when has this not been true? Who's to say these events aren't just normal acts of God? Which, I might remind you, is standard terminology in the insurance industry. Terrible things happen. Don't get me wrong, these events are terrible indeed. But who's to say—"

"There's a huge amount of data coming in," said the student. "Scientists all over the world—"

"Scientists have their theories, don't they? I don't have any problem with that. But that's the point. They have *theories*. Global warming is just a theory."

The candidate and his youthful questioner continued with their thrust-and-parry for a while, the duel gradually shifting into an outright argument. The audience grew restless. The young man clearly had sympathizers among the students and faculty, many of whom Frank knew had strong feelings about environmental issues; but the candidate, too, had partisans among the campus Young Republicans and some others present. Then, prompting a few catcalls, the candidate said, "Besides, who's to say that even if there is global warming, it's something we should stop? What if it's all part of a larger plan? A plan beyond our understanding. Who are we to question that?"

Frank glanced at Marissa, who looked back at him uncomfortably. They both knew that this candidate had touted his evangelical *bona fides*—he was active as a lay minister—and his denomination happened to be the same as hers. Frank was well aware, however, that Marissa rejected this man's opinions on environmental issues.

The student now grew hostile: "Are you saying environmental problems are God's will?"

The candidate responded cagily: "Who's to say they're not?" He even chuckled after asking that question. "Maybe these problems—all of these many problems—are simply part of what we have coming. Part of what we *deserve*."

Frank, more and more exasperated, couldn't restrain himself any longer. Standing, he waved genially and said, "Quick follow-up question."

"Be my guest."

"Are you implying that climate change and other global problems could in fact be part of the so-called Tribulation?"

"I like how you put that—*so-called*."

"Meaning, you do make that assumption?"

The candidate seemed to be restraining his derision. "As a Christian, I feel it's my duty not to second-guess God. God is the one in charge. When I see all these terrible things happening—wars and rumors of wars, famines, natural disasters, and all the rest—I have a responsibility to read the writing on the wall. To read what's there. The problem with you atheists is that since you're blinded by your unbelief, you can't even see the writing on the wall."

"But isn't it rather arrogant," Frank said, "to assume that *you* can? To assume that you're privy to what God has in mind? To act as if—"

"Next question," said the candidate.

15

ow, then, should we respond?" Frank asked the congregation as he concluded his homily. "How should we react as Catholics when we hear fellow-Christians predict the imminent end of the world? When we read of pastors who announce that the Tribulation will begin next Wednesday? When we watch on TV as people sell their possessions, quit their jobs, and prepare for Judgment Day? What are we supposed to think? What are we supposed to do?"

Dead silence. Frank's sermon had run longer than usual, three minutes instead of one, yet the large gathering that Sunday seemed fully attentive, not the least bit distracted or restless, as he gazed out over the parishioners watching him.

"Here's what I'd say. To all of you who feel anxious about the situation, and to all of you who don't . . . To those of you who have come to Pete and me with concerns about what you hear in the news or what you wonder about . . . To those of you who worry that the Last Days are upon us . . . To all of you—and to myself, too, for that matter—I'll say this: let's get back to work. Let's look after one another. Let's feed the hungry and clothe the poor. Let's offer comfort to the lonely and solace to the sick. Let's respond to the world's needs. So, yes, we wait in joyful hope for the coming of our Savior, Jesus Christ. But in the meantime— however long a time that may be—let's get to work."

16

Laurie, Frank, and Tyler rushed into the house, down a staircase, and into the basement, where they found the patient face-up on a concrete floor. Frank guessed the woman's age at over seventy—waxy white hair, yellow-gray skin. She wore only a pink nightgown. Two cops were doing CPR on her. A younger woman, forrty or forty-five, stood near the staircase with her hands clasped together and wailed, "Oh my God! Oh my God!"

"What's her down time?" Laurie asked the cops as she and Tyler took over the CPR.

"Unclear," one of the officers replied. "Could be ten minutes, maybe longer."

Laurie placed the ventilation mask over the woman's face and squeezed the black rubber bag; Tyler did chest compressions.

Frank stood nearby but didn't know what he should do. The longer he took in the scene, the more alarmed he felt—queasy, dizzy, short of breath.

Laurie told him, "Get me an oral airway."

Frank obeyed, fumbling. He opened the CPR kit, found the set of curved plastic airways, picked out the right size, and handed it over. Laurie inserted the airway as if sliding a question mark down the woman's throat. At once Laurie put the mask back onto the patient's face. "Here," she told Frank. "Take over bagging."

Frank hesitated.

"Take the damn bag!"

He forced himself to move closer, kneel, and start squeezing the ambu-bag. He was ventilating the patient! He had never performed CPR on a human being before, only on practice dummies, but now this was the real thing.

Laurie scolded him: "Thirty to two!"

Frank was using the wrong ratio, so he corrected himself: two breaths for every thirty times that Tyler compressed the woman's chest.

Now Laurie was preparing the AED, the little computerized defibrillator. After using EMT shears to cut open the woman's nightgown, Laurie stuck the electrodes onto the woman's chest. She powered up the AED. The noise all around grew intense: the daughter's wailing, the cops' calming words as they led her upstairs, Laurie's and Tyler's shouts back and forth, and now the AED's robotic voice: *"Check for pulse!"*

Tyler stopped doing compressions and checked the woman's neck for a carotid pulse. He shook his head.

The AED: *"Analyzing rhythm!"*

Frank was appalled and fascinated. Some words echoed in his head: *Lord have mercy. Christ have mercy.*

The AED: *"Clear the patient!"*

"Stand clear!" Laurie shouted.

Everyone backed away from the woman.

Frank expected her body to jolt—legs and arms flopping, torso twitching—as if a little explosion had detonated deep inside her. Nothing happened. The woman just lay there. For some reason the AED hadn't shocked her.

"Analyzing rhythm!"

"Okay," Tyler said, "stand clear."

"Clear the patient!"

"Everybody clear."

Everyone pulled back, waited, and watched.

Again Frank heard his own internal voice: *Lord have mercy. Christ have mercy.*

Once again there was no shock.

Frank felt puzzled when Tyler started doing compressions again. Laurie, speaking into the walkie-talkie, consulted with someone, maybe one of the E.R. doctors. Frank couldn't follow the exchange. There was too much static, too much background noise—the police radios somewhere and the daughter's shouts upstairs. Laurie shouted, "Where's the medics!" Almost at once she got a garbled answer. Then, irritably, she said, "Twenty minutes off."

Tyler signaled her, they stopped doing CPR, and Laurie turned on the AED again.

"Analyzing rhythm."

Within seconds Laurie told Frank, "Get the Reeves." She took over doing the ventilations.

Frank hesitated again, this time trying to remember what the Reeves might be. Then he left at once—slipped past the cops, stumbled his way up the stairs, rushed over to the rig, and fetched what he now recalled: the rolled-up flexible stretcher. Already out of breath, he raced back to the house and half-stumbled down the stairs.

By the time Laurie and Tyler had slid the woman onto the Reeves and carried her upstairs, some of the cops had wheeled the gurney from the rig over to the driveway. Together they transferred the woman onto the gurney, then loaded her aboard the ambulance, with Laurie bagging her and Tyler doing compressions the whole time. Then suddenly the doors slammed shut, Laurie and Frank were in the compartment with the patient, and Frank found the ventilation bag in his hands again.

"What are you waiting for!" Laurie shouted.

Frank stared at her for a second, then snapped back to his senses and started frantically squeezing the bag.

"Slow down! Thirty to two!"

He restrained himself, squeezing twice each time after Laurie had done fifteen compressions.

The rig jolted. Tyler drove so fast Frank could scarcely stay seated. How Laurie managed to keep doing com¬pressions, he had no idea. As the rig veered and swayed, she sometimes clutched a metal bar overhead with one hand while shoving the other hand against the patient's chest. Not exactly how they demonstrated CPR in class . . .

The whole time they lurched through town, Frank chanted to himself: *Lord have mercy. Christ have mercy.*

* * *

The patient died. Tyler raced the ambulance to the hospital, the E.R. docs and nurses shocked her again and again, they injected her with cardiac drugs, they bagged her, they did compressions for almost half an hour, but she died. Frank watched at the edge of the E.R. cubicle as the staff went through their procedures. Eventually one of the doctors pronounced the patient dead. The E.R. staff members started to leave.

After that, Laurie spent a long time with the daughter, explained what had happened, and consoled her, even letting the woman cry in her arms.

Frank, eavesdropping outside the room, felt shaky and sad.

"—we're just so sorry. We did everything we could for her, believe me."

Then Tyler signaled Frank with a single twitch of his thumb, Frank pulled away from the E.R. booth, and the two men packed up the squad's equipment.

Laurie joined them a short while later in the rig. As she drove to the squad house, she turned to Frank where he sat beside her: "You did good."

"Doesn't feel so good," Frank told her.

"For a first CPR call, I'd say you did great."

"The patient died."

Laurie swung the ambulance onto Forty-fourth Avenue. "Frank, nothing in our power could've saved that woman."

He couldn't help but turn and stare. "What are you telling me?"

"She was a goner. The cops said she'd been lying on the floor ten, maybe fifteen minutes. That's way too long to bring someone back."

"Is that why the AED wouldn't shock her?"

"You got it. The gizmo couldn't detect a rhythm worth shocking. No V-tach, V-fib—zippo."

"Then why bother at all?"

"'Cause sometimes it's not the patient we're treating."

Frank felt so stunned that he couldn't respond.

Now Laurie turned onto Ward Road. She said, "The daughter found her mom lying on the basement floor. How long? Who knows. She'd been there long enough that her skin was starting to discolor. Remember the technical term? Lividity. *Nothing was gonna revive that gal.*"

"I don't get it. All that CPR, the AED, the whole nine yards."

"It's important for the family—"

"The family!"

"—so they feel something's been done."

"We just went through the motions?"

"Sort of."

"For *legal* reasons?"

"Partly—but mostly so they won't feel so futile."

Frank didn't know what to think. "All that work so the relatives can feel better?"

"When we do CPR," Laurie said, "sometimes it's not just the *patient's* heart we're trying to resuscitate."

17

*N*ot just the patient's heart we're trying to resuscitate . . .

He sat immobile at his desk for a long time the following day as those words echoed inside his head. Not just the patient's heart . . . Whose, then? Clearly the relatives'. But someone's beyond the relatives, even? The EMTs' themselves, perhaps. Was it possible that Laurie referred to herself, given her state of mind, her fatigue, her smoldering PTSD?

Images kept coming back to him: how strenuously Laurie had persisted in doing compressions even when she understood their futility . . . how long and how generously she had let the dead woman's daughter sob in her embrace . . . how calmly she had discussed the situation with Frank in the ambulance afterward.

Other words troubled him, too, words courtesy of Pete earlier that day, once Frank had returned to the RMU area, had worked his way through the day's tasks, and had returned to the rectory: "You have a commitment to serve others."

"Maybe I've missed something," Frank said as an argument took shape, "but isn't that what I'm doing?"

"Not really. Not if you're neglecting your congregation. *Our* congregation."

"Which I'm not."

"I think you are," Pete said.

"Oh? How is that?"

"By spending so much time with that ambulance crew."

Frank didn't hesitate before letting loose: "I don't know what you're talking about. So much time! I'm only on duty during my day off. How is that a problem?"

123

"It's not a question of your day off. Do whatever you like on your day off. But with the squad you're up all night, then exhausted the whole day after, and you're both edgy and distracted clear through the weekend. Even when you're *here,* you're not really here. That homily you gave on Sunday—it wasn't just members of the congregation who were nodding off. I thought you were gonna pass out and take the lectern down with you."

"That's ridiculous—"

"Which reminds me. One of the older parishioners told me that when you heard her confession a couple of days ago, you fell silent for a long time, and when she spoke to you—*"Father? Father?"*— she heard you snoring."

"I wasn't snoring."

"She said the sound was unmistakable," Pete said. "She made multiple attempts to get any response from you. So don't tell me you can do whatever you like on your day off."

Very well, then, he thought that night as he lay in bed surrounded by darkness and silence. I won't tell you that. I won't tell you anything. *No te digo nada.*

18

Each night he climbed into bed as if boarding a powerful but unreliable spacecraft; he reclined into his ergonomically designed astronaut couch; he pulled up the blankets like a hatch until they sealed him tightly into place; and, following a few technical delays, he blasted off into space on a hazardous and unpredictable voyage to the strange, often hostile environments to which Mission Control had sent him.

One night he dreamed of his years in Oaxaca, of the parish that he had helped to run, of people there he had known there—Father Mariano, director of the rural health center, who spent his own meager salary to feed the patients; Justina, a young mother who had lost premature twin girls; Graciela, a teenager dying of leukemia; and Armando, an ten-year-old boy who followed Frank around all day asking *¿Cómo te ayudo, Padrecito?*—How can I help you, Little Father?—and who eagerly, happily performed any chore that the priest asked of him.

One night he dreamed about visiting with St. Augustine, who served him coffee and a tasty Austrian-style fruit pastry. "Pear *stollen?*" asked Frank. "No," replied Augustine, "stolen pears."

One night he dreamed about Erin, still twenty-two even though Frank was now just three years shy of sixty, and he asked her with deep curiosity and intense longing where she was and what her life was like. "Well, I'm dead," she replied, "so there's not really much to tell." "But you look *alive*—so beautiful and young." She smiled and Frank awoke.

The dreams grew more frequent, more tense, more unpleasant, more alarming now that Frank had begun riding with the Foothills EMS Squad. Even a relatively uneventful shift left him keyed up, often unable to sleep without reading or doing paperwork for several hours first, then more likely to have strange dreams even once he settled down sufficiently to doze off. An active shift caused yet more problems. Frank took a long time to fall asleep, sometimes hours, and before sliding from awareness his mind replayed clips of whatever events had transpired during his time on duty. A messy CPR call. The aftermath of a car-truck collision. A nine-year-old girl mauled by a dog. A woman who claimed to have fallen down some steps but who had probably been beaten by her husband. Mulling over these calls made it difficult for Frank to relax, much less to surrender unto sleep. Then, once relieved at last of consciousness, Frank discovered that he hadn't escaped the squad after all, and he found himself confronting some of the scariest, strangest situations he had ever experienced in the deeper reaches of his mind.

Doing mouth-to-mouth rescue breaths on Stacey, he suddenly found the young woman's lovely face morphing into the wrinkled, baggy visage of Margaret Beach.

A baby had stopped breathing. When Frank grabbed the vacuum wand to suction the child's mouth, he cleared the obstruction easily. But at once the metal tube sucked in the baby's face, then the whole head, and then, with a horrible slurping sound, the entire child.

Frank struggled to gain access to a smashed-up car. Someone was inside: he could hear a woman's voice. He could see her motions through the crazed windshield and windows. "Help me!" she cried. "Help me get out!" The badly mangled doors wouldn't open. Frank alone could rescue her, so he grabbed a rock and tried to smash a window, but the impact of stone against glass sent sparks flying; the car—foom!—burst into flames; and Frank saw only too late through a shattered window that the burning woman inside was . . . *Laurie.*

19

Sweaty and breathing hard, Frank worked out at a private fitness club not far from Foothills EMS. He could have used the RMU gym for free, of course, but that option felt unbearable: too many students and professors present, most of them aware of his role at the university, many certain to feel amused by the sight of a pudgy, out-of-breath priest among the buff jocks and the svelte coeds. In this private club, however, he could hide among the spry retirees, the suburban executives, and the soccer moms. Frank was just another Boomer throwing off the day's tension and struggling to stay in shape as he pedaled a stationary bike.

At least a dozen people surrounded him on other machines. A thirtyish African-American fellow worked the StepMill next to Frank. The slim blonde right ahead of Frank ran with perfect form on a treadmill. Two corporate types strode intently, side by side, on elliptical trainers. Others went about their business on other machines. Some people read; others listened to music through earphones; still others watched the bank of TVs up ahead, the monitors variously displaying the twisted wreckage of a car crash, a man motioning toward a weather map, two women in robes and Islamic head scarves kneeling beside a corpse, a reporter gesticulating toward a parched landscape, a lovely blonde swirling her hair in slow motion . . . Most of the people working out here looked serious, focused, even grim. No one spoke to anyone else. The only sounds derived from the thump of running shoes on rubber conveyor belts, the rhythmic huffs of exhalations and inhalations, and the whir of machinery.

How odd, this journey to nowhere. If he were riding a bike outside, Frank wouldn't have felt so ridiculous. The effort wouldn't have seemed so preposterous. Who knows, he might even greet a passing fellow-cyclist without the other person perceiving his words as intrusive. Here they may as well have been following the Carthusian Rule. Frank pedaled onward, too, without speaking. Just as well. The weather was too cold today for him to feel comfortable out of doors. Better to endure this ordeal in close quarters than to skip it altogether. But ten more minutes passed—twelve, fifteen?—and soon he couldn't stand his restless mind or his burning thighs, so he slowed down, ambled along for a while, and dismounted, delighting at once in the sensations of stasis.

Frank knew he should now shift to his strength-training workout. He started with the chest press machine, fifteen reps at forty pounds. He proceeded from there to the row and the lateral raise, another fifteen reps apiece. Then he endured the bicep curl and the triceps extension. After that he muddled through the leg press, the seated leg curl, and the leg extension. He had to lower the weight at each machine from whatever the previous person had set it for. Even so his muscles soon smoldered and sparked as he exerted himself. A sign on a wall elsewhere in the gym read: PAIN IS THE BEST INSTRUCTOR. These words could have been the motto carved above the door in a medieval cloister. *Dolor magister optimus.* Or in his own boyhood parochial school—how the nuns made him suffer! "Pain will guide you on the straight-and-narrow," Sister Mary Bridget had repeatedly intoned. At least here he could suffer in private. The patron saint of the overweight, whoever that might have been—who knows, maybe Aquinas himself, given St. Thomas's vast girth and his legendary appetite at table—well, surely someone had interceded on Frank's behalf, since he now discovered (with deep relief) that he'd gain access to most of these machines without having to wait for someone else to finish. As he proceeded, though, other people started lining up to take their turns while he struggled against his wimpy burdens of forty or forty-five pounds. He noticed on finishing that the next person, an astonishingly muscular but still curvy blonde in T-shirt and shorts, took the seat and, looking amused or impatient, adjusted the weight to ninety or a hundred.

These are the new Stations of the Cross, he decided abruptly. This is the pilgrimage we're taking. Just as Frank once moved through half-illuminated, incense-palled churches and tried to deepen his awareness of Christ's suffering, now he worked his way through this other temple, this mirror-walled, brightly lit, rock- and rap-pounding nave, on another quest. The sound system blared a woman's crooning, moaning voice: "It feels so *good* . . . It feels so *good* . . . It feels so *good* . . . " Yet even as he listened to this inescapably loud, lewd song, Frank couldn't avoid remembering how his grandmother led him from one station to the next at Our Lady of Guadalupe Church during his boyhood in west Denver and taught him how to pray. *Mira, Paquito,* she told him. *Aquí Jesús es condenado a morir . . .* And: *Aquí Jesús carga su cruz al Calvario . . .* Even now, surrounded by sweaty suburbanites, he imagined for an instant catching a whiff of something redolent of votive candles.

He moved over to the bicep curl—wasn't that what the trainers called this machine? Achy and sweaty, he couldn't understand what prompted him to keep tolerating such torture. Yet he must. If he were to have any chance of surviving the squad . . .

Adrenaline is the medication released by an epinephrine auto-injector—true or false?

Which muscle type has the unique property of automaticity?

List the three layers of the skin, from superficial to deep.

List the signs of adequate breathing.

These questions and demands started assaulting his mind like a new and unfamiliar catechism. He couldn't avoid this internal inquisition. Just as he needed to make his body fit, he must train his mind to respond quickly and accurately. Frank asked himself the questions; he recited the answers.

The chemicals released by the endocrine system are called what?

An unresponsive patient without a suspected spine injury is placed in which position?

Describe how to measure and insert an oropharyngeal airway.

The Q-and-A was demanding in its own right, even tedious; but, like exercise, perhaps it offered a path to some kind of salvation. Physically tired, Frank had started drilling himself off and on through the course of each day—while showering each morning, while doing the dishes after breakfast, while walking to the Center, while biding his time between sessions . . . and now even while flagellating himself at the gym.

What is the term for undesirable actions of a medication?

Describe the complications of near-drowning.

Abdominal rigidity and tenderness are possible signs of what physiological condition?

Infants are at less risk than adults for hypothermia—true or false?

If the pulse distal to the injury is absent, what should be applied gently to the extremity?

After so many years of attending to his parishioners' spiritual concerns, so many years of looking after their souls, it amused and amazed Frank to find himself attending to the human body and the perils afflicting it. To find himself pushing hard to master a new corpus of knowledge, not the minutiae of theology or the fine points of church history or even new techniques for practicing marriage therapy, but simply the necessary steps for stopping a hemorrhage and the methods for preventing shock.

He realized abruptly that he was soaked with sweat, out of breath, and shaky. Enough. He suddenly felt tired of these machines, the gym, and the other members. Time to clear out and shower and go back to the Center.

Easing himself off the seat, he noted with dismay and surprise who had emerged from the men's locker room into the gym: Tyler. Frank faltered. For a moment all he could do was stare. The guy's shorts and T-shirt didn't look intentionally tight or skimpy in the common style among guys showing off their muscles, yet Tyler's physique was remarkable even at a glance. His arms and legs were sinewy, his chest broad, his back as solid as a brick wall. Frank noticed some of the women present visibly perk up as they spotted Tyler, and a few of them discretely tracked his path across the gym. Frank watched him, too, plotting his strategy for avoidance. Forget the workout; his only desire was simply to dodge Tyler. How, though, given where the guy was walking? Then Tyler stopped. He was facing the other away now. Perhaps that moment of hesitation offered safe passage. Or not: all the mirrors in this place would make stealth impossible. Frank's only hope was that Tyler might be too engrossed in his own activities, or in himself, to spot the priest. Otherwise Frank couldn't risk making his move. For now he saw no alternative but to pick another machine, keep working out, bide his time, and wait for another chance.

Tyler took a few steps to his left and started lifting free weights. What did they call that? Curling? Pressing? Frank couldn't recall. So much terminology—as precise as medieval theologians' schemata! He couldn't care less about all this fitness jargon, but neither could he avoid watching Tyler as he started to work out. Even while just warming up, Tyler had picked a barbell so huge that it resembled the axle and metal wheels from a good-sized mining cart. How could any human being lift such a massive object? Yet now Tyler began hoisting it repeatedly.

He belonged to a different species, Frank decided. A different order of human being. Was this what people call a Real Man? Was this what a man *ought* to be? What women admired? What they desired? If so, Frank shouldn't be surprised that Tyler smiled that faint, derisive smile whenever he looked at him. No surprise, either, that Laurie often gazed at Tyler with that sheen of hunger in her eyes. Maybe this strength, this physical might, was simply what women wanted. If so, small wonder that Tyler smiled at the sight of his lover's eyes when Laurie stared at him.

An image of Laurie in Tyler's embrace flitted into Frank's mind and prompted him to shudder. At once he pushed the thought away—not because it was obscene, but because Frank understood just then how much he envied Tyler.

The guy went on and on, releasing a feral grunt each time he hoisted the barbell. Up and down, up and down. At last he released it to the padded floor with a clank. He paced for a while, still pent up, before repeating the cycle.

How long must this continue? Frank asked himself. How long must he watch this strange drama?

Abruptly Tyler walked to his left. Frank made his move. He stepped away from the elliptical trainers, cut through the row of exercise machines ahead of him, and walked straight toward the locker rooms.

Tyler turned unexpectedly and headed in the same direction.

The two men crossed paths near the entrance to the men's lockers.

A quick nod. "Padre." *Paw-dray.*

"Tyler."

"Never thought I'd see *you* here."

"Doctor's orders."

"Yeah, I bet."

Frank could see that subliminal smirk. He told himself to ignore it. On impulse he said, "Plus, I suppose I should get in shape for the squad work."

"Good idea."

Maybe he could disarm the guy—transform his contempt into something more useful for both of them. "Any suggestions?"

Tyler's nostrils emitted a tiny puff of air, an almost inaudible snort. "Not off hand."

"Just wondering."

"Hire a trainer."

"I already have."

"Well, then—good luck."

"Thank you."

"No problem."

Nobody said there was a problem, Frank noted.

They stood there a moment without speaking. Frank could feel his sweat turning cold. Neither man seemed able to disengage. Tyler broke the tension when he stepped over to the water fountain, took a long, slurping drink, and wiped his mouth with the back of his hand. "Well," he said, "back to the ol' salt mine."

Frank gestured toward the locker room. "I'd better go."

"You betcha."

20

A lot of people were milling about by the time Laurie, Tyler, and Frank reached the accident scene. Some were motorists who had pulled over and now stood near the wreckage, where they clustered gawking in little groups or else approached the car, peered into it, tugged at the door handles, or called out to the driver inside. Just as the ambulance pulled over, a police car did, too, and Frank saw two officers emerge. Then, as Laurie parked the rig, Frank got a better glimpse of the accident. The car's front end had compressed and buckled. The passenger compart¬ment was smashed up, especially on the right, as a telephone pole now lying lengthwise across the car had flattened the right half of the vehicle from front to back. The impact had spun a web of cracks over every window. Frank couldn't imagine how anyone inside could still be alive.

He felt shaky as he stepped out of the ambulance through the side door.

Laurie said, "Frank, bring the green kit. Tyler, backboards and C-collars." A few moments they walked toward the wreckage.

Laurie turned to Frank. "You okay?"

He forced himself to nod.

The scene was so crazy that he couldn't fully track all the action. Some police officers yelled at the onlookers to back off. Laurie and Tyler started sizing up the situation to determine how many people were inside the car and how badly they might be hurt. Just then some fire department vehicles showed up: a fire engine, a rescue vehicle, and the chief's SUV. ALS ambulance arrived next, two medics joining the effort. By now sixteen or eighteen people swarmed around the car. Everyone seemed to be talking at once. Frank felt so confused that he backed off a few yards.

Using pry bars, the rescue team and fire fighters pried open the driver's-side door, revealing the only person inside the car: a middle-aged woman slumped against the steering wheel. She looked strange, her whole body quivering, an awful sight. Frank couldn't imagine what even all of these emergency personnel could do to help her. When the rescue team succeeded in opening the left-rear door, Frank saw that nobody else was in the car.

Frank came to his senses. Laurie held up a heavy turnout coat that would protect him from broken glass and torn metal. "Put this on," Laurie said. "You'll do spinal stabilization."

Frank hesitated for a moment. *Spinal stabilization* . . . Of course: supporting the victim's head to minimize the risk of paralysis. He slipped his arms through and pulled on the coat. Heavier than he had expected . . . At once Laurie handed him a blue hard hat, a pair of goggles, and some bulky leather gloves. He put on all this gear feeling more and more alarmed, but he felt too stunned to resist. By the time Frank fully grasped the situation, Tyler and Laurie had eased him next to the left-rear passenger seat, nudged him till he was sitting, and tucked his legs right behind the driver's seat.

Tyler said, "Okay, do your thing."

Frank's mind went blank. *Do my thing . . . ?* Then it clicked. Whether this woman had suffered a spinal injury or not, the EMTs would assume that she had throughout the effort to extricate her. Frank would support the woman's head while the others protected her from further damage by putting a cervical collar around her neck, strapping her into an extrica¬tion device, and getting her out of the vehicle.

Frank reached around the driver's-seat headrest—one hand to the left, one to the right—and he grasped the woman's head to cradle it with both hands.

In a calm voice Laurie said, "You're a lucky guy, Frank. You'll sit there nice and pretty while the rest of us do the heavy lifting." Then, speaking louder and more slowly, Laurie addressed the patient: "Hey, how ya doin' there?"

The woman moaned.

Frank could see Tyler reaching into the car to putting the plastic collar around her neck, and he felt the heavy head shifting as he tried to support its weight.

Tyler said, "We'll get you out in a jiffy."

No response. Frank felt the woman resist him.

Laurie said, "Talk to her, Frank. Keep her awake. Don't let her doze off."

He felt a twinge of panic. Glancing to his left, where big black and yellow coats shifted about as the firefighters came and went, he wished he could be anywhere else but stuck inside this car. The thought crossed his mind that this woman might literally die in his hands.

Laurie again, speaking once more to the patient: "What's your name?"

Frank couldn't understand the response.

"Ma'am, what's your name?"

The answer sounded like "Sandy."

"Sandy?"

He could feel her nodding.

"Don't move your head—stay still. We're gonna get you out quick as a flash. Sandy, this is Frank. He's the person holding your head."

Frank said *Hi*, though his voice didn't do much more than a squeak.

Laurie said, "Talk to her."

For a moment he couldn't speak. He couldn't even breathe. A weird metallic odor filled the whole place and left him on the verge of vomiting. Despite the collar around Sandy's neck, he worried he would lose his grip and leave the patient paralyzed. Most of all he felt afraid that Sandy would end up dying.

"How's it going?" Frank asked, then cringed at the stupidity of his question.

He heard Tyler at that moment—"I'm going to take your blood pressure"—and Frank saw him on the left wrapping a cuff around the woman's arm.

"We'll take good care of you," Frank said. "Just hang on, Sandy. We'll get you to the hospital."

Frank stayed inside the car for what seemed like an hour, though he found out later that the span was less than ten minutes. The crew strapped Sandy into a papoose-like KED that kept her back and neck rigid. Then the rescue guys helped the EMT's lift her out of the car, they secured her onto a plastic long board, and they loaded her into the ambulance.

She died a few minutes later. Before Tyler could even pull the rig away from the scene, Laurie noticed something about the woman's appearance, checked her carotid pulse with two fingers against her neck, and said firmly: "Tyler, she's coding."

Frank felt a surge of alarm. Cardiac arrest . . .

At once Tyler stepped out of the cab, walked around the ambulance, and entered through the back. He and Laurie then started CPR, defibrillated the patient, and "worked on her," as Tyler put it later, with Frank watching awkwardly from his seat at the front of the patient compartment.

"What can I do to help?" he asked at one point.

"Just keep out of the way," Tyler told him.

He was embarrassed and annoyed at himself when, after Laurie and Tyler had given up, bundled Sandy in a sheet, and prepared to leave the scene, Frank started to weep. Tyler was filling out the call sheet in the driver's seat, fortunately, and couldn't see him. Best of all, Tyler couldn't see Laurie walk over to where Frank stood and suddenly embrace him. He hesitated a moment, then hugged her right back. As splendid as it was to hold her, he felt relieved when she gently pulled away. "You know the Two Great Rules of EMS?" she asked.

"The what?"

"The two Great Rules of EMS. Rule Number One: Sometimes people die. Rule Number Two: No matter how hard you try, you'll never change Rule Number One."

"What are you telling me?"

"Don't beat up on yourself."

"I'm not."

"You are."

"I wish we could've made more of a difference."

"Of course. But you know what I think? I think you're trying to change Rule Number One."

21

A minister, a rabbi, and a priest walk into a bar . . .

      Perfect setup for a classic joke, Frank told himself as he nursed his Belgian beer. Better yet: *A beautiful blonde minister, a gorgeous pregnant rabbi, and a dumpy over-the-hill priest walk into a bar . . .* Scaldis, the label said, tasty but a little strong for that early hour—"12 percent alcohol by volume"—what with so much paperwork awaiting him back at the parish house. Somehow he would muddle through. What was the punch line to his joke? Frank didn't care. He was content simply to sit here with Marissa and Jenna, to enjoy bantering with them, to savor this hour away from Pete and the many tasks ahead.

"—going okay?"

Marissa was asking him a question. "Sorry," Frank said, "I couldn't hear you over all this racket." He gestured at the other people around them in the Campus Lounge, a local watering hole.

"I said, Is your EMT work going all right?"

"Just fine. Challenging. Exciting. Scary as hell!" he exclaimed suddenly, punctuating his final comment with a laugh so abrupt that he startled the trio of undergraduates in the next booth.

"My hat's off to you," said Marissa, "that's for sure. I could never do what you're doing."

"I couldn't either," Frank told her.

"You are doing it."

"True."

"So don't say you're not."

"What I mean is—if I actually knew what I'd face each shift, I couldn't do it. Or even show up. Too scary, too threatening. Precisely because the situation is so unpredictable each time,

I have no choice. I show up, stuff happens, and I cope. Heart attacks. Burns. Car wrecks. Pediatric injuries. All kinds of crazy stuff. There's no way of knowing what's coming at me, which is the only way I can handle it."

"Have you delivered any babies yet?" Jenna asked.

The thought appalled him. "No, thank God!" Frank found his gaze involuntarily lowering to Jenna's belly. How far was she along now? Seven months? More? Her abdomen was so massive that Jenna sat sideways at the booth's edge to give the swollen belly clearance from the table. This sight made him tense and anxious. He couldn't imagine the stress of delivering a baby.

"Just wondering."

Marissa looked pensive. "This is so interesting, what you're doing. It's so easy for all of us to settle into our routines, to do what's predictable and familiar. Sure is for me, anyway. And here you are, Frank, at age whatever—" At this moment she laughed, held up the palm of her right hand as if to stop him, and said, "Don't tell me! I'm not pressing for details! All I'm saying is, it's pretty darn amazing for you to go out on a limb and perform a service that's so stressful, demanding, and difficult."

What could he say to them? He found it touching to hear this acknowledgment—this praise, even—after so much carping, implicit criticism, and dismissive silence from Pete.

"Tell me something," Jenna said. "What are the people like? The squad members?"

"That's an good question," Frank said, "one I can't answer very well, to be honest, because I've met so few of them. Each shift has its own crew, so I'm well-traveled on Thursday nights, so to speak. I interact with the same two people every week."

"And?"

He couldn't help but conjure Laurie's image. Tyler's, too, lingered at the edge of his consciousness, at once vague and unpleasant, like a passing wave of nausea. Laurie, though: vivid and delightful. "It's complicated," he said. "Both are remarkable, and each is a real handful. But one is hard to tolerate, while the other— The other—" He cut himself short.

Jenna listened, watching him closely. A smile eased onto her face. "Interesting! Let me guess. The one who's hard to tolerate is a guy, while the other—the one who Frank can't quite describe to us—is female."

"That's what I was thinking, too," said Marissa.

Frank didn't know how to respond.

"He's blushing."

"He's definitely blushing."

The two women watched, smiling at first, then snickering.

"Tell us about Ms. Not-so-hard-to-tolerate," Marissa said.

"There's not much to say."

"You're *still* blushing, Frank."

To make matters still worse, Jenna said: "Here's what I think. I think you have a thing about the female EMT—in fact, you have a real crush on her. Why else would you, of all people, find yourself so tongue-tied? And you find this situation awkward in more ways than one."

He decided not to resist. "What am I supposed to say?" he asked. "First you expose my soul with your female CAT-scan telepathy and leave me no place to hide. Second, you hand me the diagnosis I've been dreading. Third, you remind me of the worst possible aspect of the whole situation: there's no cure for this disease! I'm a priest, damn it—a Roman Friggin' Catholic priest."

"True," Jenna said.

"Any suggestions?"

"A hair shirt?" Marissa said. "Self-flagellation?"

"Living with my confrere is sufficient mortification of the flesh, thank you very much."

None of them spoke for a while. Then Jenna said, "I guess the situation would be easier, wouldn't it, if this woman were already in a relationship."

"Right again," Frank told them. "How did you know?"

"Just a hunch."

"You're on the mark."

"And let me guess," Jenna went on. "Her relationship is with the other EMT."

142

22

How odd, then, to find himself cooking dinner for Laurie; cooking in her own kitchen; cooking with ingredients not easily available in the RMU neighborhood, thus prompting a drive clear across town a day earlier to purchase items at a Mexican *bodega;* cooking now after several hours of initial preparations at the parish house, an effort so complex that Pete had wondered out loud about "such a big production"; cooking in ways that Frank had described to Laurie as quick and easy but that in fact now required subtle, late-phase alchemy to transmute several dozen ingredients into the feast he had envisioned. How odd. What, Frank asked himself as he stood at the stove in her apartment and prepared to steam a half dozen *tamales de camarón a la yucateca*—what exactly was he doing?

He was . . . cooking. "How about let's grab a bite sometime," Laurie had said one morning as they crossed the squad parking lot after a shift, "and we'll catch up a little." One thing had led to another in the intervening week. Here they were, about to grab a bite. As far as *catching up a little* . . . Frank, shifting now to preparing the soup—the creamy, savory, smoky *sopa tarasca estilo de Pátzcuaro*—listened to Laurie answer his question about her past.

"—and a fairly normal childhood until I was fifteen or so. Except, of course, when you figure that my parents hated each other and had a terrible marriage. But that's not so uncommon, is it? I can't say I had it rougher than anybody else. Then suddenly— and I do mean *suddenly,* no warning at all—my father walked out of the house and never came back. I didn't have any contact with him for many years after that. He simply abandoned my mother and brothers and me. Then, to complicate the situation, my mother had a nervous breakdown after Dad took off."

143

"I'm so sorry," Frank said uncomfortably. It felt ridiculous to putter at his culinary tasks as Laurie told her tale, so much more revealing and difficult a narrative than he had expected. He shouldn't have assumed that her response would be upbeat or easy . . . Yet she told her story in such a calm, flat tone that the telling somehow disarmed his unease.

"There's nothing to be sorry about. It's just the hand I got dealt. But the question I had to answer was: what should I *do* about it? I was sixteen years old. My mother was incapacitated. My brothers were eight and twelve. Since my dad had simply disappeared—no divorce, no alimony—we had no income. The department of social services would've swooped in within a couple of months, split up the family, and farmed us kids out to foster parents. No doubt about it. But you know what? I wasn't going to let that happen. I just wasn't. So I hassled my relatives for cash, I got a job at the local supermarket, I pulled in whatever income I could, and I kept us afloat."

"Incredible."

"Frank, it wasn't incredible. It was just—what it was. What else could I have done? I didn't want my mother to get stuck in a loony bin or my brothers and me to end up parked in the homes of strangers who didn't give a damn about us. No way. So I went to school every day like any other sixteen-year-old, I walked home after school, I helped my brothers do their homework, I fixed dinner for my mom and the boys, and I went off to the Safeway to stock the shelves all evening. Then I walked home, did my own homework, and got a few hours' sleep until the whole routine started over the next day."

"I still say it's incredible."

"Bullshit."

"Then you are incredible."

"Also bullshit."

By then Frank had put the soup to simmer, so he proceeded to brown slices of turkey breast for the *mole coloradito de guajalote.* "What can I say?" he asked her. "In some respects I'm not surprised. Your story makes sense, now that I think of it. I see you in action every shift, I see you looking after so many people in need, I see you focusing with such care and expertise, and it's clear that you're really, really good at helping others. That's wonderful. It's a rare thing. At the same time, I can see now where your skill and warmth and focus come from—it's clearly what you've always done."

"Thanks for the free psychotherapy." A sudden smile. Tiny crinkles sprang up around her eyes.

He caught himself wondering why anyone would want to Botox those subtle, expressive lines into oblivion. How splendid that she hadn't. Yet he saw at once that he'd overstepped, that he'd offended and perhaps even hurt her.

"I didn't mean it like that," he hastened to say. "I'm speaking as a friend, not as a therapist."

"I know it must seem like I'm always trying to save the world."

"Not at all."

"Isn't that how you see me?"

"Look—all of us are shaped by the demands we've faced early in life. I could tell you a thing or two about my own. Do those demands fully explain why some people feel drawn to help other people? I'm not so sure. There must surely be other factors. Other motivations."

She watched him as he seared the turkey.

He wanted to say more but made himself stay silent.

Frank proceeded with his cooking tasks. Laurie kept watching him. Such close attention from anyone else would have made him self-conscious, would have complicated his task, but he somehow felt relaxed and pleased to be the object of her gaze. He was cooking for *her*. So much the better that she would observe so closely. The act of observation itself was a gift that he accepted and appreciated, just as Frank's cooking was a gift that he offered and that Laurie now clearly accepted and appreciated. Her attention was so steady and her smile so warm throughout these final phases of his effort that he couldn't help but feel gratified.

They kept chatting as he worked. Laurie told him more about her brothers. She asked about his family and about his growing up in a Chicano neighborhood west of downtown Denver. They gossiped briefly about the squad. Then, after Frank had made some final adjustments to the *coloradito,* poured the reddish-brown sauce onto the turkey, and settled the pan into the oven, he ladled out two bowls of sopa tarasca. Laurie poured another round of beers. They carried the food and their beverages to the table.

Sitting, she raised her glass. "To . . . " She couldn't seem to finish.

"To the pleasure of each other's company," Frank said. *Click!* *"Buen provecho."*

"Meaning?"

"That's the Mexican equivalent of *Bon appétit.*" He waited as she took her first taste of the soup.

A look of surprise. "Oh my God!" she exclaimed, then looked up at him. "This is incredible!" Taking another spoonful, she closed her eyes and smiled. "What *is* it?"

"Peasant-style soup from the state of Michoacán."

"I've never had anything like this. Frank, this is *Mexican?"*

"El mero mero."

"Translation?"

"The real deal."

She set to work, eating eagerly. Frank ate, too, but his pleasure wasn't the food so much as Laurie's obvious delight. Such a beguiling mix of energy and sensuality . . . He felt pleased, too, that the meal itself so fully and immediately vanquished the unease of their exchange right before he served.

After eating for a while in silence, Laurie took a guzzle of beer, paused as if preparing to say something momentous, and asked, "Does Pete know how lucky he is? To have you in the kitchen?"

"He doesn't feel so lucky."

"Really!"

"He's a classic American meat-'n'-potatoes man—"

"Too bad for him."

"—and, truth be told, he finds my food downright repulsive."

She fiddled with her glass, swirled the beer to stir up the bubbles. "How do you put up with him?"

"I have no choice."

"I know you work with him, but do you really have to live with him?"

"Our order is more democratic than most within the Church, but we basically do what we're told."

"Pity."

"You know about the vows?"

She smiled. "I've heard rumors."

"Poverty, chastity, and obedience."

"Gives me the creeps just to think about it!" she exclaimed with a laugh.

He couldn't help but respond mischievously. "You know which vow I find the most difficult? The most—to put it bluntly— *unbearable?*"

"Yesssssssssss?" she said, raising her left eyebrow.

"Guess."

"No, you tell *me. Confess* to me, Frank."

"Obedience."

"You can't be serious."

"Dead serious."

"You're lying. I don't believe you. You're kidding yourself— or you're— What would you therapists say? You're *repressing* yourself."

"Now wait a minute," he said. "I said, which do I find most difficult. Did I say the others weren't difficult? Did I say they don't all drive me crazy?"

"Okay, that's better."

"As far as Pete— Look, the order has thrown Pete and me together, end of story. I'm stuck with him. He's stuck with me. We get along, more or less, because we're both decent human beings, we both want to serve our parishioners, and there's no alternative. But yeah, the standard issues come up, including differences of taste."

"Including taste in food."

"We share the evening meal two or three times per week. I try to accommodate him. I'm the better cook, so I'm more adaptable than he is. I can fix both what he likes and what I like. To be honest, it's frustrating. I feel as if I'm cooking for a high school jock. I could really do us proud, but he's not interested, so I end up fixing burgers, fried chicken, pizza, all the stuff you'd serve a kid."

"You can come cook for me any time."

"I'll keep that in mind."

Soon the *tamales* tinged the room with their aromas of shrimp and spices, so Frank got up, returned to the kitchen, and served them. When Laurie saw the little packets on her plate—two rectangles of corn *masa* wrapped in a steaming dark-green banana leaves and tied up with fibrous bows—her expression once again showed amazement and delight. "What are they?"

"Try them and find out."

"They look like little Christmas presents!"

"Pull them open." He showed her how.

Exposing a square of dough, she took a forkful, tasted it, and said, "It's— It's—"

"Go ahead." Amused, he savored the sight of her expression.

"How did you learn to *make* this stuff!" she exclaimed with her mouth full.

"Let's just say I had two great teachers."

"Your parents?"

"My mother and my grandmother." It occurred to him just then how startled those Catholic matriarchs would feel—his grandmother, especially—to see their little Francisco, now a priest, delighting a beautiful young woman with their family recipes. What would they think he was doing? What was he doing?

He watched her eat for longer than felt appropriate. Then, as if to disrupt his train of thought, he said, "I need your input on something. More accurately, on someone."

"Oh yeah?"

"Tyler. I'm getting bad vibes from Tyler."

She exhaled abruptly, smiling. "Tyler, Tyler, Tyler. What can I say about Tyler?"

When she didn't continue, Frank waded deeper into the dark water of this new topic. "Such a smart guy. Lots of raw energy. Even a newcomer like me can see he's an incredible EMT."

"All true."

"Tyler 'Dyne-o-Mite' van Dyne . . . What a perfect nickname—he's powerful but such a powder keg."

"Also true."

"So can you— Sorry to press the point, but I'm really curious, and it's not idle curiosity. I'm trying hard to get along with him."

"You aren't the only one!" she said with a laugh.

"I don't think he likes me."

"It's nothing personal."

"The priest thing?"

"That's part of it."

"I don't blame him," Frank said. "I don't like priests either."

"He's also got a bad attitude about Hispanics."

"I noticed."

"Especially the Hispanic who's his ex-wife. "

"*Interesting,*" Frank noted.

"There's a big custody battle in progress."

"I'd forgotten he's a dad."

"He and his ex, Gabriela, have an eight-year-old son."

"Obviously a side of him I haven't thought about."

"Tyler has many different sides, believe me."

"Of course. I shouldn't be so presumptuous. Still, I can't help but feel there's something personal in his animosity."

"Maybe so," Laurie told him, "but believe me, it's not just you. Tyler doesn't like lots of people. "

"Just the nature of the beast? Mr. Macho?"

"That's part of it, plus the divorce, plus some other stuff that's happened to him." After pausing a moment she said, "He's had a few squad calls that changed him beyond the normal wear-and-tear. His little Nine Eleven junket, for instance."

"The Trade Center attacks?"

"He went to New York right after the planes hit."

"I see."

"Along with every other EMTs in the whole damn country! Except for me and maybe three others, I guess. You'd think nobody was on duty for weeks except at Ground Zero. A few of use figured we'd better stay home and mind the store."

"What happened to Tyler?"

"Nothing. Or almost nothing. Little by little, though, he got more edgy."

"I guess we all did."

"True. But I'll tell you this: Tyler is complicated. It's not just one thing. And whatever else, he's always got a chip on his shoulder."

"I noticed that as well."

"Especially toward other men."

"So what should I do?" Frank asked. "I defer to him. I try not to step on his toes. I have to say, though, even my best efforts seem to cause offense."

"Ignore him. Don't let him get your goat. You have as much right to be on Foothills EMS as Tyler. If you don't take his bull-shit personally, he'll calm down little by little. I've seen it time after time."

"I'll do what I can."

"Tyler's a good person. He just doesn't know that yet." Then, slicing the air with her knife, she said, "Enough about Tyler! I don't want to spend our whole conversation yakking about Tyler! What about you, Frank? I want to hear about you."

He felt pleased but embarrassed. "And you."

"Okay then!"

So they talked about themselves, they asked questions, they rambled, they teased, they interrogated each other, and, as Frank noted with growing enjoyment and growing unease, they flirted as the meal continued, the *coloradito de guajalote* now rich and savory before them. The beer flowed, too, the contents of a third bottle entering his glass and quickly disappearing. Small wonder that the conversation grew so intense and open . . . Small wonder that he found himself asking more and telling more than he would ordinarily have thought prudent. Small wonder that Laurie did, too.

"Here's what I don't understand about you priests," Laurie said, staring at him with a warm gaze that he found almost unbearably beautiful. "I mean, no offense, right? 'Cause I have no doubt whatever—not the least!—that you're fabulous in your line of work. What you do for people at the university. Other people too, Frank. But damn it, Frank, how can you relate to normal— I guess what I'm trying to say is, since most people have the standard set of biological—"

"Urges?"

"Right. Urges." She smiled, averting her gaze for just an instant.

He said, "How, you wonder, can a priest understand what people—we'll call them Normal People—experience?"

"Right."

"Maybe you'll believe me when I say I wasn't born a priest. In fact, I took my vows late. I was almost thirty. And before that I wasn't exactly wearing a hair shirt and praying the Rosary all day long."

"Or all night."

"Or all night. I was a normal American male. I went off to college in the late Sixties and didn't even start my seminary training until 1976. You can understand the implications."

Laurie snorted. "Must've been quite the man about town."

"I take the Fifth."

"Don't you miss it?"

"Getting laid?" asked Frank, meeting her gaze.

She nodded.

"Of course I miss it. But that's not the point."

"It's not exactly irrelevant, Frank. To most people."

"True."

"So then?

"I've made a different commitment. I have obligations to focus one hundred percent on my congregation."

"Well, what *I* think—" She looked away abruptly. "Oh, never mind."

"I know what you're going to say. Chastity and celibacy are unnatural. They distort the personality. There's no reason that a member of the clergy couldn't honor both his commitment to his congregation and a commitment to a more intimate relationship. Ministers and rabbis succeed at both. Why not priests?"

"That's not what I was going to say."

"What were you going to say?"

She smiled. "Never mind."

"Tell me."

For a long time Laurie stared at him, stared with a calm intensity that troubled Frank yet beguiled and reassured him, as if he could warm his hands, or his mind, at least, before the fire of her beauty and her obvious affection. She said, "Here's what I was going to say: I think you should give me a back rub."

He faltered. "A back rub . . . "

"That's all. That's not so terrible, is it? Right here. Sitting. Just like this. Fully clothed."

"Well—"

"Surely there's no vow against *that*."

What should he have said? Should he have quoted Paul in First Corinthians—*It is good for a man not to touch a woman*—surely one of the most harebrained utterances in all of human history? Frank felt a dizzy as he contemplated the situation facing him. As he contemplated the woman before him . . . There was no vow against back rubs. *"Pues, ¿cómo no?"* he told her. How convenient, he told himself, that Spanish allows saying yes by saying no.

"Plain English, please."

"It's a roundabout way of saying *of course*."

Frank stood, Laurie scooted her chair away from the table, and he walked over to stand behind her. She eased the already wide neck of her blouse a little wider. Then he rested both hands on her shoulders. Just placing his palms there made him shiver with delight. The warmth of her skin, the simultaneous give and firmness of her muscles, the solidity of the bones beneath—what more convincing evidence could he want that earthly life is a locus of grace?

"I guess I'm always kind of tense," she said as he started kneading the ridge of her shoulders.

"Not surprising, given your line of work."

"The tension just *hides* in those muscles and won't come out."

"I know the feeling."

His thoughts turned to Erin, to the relief and solace she had found in the massages Frank gave her. So much the easier, then, for his hands to recall what Frank had done so well many years ago.

"That's good," Laurie said. "Keep doing that."

For as long as you like, he thought. Only her lush hair presented a problem—but what a problem!—this sheaf of soft straw that kept entangling his fingers. Frank gathered it up, shifted it around the left side of her neck, and let it drape against her chest while he worked on her right shoulder; then he eased the remarkably thick mass around to the right while he focused on her left shoulder. Laurie chatted for a while—"I knew you'd be good at this"—but then fell silent.

He kneaded her muscles for a long time, moment by moment savoring the feast of textures.

"Tell me something you do in private," she said abruptly.

"In *private?*"

"Right. Something you wouldn't do with anyone else around."

He couldn't resist chuckling. "Well! Your question is rather—"

"Nervy? Ballsy?"

"Both."

"You don't have to answer. I'm just being obnoxious." At once she snickered. "Tell me anyway."

Frank, now using his thumbs to stroke the column of her neck, hesitated initially but then decided to respond. No point in seeming standoffish. What to say, though? Even if he revealed his darkest secrets, Laurie would find his activities so dull and ordinary that she'd assume he was—was *repressing* himself. "Okay," he said at last. "I stick pins in a wax doll of the bishop."

"Seriously."

"I surf the Web for pictures of nuns in full habit."

"Yeah, right."

"I face Mecca five times a day, kneel on my prayer mat, and chant *Allahu akbar.*"

"Come on."

"I do what most people do. I watch TV, listen to music, read mysteries, stuff like that. I tend my garden. I stare out the window and wish I didn't have to do the stuff I'm supposed to be doing."

"What else?"

"I cook a lot."

"What else?"

"Nothing else."

"No special private priest stuff?

"Well, I pray—but not as much as you might imagine."

"I'm shocked."

"Don't tell Pete."

"My lips are sealed." She fell silent for a moment. "That's it?"

"I'm a total bore," he said. Then, perilously, he asked: "And you?"

Another smile. "Okay, here's my secret: I sit in bed and eat chocolates and stroke my breasts."

"A tough job," Frank said, amused, "but someone's gotta do it."

"Sort of like having a pet I can—pet."

"Two pets."

"They don't call 'em puppies for nothing."

"Apparently not."

"Woof."

"Woof indeed." Flustering, he felt his cheeks flush. Sweat prickled on his forehead. How remarkable to find himself exchanging ribald banter with this beautiful woman—a woman literally at his fingertips! If she talked like this during a back rub . . .

The phone rang.

Frank felt as if he'd been punched. He could feel Laurie flinch.

Again! The damn phone!

From down the hall Frank heard a recorded voice speaking in the same clear, calm, emphatic tone he might have heard from her during an EMT call: "This is Laurie. Leave me a message."

Beep!

Now the caller's voice: male, low-timbered, and abrupt. "Laurie, pick up the phone." Frank recognized it immediately as Tyler's. A pause. "Pick up the phone."

Laurie turned her head to listen more closely. The muscles of her back and shoulders didn't tighten so much as *solidify*. Frank felt dismayed by how rigid, how much less supple, her body felt.

"Pick up the phone."

She stood suddenly, prompting Frank to pull his hands away and step back. She strode through the kitchen and into the hall. Frank lost sight of her and heard no verbal response to Tyler's command.

"Pick up the phone, Laurie. I know you're there. Listen to me: *pick up the goddamn phone."*

Silence.

Tyler again: "This is an emergency. Something's happened. *Talk* to me."

Laurie's voice, sotto voce: "What's up?"

With the machine now interrupted, Frank could hear Laurie's voice alone, and not too clearly: "I was soaking in the tub . . . Yeah. Damn right you are." A long silence. "—well maybe so, but doesn't mean you just fuckin' order me around— Okay, okay. No. *No.* Absolutely not. No— Tyler, you have no right to say that."

Frank, still standing next to Laurie's chair, grew more and more uncomfortable as he listened. Maybe he should start cleaning up the kitchen? They weren't really finished with the meal, were they, so cleanup might seem presumptuous, even insulting, to his hostess. Worse yet, he would have to move closer to the hallway to gain access to the sink, so Laurie might mistake his actions for an attempt to eavesdrop. Worst of all, Tyler might hear the click of plates and cutlery or the clank of skillets as he washed them.

"—later."

Frank heard a sudden clack: the phone shoved into its stand.

He expected footsteps but heard nothing.

Should he check up on her? Return to the table and finish eating? Check his own phone for messages?

"Sorry about that," Laurie said, returning abruptly to the kitchen. "Tyler, as you might have noticed."

"Is everything all right?"

"Apparently there's a personnel issue at the squad, but Tyler won't explain what's going on, and I'm not convinced it's such a big deal that he needs to bother me on my one evening off this week. No, it's really not quite so serious as that."

"If you have to go—"

She looked glum and distracted. "I— Damn. I guess I should. Not that I want to—" She walked over to the table. Sat again. "In a few minutes— Ten, fifteen—" She stared at her food. "Frank, I'm sorry. You know what it's like with the squad." Another pause. "Where were we?"

The shimmering bubble of the moment had burst. They resumed talking, but of course the real response to *Where were we?* wouldn't have been words, wouldn't have been an unsettled silence, either, which was what now fell between their sporadic bits of conversation. A true response to *Where were we?* wouldn't have been feasible, either: Frank returning to knead those marvelous shoulders, easing her tension, and letting his hands proceed to offer solace of other sorts. Maybe not just his hands . . .

Now, following five or six minutes of awkward exchanges, Frank said, "I shouldn't keep you. I'd better go."

"Maybe so."

"It's later than I thought."

"I should figure out what's bugging Tyler."

"Good luck with that." Getting up, Frank added, "I guess it's not ideal for me to say, *Tell him hi from Frank.*"

"Probably not." She smiled but avoided his gaze.

"Well, then." He looked around, couldn't spot the sweater he had brought with him, decided it must be on the sofa, and walked to the living room. On finding it there, Frank decided to use the toilet, so he went around the corner to the bathroom.

He locked the door, stood in the dark. Head pounding. Pulse echoing in his ears. Frank couldn't imagine leaving yet felt a sudden urgency to flee, to seek the calm routine of the parish house. What accounted for the vertigo swirling through his entire body? He hadn't really drunk so much—three beers, or was it four? Maybe that explained it. Or not. Whatever. No matter what the cause, this wasn't a good state of mind.

He tried to steady his nerves. He took long, deep breaths, just what he'd urge an upset client to do. Was he upset? No, far from it. Not upset. *Jangled.* The lingering, still intense exhilaration he had felt before Tyler intruded with his phone call— Massaging Laurie's back, for pity's sake! So slight an event, really nothing at all, yet a strange feast that left him at once sated and ravenous. What exquisite textures, what perfection of smoothness! What clearer sign that being alive was good, rich, and full? Standing there, Frank reveled in the memory of touching her and marveled that even if this occasion had now been disrupted, Laurie herself remained on the other side of this door. Laurie, still there—

Dizzy, he recalled why he had stepped into the bathroom. His bladder and indeed his entire pelvis ached as he stood there in the dark. How strange, he thought, how risible, this periodic necessity of unloading liquid from the human body! Frank flicked on the lights. And how remarkable now to discover as he unbuckled his belt, unsnapped his pants, and unzipped his zipper that his bladder wasn't the sole locus of discomfort. Clumsy from all that beer, he let his pants fall to the floor. How could he have been so unaware?

He faced a far different sight from what he expected to find in the full-length mirror mounted on the bathroom door. Not just the round-shouldered man there, his paunch looming over his fat thighs, the hair on his legs as salt-and-peppery as his beard. All of those features looked familiar. No, what surprised Frank was the erection poking up over the rim of his underpants and nudging against the bulge of his belly. Small wonder, though, given his conjuring of Laurie's image.

To his further surprise, the hard-on didn't wilt. Seeing it reminded him once again of Laurie, of his longing for her, of the woman herself a few feet beyond the door, of his having caressed her, and these thoughts kept his flesh inflated.

He stood there and stared. What a sorry sight. Maybe it's just as well that he had taken his vows. If he were an available, almost-sixty-year-old bachelor, who would want him—a pale, furry, big-bellied tub o' lard? If he were instead a long-married husband, what wife would stay patient with such a dumpy guy as he quickly went to seed? Better to keep himself and his this unbidden boner out of circulation, out of trouble, out of commission. "At ease, private," he said. "Stand down and await further orders."

Somehow his dick wouldn't deflate. The more Frank urged it to diminish, the more he thought of Laurie. Not just the thought of her beautiful body, at once muscular and soft to the touch. Not just the fantasy of holding and stroking her everywhere. Of feeling her breath against his face. Of tasting her skin, her lips, her tongue. Of embracing skin to skin, of holding each other chest to chest.

"Hey, Frank—you okay?"

Laurie's voice revealed puzzlement and even a little concern.

How long had he been standing in the bathroom?

"I'm fine. I'll be out in a jiff."

"Okay, just checking."

He came to his senses. Waddling over to the toilet, he almost tripped over his pants. He stood there. Tried to aim downward but couldn't. Waited and waited. Still couldn't.

How annoying: his pecker wouldn't soften but stayed hard and vertical, ignoring his entreaties—as rigid, upright, and useless as a plaster saint.

23

For days after that Frank felt out of sorts—uneasy, unnerved, uncertain. The hours with Laurie had been the most enjoyable occasion he could recall in many years, yet in retrospect the time together had also been a harrowing close call. Such a wonderful evening. Such a sense of closeness. Such a brush with disaster. In an odd way, Frank owed a great debt of thanks to Tyler for inadvertently crashing the party. Then at once a thought occurred to him: was the phone call truly accidental? Did Tyler perhaps have some notion of what was occurring that night and had thus chosen to disrupt it? In addition to all the other emotions swirling through his mind, Frank felt deep foreboding about this possibility. Personnel problem, indeed! What ever had prompted him to spend an entire evening with a young woman in the privacy of her own apartment? To drink so much beer that he had loosened up, had set aside his better judgment, had indulged himself in physical intimacy with her? Innocent enough, he told himself—just a back rub! But one thing could easily have led to another. In fact, the delightful but perilous sequence of steps had already commenced by the time the phone rang. Would that have been so terrible? he wondered. He didn't even feel comfortable answering that question. Whatever the moral issues involved, the looming presence of a third party in the background filled Frank with anxiety and alarm. What if Tyler hadn't phoned but had stopped by the apartment instead?

"Is anything the matter?" Pete asked when he and Frank crossed paths on Monday evening.

"No—why do you ask?"

"You seem rather subdued."

"I'm fine. Tired but fine."

"Okay, just curious."

Frank felt relieved when Pete, fixing himself a sandwich, retreated to his study to catch up on paperwork. He simply wanted to be alone for a while. He wanted to think through what had happened, to make sense of what he was feeling. Fat chance of that, given all his obligations.

Worst of all, he found himself longing for Laurie with such intensity that his whole body ached . . . while at the same time he contemplated the option of calling in sick for his squad shift on Thursday, all the better to avoid her just a few days longer.

24

Unbidden, an odd event.

Frank had given up visiting the gym in Arvada. Even before the recent turn of events, he hadn't wanted to risk bumping into Tyler. He would be better off resorting to the university's athletic complex instead. Although he didn't look forward to working out among the faculty and students there, the dangers of feeling awkward on campus now bothered him far less than that other, more troubling possibility. Attending Family Day at the facility's pool would be a low-stress alternative: faculty and staff would be present, along with their offspring; the RMU students would probably stay clear; and in this setting Frank would have an easy way to get some exercise. The Olympic-sized, dome-covered indoor pool would offer a setting on that particular day far more attractive than a gym full of yuppies and undergraduates.

Initially the situation didn't work out as planned. The pool was much more crowded than he had anticipated. Frank tried to swim laps but couldn't—too many people in the water. Dozens of teens and preteens horsed around, the boys playing raucous games, the girls socializing loudly in clusters. A few adults navigated among the adolescents, most of them either stroking their way alone through the pool or else teaching their young offspring how to swim. Other kids, too, were present in profusion: they bobbed and splashed all around, zig-zagged through the water, swam under the surface, and breeched without warning, as frisky as harbor seals. The din was intense.

"Caitlin! Caitlin! Caitlin, over here!"

"—if you do that again!"

"Yeah!"

"—and Jerry—"

"Stop *splashing* me!"

"Michael!"

"*—sea monster!*"

Frank grew annoyed. In another twenty minutes the Adult Swim would start, but he might have to leave earlier, so exhausting was this aquatic free-for-all.

Then, abruptly, the clouds shifted, the rich blue Colorado sky opened up, and sunlight poured through the dome and suffused the water. The light was so intense that it became the water and the water *became* the light. All those bodies now appeared to be held in the light, suspended in it. Somehow what had felt oppressive until that moment—so many human beings in motion all around him—suddenly felt comforting, even delightful. The thought struck Frank just then that maybe this is what heaven would be like: everyone at once fully individual yet fully together, untrammeled by gravity, unburdened, free of loneliness, illuminated, joyful.

25

Two days later, when Frank decided to proceed with his regular shift, he sat with Tyler and Laurie as they grabbed a quick supper at the local Denny's. Tyler, smirking, asked: "So: you know why Mexicans refry their beans?"

"Go ahead," Laurie told him wearily, "just get it over with."

"'Cause they're too stupid to do it right the first time."

Frank couldn't believe that Tyler would resort to telling that pathetic old joke. Would tell it with clear intent to pick a fight. Did the reference to Mexican food imply an awareness of what had transpired so recently at Laurie's apartment? Was this the opening skirmish in a wider battle? Frank gazed out the window, sipped his coffee, and pretended not to give a damn.

Tyler wouldn't let up. "*Refried* beans! Unlike *some* situations I could mention, you'd think once would be enough."

"Just ignore him," Laurie told Frank. "The guy obviously has a problem with Mexicans, but you know why? It's not you. It's the Mexican who divorced him."

Old news, Frank thought, but good to have her state it openly.

Snorting, Tyler said, "Well—my ex sure as hell is *one* of the problems."

"The joke would be funny," Frank said abruptly, "if it weren't based on a mistranslation. Everyone assumes that refrito means 'refried,' but it doesn't. In Mexican slang, *re-* is a prefix that means 'very.' So *frijoles refritos* aren't 'refried beans' at all—they're 'very fried beans.'"

Tyler's expression revealed his struggle to stay patient. "Very fried beans. What the fuck are very fried beans? If that's the situation, I say just go ahead and fry 'em twice."

Before Laurie could intervene, the radio's alarm went off. The dispatcher's voice: *"Pediatric emergency—"*

"Great," Tyler said. "Always a joy."

"—possible gunshot wound—"

"Shit!"

Startling the other customers, the EMTs got up from their booth abruptly, grabbed their jackets, and strode out of the restaurant. Tyler had parked the ambulance right in front. He took the driver's seat, Laurie got in next to him, and Frank sat back in the compartment.

Tyler pulled out and drove way over the speed limit.

"Slow down," Laurie said.

He ignored her. Frank knew by now that nothing could restrain Tyler on a pediatric call.

Laurie twisted around to speak with Frank in the compartment. "If it's what the dispatcher says, it's gonna be bad. Here's the plan. Tyler and I will focus on the kid. You interact with the parents, okay? Do whatever the cops tell you. If it's possible to engage with the mom and dad, that's your assignment. They'll be upset, I guarantee it, so try to calm the situation."

Frank felt his stomach tighten. *Possible gunshot wound . . .*

A long stretch, a left turn, then straight again for many blocks at near-highway speed. Rush hour had eased, so at least traffic wasn't a problem. After a few gut-wrenching turns, Laurie told Tyler once again to ease up. Once again he ignored her. They headed west and entered one of the newer subdivisions. Tall houses, big yards, three-car garages. As Tyler parked the rig in a driveway, Frank looked through the side door's window and spotted three squad cars in front.

The situation inside the house was even worse than what he'd expected. Cops swarmed through the place, six or seven officers. Two cops inside the house were doing CPR on the victim, a girl maybe six or seven years old, who lay on her bedroom floor. Frank couldn't believe the amount of blood—blood on the floor, blood on the bed, blood on the cops' hands, blood soaking the girl's Hello Kitty pajama top. The kid was motionless and blue-gray. In the doorway between the hall and the bedroom, a man and a woman thrashed and hollered as three officers attempted to restrain them. So many people were shouting that Frank needed a moment to grasp that parents were speaking Spanish.

"¡Te dije!" the woman bellowed. "¡Te dije que guardes esa pinche pistola!"

Laurie told Frank, "Do your thing." Then she and Tyler walked over to the cops crouching beside the girl.

Frank heard one of the officers speak to them: "—kid brother found a loaded pistol—"

Frank could scarcely move, he felt so overwhelmed, but he forced himself to retreat into the hallway. The parents screamed and struggled with the cops.

"¿Cómo les ayudo?" Frank asked.

They didn't even acknowledge his presence.

Then, abruptly, three more people barged into the house: two men and a woman in dark blue uniforms: medics. Frank felt relief so intense that it dizzied him.

The medics pushed into the hallway and entered the bedroom. Frank couldn't see well enough to follow the action, but he could tell that for several minutes they attempted to treat the child. Then, abruptly, one of the medics carried the girl out of the bedroom in his arms. At the exact moment of his walking past the parents, the mother broke away from where she had been standing with Frank and the officers, she lurched over to the medic holding her daughter, and she started tugging at the girl's limp body. "Ay, Dios!" she wailed. "No— No, no— Ay, por Dios—no! Por favor, Dios mío—no, no, no!" Two cops grabbed the woman and pulled her away. Then all the medics left the house with the child, Laurie and Tyler followed, and a short while later Frank heard an ambulance pull out, sirens blaring.

The parents followed soon after, the mother and the father in separate squad cars, each with a separate pair of cops.

The sirens faded. Noise continued inside the house: a child wailing, an older woman's voice shouting in Spanish, police radios jabbering.

Frank looked at Laurie and Tyler standing in the doorway.

"Fuck!" Tyler shouted. "I mean—*fuck!*"

"We did what we could," Laurie told him.

"Yeah? Well, I say *fuck!* That was the biggest crock-of-shit call in my whole sorry career. I mean, what the hell makes these people think they're parents, allowing kids access to a loaded gun?"

Recoiling from what he saw, heard, and smelled in this wretched place, Frank suddenly needed to be somewhere else. Anywhere else. He left the hallway, crossed the living room, and stepped out onto the front porch.

Tyler followed him. "Go back and get our stuff," he said. Then to Laurie: "Gunshot wound to the chest! Little bro plugs his sister right through the heart. Lucky for us the medics came riding over the horizon."

Standing on the lawn near some bushes, Frank needed a moment alone before he realized how awful he felt. Not just upset—bilious, faint. He fought the urge to vomit. Something swelled inside his chest, a fist-sized stone or brick lodged there. He began to grasp that he might pass out. He turned to Laurie and Tyler. "I'm sorry, but I need to talk with you."

Tyler stared at Frank, his face tight with anger. "I said *go get our stuff.* Shall we hang here all night? Maybe join the family for some target practice?"

Frank's own words surprised him: "I think I'm having chest pain."

Laurie looked at him with an expression he couldn't fathom: surprise, alarm, or both.

"*Chest pain,*" Tyler echoed. "We're finishing up the worst-ever pediatric call and you decide you're having *chest pain.*"

Frank took a few steps toward the ambulance. Bracing himself with one hand against the rig's side door, he used the other hand to rub his chest like someone kneading a cramp.

"Come here," Laurie told him. She took his arm and guided him toward the door. Opened it. "Sit down." She helped Frank sit on the rig compartment's floor.

Tyler stepped closer. "Un-friggin'-believable."

"I'm sorry," Frank said.

"Don't be sorry," Laurie told him. "Just tell us what you're feeling."

Tyler intervened. "Let me say this: if you're gonna fuck up a call as fucked up as this one, you sure as hell better be having some actual fuckin' chest pain." Then, as Tyler looked at him more closely, Frank observed a change in his expression. He saw what Laurie called Tyler's EMT Look: the line of his lips softening, the light in his eyes shifting. His tone of voice, too, began to ease. "Talk to us, bro. What's happening?"

"I don't know," Frank said. Fire kindled in his chest. Flames spread.

Laurie and Tyler assisted Frank into a standing position, stepping into the rig, and sitting on the gurney. Unbuttoning his shirt and rolling up his sleeve, they took his vital signs and prepared to run the EKG machine. Neither of them commented on his vitals or on the EKG strip. Spreading, Frank's pain raged throughout his torso.

Laurie asked Tyler, "Who's driving?"

"You," he said. "I'll stay here and give Frank some TLC."

Hearing Tyler express *tenderness,* of all things, worried Frank most of all.

Frank looked at Laurie. He wanted her to stay, wanted her to be the person attending to him. "Can't you—?"

"You'll be fine, I promise," she told him. "Let's go get you checked out."

III

FALL INTO WINTER

26

This is an old story, " Dr. Bedarian told Frank in her examination room the day after his long night at the Emergency Department. "Which I realize doesn't make it any less terrifying, of course—how closely and intensely heartburn can mimic the signs and symptoms of a heart attack."

"Heartburn," Frank echoed wearily.

"In a city this size, what you experienced probably happens to several dozen people a day. It's a standard E.D. scenario."

So reassuring, these words, but they still left him feeling like an idiot. "A standard scenario," he said, "but I wasted a dozen people's time, energy, and concern over nothing."

Dr. Bedarian reached out to rest a hand on his forearm. "Frank, don't beat yourself up. You did the right thing. How could you have known?"

Such a warm touch, literally. A touch he found calming as he sat on the examination bench, once again attired in the ridiculous patient gown, once again feeling both absurd and delighted as he spoke with this kind physician. "I'm an EMT now, right? I damn well ought to know the difference between heartburn and a heart attack."

"Nonsense. Even cardiologists can have difficulty telling one from the other until they do an EKG and see the lab work."

"Still—"

"There's no *still* about it. You were absolutely right to check out the situation rather than assume there's no problem. What if you were having an M.I.? Would it have been better to whistle in the dark? Okay, it was a false alarm. You experienced just about the best-case outcome. Nobody holds that against you. Now let's move on."

"Gladly."

She paused for a moment. Despite the affection obvious in Dr. Bedarian's smile, her eyes revealed a shrewd, clinical scrutiny. "Which doesn't mean I'll let you off the hook," she told him. "Better gastric-esophageal reflux disease than a myocardial infarction. True. That said, what you experienced is a problem in its own right. We have to take it seriously. It's not a major issue at the moment, but GERD can cause lots of damage, including esophageal cancer. I can't ignore the risk, and you can't, either. We should have a specialist do an upper G.I. endoscopy—"

"Agreed."

"We should also assess your diet for the so-called 'trigger foods'—"

"Fine."

"And forgive me for repeating myself—"

"You want me to lose weight," he said impulsively.

She smiled. "I sound like a stuck record."

"Don't apologize. After last night, I'll do anything you tell me to."

He returned to the parish house. Pete, eating lunch at the kitchen table, asked, "How'd it go?" and Frank said, "Just fine. Nothing serious." That was the end of it. Pete knew about the appointment, since Frank had requested help pinch-hitting at the Center that morning, but he wasn't aware of the E.R. visit the night before. Best to keep it simple. No need to cause even more concern about The EMT Thing.

Frank heated water in the kettle, warmed a cup of milk, fixed himself a caffè latte, carried the mug through the house to the back door, and stepped outside. Late morning. Sky overcast, air cool and still. By now the garden had been totally Novembered— the greenery gone, the plants withered, the few pumpkins half-rotted, the last tomatoes reduced to flat brown bags. The lawn was gray-tan. The coeds' next-door yard lay empty, the young women's sleek, slick bodies now a faded memory. Frank turned to gaze in the other direction and caught sight of Margaret Beach watching him through her kitchen window. Tempted briefly to wave, he simply turned his back on her.

What are you feeling? he asked himself—the same question he routinely posed to confused counselees. Once again he felt the slap of embarrassment over the E.R. visit. So many people sizing him up! Poking and prodding him! Connecting him to high-tech machines! Skewering his arm to take blood! He recalled his boredom as well. After the initial rush of activity, hours of waiting. Hours that Laurie and Tyler could have spent caring for people in the community rather than sitting with Frank in the examination booth. Hours they could have devoted to saving lives rather than killing time. He felt a lingering sense of fear, too, each minute suffused with dread. Dread that he would die. Worse yet, dread that he would die in this noisy, too-bright E.R. Worst of all, dread that he would have no final time alone with Laurie, no last chance to speak with her in private. Tyler, of all people, stood nearby, expressionless. And the cause of all this embarrassment, boredom, and dread? *Heartburn!* All this commotion over a case of indigestion.

The other question he asked himself: *What's the big picture?* Once again what he would have asked a befuddled undergraduate. *Let's pull back and get the wide-angle view. What does this situation show us overall?* Well, he told himself, invoking the current cliché: *You dodged the bullet.* Bullet indeed! The pain last night felt as if someone had shot him through the heart. Someone? No, the would-be assassin was Time, the ultimate gun nut. Only blanks that night, not live ammunition . . . but warning shots all the same. Frank was four months shy of fifty-eight. Papi had dropped dead at fifty-four, Mami at sixty-three. How many middle-aged relatives, friends, and parishioners had died over the years? Dozens. It wasn't hard to connect the dots. The diagnosis of heartburn let him dodge the bullet, true enough, but many more rounds would be waiting in the clip. Unlike the psychopathic young males unloading their guns in workplaces, shopping malls, theaters, and schools, Time would never run out of ammo.

Frank shifted his thoughts to the patient from the call last night. What of her? Nausea welled up again as he recalled that pathetic child. A little girl dying of a gunshot wound was bad enough. Worse yet, dying at the hands of her three- or four-year-old brother! And what of the little boy? How would that child manage to carry the weight of having killed his sister? Even a sleepless night of revisiting the whole wretched incident let Frank scarcely begin to grasp what had happened. The more he tried to shove the images away, the more they spread and festered in his mind. The gray child. The blood all over everything. The frantic parents. The mother's rant against her husband: *"I told you! I told you to hide that goddamn pistol! And now— And now—"* The sight of the husband, frantic and flailing, not exploding but imploding. Frank found solace in knowing that his own medical crisis hadn't deprived the child of the care she needed . . . though if his symptoms had started earlier, his problem—indigestion!—surely would have. Then what?

The squad. What to do about the squad . . . He had disrupted a shift, had almost deprived a horribly injured child of medical attention. He had alarmed Laurie and exasperated Tyler—had inspired pity in the former, contempt in the latter, and surely abundant doubts in both regarding his presence on the squad. How should he respond? He recalled Laurie's final comments following his discharge from the E.R.: "Take whatever time you need to recover from this g.i. problem, okay?" But as Dr. Bedarian had explained the following day, reflux was a chronic issue, not an acute problem, one that wouldn't require high-tech treatment or a suspension of activities. What, then, was Laurie suggesting? *Take whatever time you need* . . . Was she hinting that Frank should back off for a while? Should resign, even?

Frank thought over Tyler's parting remarks as well. Arriving back at the squad around four a.m. after leaving the hospital, Frank stepped down from the ambulance and stood in the parking lot. He had already thanked both Laurie and Tyler, he felt tempted to do so again, but he knew that succumbing would backfire. They lingered awkwardly. He said, "I'll see you soon."

Laurie nodded. "Get some rest."

Tyler had already sauntered off.

Frank turned away when Laurie followed Tyler toward the squad house. He walked over to his car, fumbled with his keys, unlocked the door, and eased wearily into the driver's seat. Starting the engine, he just sat there.

He jolted when someone rapped on the glass: Tyler. Frank lowered the window.

Leaning in close enough that Frank could smell the guy's cigarette breath, Tyler said, "A word to the wise. If you're gonna be on this squad, I suggest you figure out ASAP how to be a care *giver*, not a care *needer*."

"I'll keep that in mind."

"Good idea."

27

What alternative did Frank have, really, other than getting back to work?

"Tell me a little about how you're feeling these days," he told Celeste during her session that afternoon.

Seated squarely in the chair, feet flat on the carpet, hands palm-down on her thighs, she showed prim body language compared to most other RMU students, who habitually sprawled or slouched. She was motionless except for reaching up once to nudge a blonde lock behind her left ear. "I'm fine."

"Coping with your academic work?"

"It's been an okay term."

"Are you sleeping all right?"

"Pretty well."

"Eating regularly?"

She nodded.

"Taking your meds on schedule?"

"Mm-hmm."

"How about activities? Are you doing things on campus? Getting together with friends?"

She nodded.

All the right answers. Frank felt uncomfortable anyway, and not just because the answers sounded perfunctory. Were these fairly positive responses the whole story? Or was Celeste merely saying what she knew he wanted to hear? Further questions didn't yield more detail. His comments didn't prompt further discussion. His purposeful silences didn't elicit what other students might have provided—a wisecrack, a counter-question, a tale about campus life. He couldn't seem to get at her. Celeste reminded him of a bead of mercury he had examined four decades earlier in a high school science class: he could push it and prod it, could even reshape it with his finger, but the strange liquid yielded to his touch without ever letting him break its surface.

They talked for a few minutes longer. From start to finish, Frank couldn't spot any signs that Celeste was troubled beyond what he already knew about. Perhaps her situation was stable. He had to take her reassurances at face value. He let the session sputter to a close. "Well, then. Good luck with everything. I'll see you next week. You know where to find me."

"I sure do."

Then his session with Mark: the usual hodge-podge of End Times anxieties.

"What I just don't understand is this," the boy said. "There's so much terrible stuff happening! Why doesn't God intervene?"

"A good question," Frank responded. "One that people have been asking at least since back when some tortured soul wrote the Book of Job."

The boy wouldn't relent. "Father, it's incredible. Just watch the news for five minutes and you'll want to puke! Wars, earthquakes, and terrible diseases! Terrorists setting off bombs! Plane crashes, floods, tornadoes! Crazy dudes shooting innocent people! Girls sold as sex slaves! Little kids getting abused! It's like evil is everywhere and out of control! I mean, why doesn't God *do* something?"

"Look. Sometimes I'd like to tell God what Sister Mary Margaret told me back in eighth grade: 'You're clearly quite gifted, but you're not performing up to your full potential.'"

The boy stared at him, clearly startled, even offended, but he didn't respond to Frank's remark. He brooded for a while, alternately staring at the floor and glancing irritably, until he announced: "Well, I think God *is* gonna perform up to His full potential. I think God *is* gonna intervene. And I think He's gonna do it really, really soon."

* * *

Then, to his surprise and relief, a more interesting client. Serena stepped into Frank's office to introduce her—"Ms. Espinoza to see you"—and then withdrew. Thirtyish, attractive, and more classily attired than most RMU students, this woman wore black slacks, a burgundy cashmere top, and a sleek wool jacket that complemented her elegant figure. Lustrous dark brown hair draped across her back and shoulders. Given her facial features and swarthy complexion, Frank assumed she was *latina*.

"Please come in."

"I'm so sorry to bother you!"

"No need for apologies—I'm here to help."

She reached out to shake hands. Warm, moist skin; firm grasp. "My name is Gabriela Espinoza."

"Frank Ochoa."

"Thank you so much for making time, Father."

"Please call me Frank."

She nodded but made no reply.

They settled into the chairs across from his desk. "Tell me what I can do for you."

She stayed silent for a few moments as if to collect her thoughts. No sign of tears, but she was clearly upset. "I just don't know how to explain the big mess of feelings in my head."

He gambled on switching languages: "*¿Prefieres continuar en español?*"

"Thank you, but I'd really rather talk in English." A long pause. "The problem isn't which language. It's— There's just too much happening for me to find the words either way. I don't even know where to start."

"Start where you feel most comfortable."

What followed was a much more articulate description than what this woman's apology had prepared him for. If anything, she was unusually organized, even systematic, in summarizing the issues she faced. She was thirty-two years old. Having grown up in a working-class family near Fort Collins, Gabriela had started college ten years earlier at the University of Colorado.

Her collegiate experience had gone well initially, although financial pressures required her to juggle two part-time jobs along with a full academic load. Then, falling in love with a man she met during her junior year, she became pregnant, decided to have the child, and married her boyfriend. Married life and parenthood started out well. She greatly enjoyed being a mother. Her husband was a devoted father. He was a frustrating, often difficult spouse, however, and in recent years the marriage had deteriorated. The couple had separated two years ago. Gabriela had filed for divorce. In the meantime, she had returned to college—she had won a scholarship for Latino students at RMU—and she was now just two academic quarters shy of graduation. "So I guess you could say there's a lot going on. Some of it's good, so I shouldn't complain. My son is wonderful. I'm about to get my degree in business administration. With any luck I'll move up to a better-paying job. I'm an optimistic person! But I just feel so . . . *stressed.*"

"With good reason."

"I'm so, so tired."

"Fair enough."

"Sometimes I just want to lie down and sleep for a hundred years."

Frank held back, giving her ample time to continue.

Instead of speaking, she made a sudden gesture: both hands raised abruptly, palms up, fingers flung outward toward him. She smiled suddenly.

"I hope you realize that your feelings are totally normal," he said. "How could you juggle so many tasks and responsibilities and not feel exhausted? Not feel stressed? Not feel upset?"

She gazed at him, then away, as her sadness welled up.

Frank let her sit with these emotions for a while. "What are you feeling?"

A long pause. "Lots! But Father, I can't afford to feel what I'm feeling. There's so much to do! There's always so much to do!"

"Always so much—absolutely. But you still have a right to be upset. Have a right to feel what you're feeling."

"My ex-husband is so *difficult.*"

"Which of course makes everything else more difficult, too."

"I'm running out of energy to cope. But if I get upset I'll fall apart, I know I will, and I'm afraid—"

He stayed silent.

"I'm so afraid—"

Again he restrained himself.

With her hands tightening repeatedly, grasping each other urgently, Gabriela forced herself to stay composed.

"You're afraid that if you fall apart, you'll never put yourself back together."

She nodded slowly, weeping now.

"Something like that?"

A nod and a smile.

"That won't happen," he told her. "You can fall apart and still be fine. You can fall apart and become all the stronger precisely because you've let yourself fall apart. Why? Because no matter what you may imagine, you won't fall apart and stay that way. Instead, you'll rearrange the pieces, you'll finish your degree, you'll get the job you want, and you'll be an even better mother than you are already."

She didn't break down; she simply sat there and wept calmly, wiping the tears from her right cheek with her right hand, then her left with the left.

"I want you to see this Center as a safe place for falling apart. For thinking through whatever next steps might be helpful. Is that acceptable? Useful, even?"

She nodded.

"The University may also have some other resources available."

"That would be nice."

"In any case, I encourage you to come here once a week so we can talk further."

"Thank you, Father."

"Please call me Frank."

28

He avoided the squad. Laurie had nudged him to "take whatever time you need," hadn't she?—"to recover from the gastric problem," or however she'd phrased it—so Frank had complied. Not for medical reasons, surely. More to give Laurie and Tyler a break from his company. To ease the tensions caused by his E.R. visit. He felt no physical distress now; popping a pill twice a day eliminated the hot-coal sensation in his chest. But staying clear of the squad house would let something else cool off, too. A quick message left on the squad's answering machine—"Sorry, guys, but I'm still under the weather"—solved the problem.

It wasn't as if he lacked enough to do. Counseling sessions, committee meetings, Interfaith Council discussions, the marriage preparation class . . . Logistical tasks for the rectory . . . Shopping and bill-paying . . . Celebrating Mass, hearing confession, marrying couples, baptizing babies and a few adult converts . . . Social obligations? Not many of those, fortunately, but the situation would change, would get complicated fast, once the holidays rolled in.

What, though, to make of the situation? What to do about it . . . whatever "it" might be. Frank had scared himself half to death, feeling pain like that, the worst he'd ever experienced. Had humiliated himself in front of her—and, for good measure, in front of the person he wanted most to impress—and, for good measure, in front of the person most likely to delight in his humiliation. Dr. Bedarian had assured Frank: "It's not a major problem at the moment." True . . . medically speaking. But beyond that?

Something nagged at him. Throughout the early phase of his "possible M.I.," as the E.R. doctors called it, Frank had been convinced he was dying. The pain, the difficulty breathing, the pressure in his chest . . . At any moment he would step across the transom into— Into what? Now wasn't that a doozy of a question! *The* question. So then what, exactly, had he been contemplating while *in extremis?* The Risen Christ? The mystery of Divine Grace? The state of Frank's immortal soul? The Four Last Things—Death, Judgment, Heaven, and Hell? None of the above. Throughout the whole incident, he hadn't given a moment's thought to what should have been focusing his mind. Spiritual concerns weren't even blips on his mental radar until hours later. No, he was thinking about . . . Laurie. Was wondering if she saw him as pitiable for being weak and pathetic. Whether she would forgive him for puking on her. What was that all about? Frank felt so uneasy about this situation that he pushed his discomfort aside.

Then, during what started as a congenial lunch at the parish house, Pete shifted the conversation abruptly: "There's an incident we need to discuss."

"I'm sorry?" Frank said. *"Incident?"*

"Something that occurred a few days ago."

"I'm not sure what you're referring to."

"Apparently you told one of your counselees that God is talented but not doing a good job."

"I may have said something like that," Frank responded, recalling Mark, the millennial alarmist. He couldn't believe this boy had popped up yet again like a neurotic Jack-in-the-Box.

"Does that comment strike you," Pete said, "as, what, rather *inappropriate?"*

"I said it for effect."

"You feel confident that a priest making that remark would have a good effect?"

"Under the circumstances, yes. The kid needed a jolt, theologically speaking."

Pete gazed at Frank with an expression that didn't seem angry or hostile so much as weary. "Look, you can hold any opinions you want, including theological opinions. I can't set you straight, the provincial can't, the bishops can't, even the Pope can't—"

"Much as you'd all like to try."

"For pity's sake, does it make sense to utter such words when a troubled soul is struggling?" Pete asked. "Really struggling? Struggling to maintain his faith?"

"Maybe."

"Oh really?"

"The kid needed a reality check. He's come down with a nasty case of eschatological hysteria. A little shock therapy seemed appropriate."

Pete sat back abruptly in his chair. "Appropriate! Do you have any idea how much your comments upset the boy?"

"We had an earnest conversation. We spoke openly about many matters. I invited him to come back—as I always do—so we could resume the discussion."

"Except that he probably won't come back. He's too upset. He thinks you've brushed him off—"

"I've done nothing of the kind."

"—so he came to me instead. Why? Because he doesn't trust you," Pete said, "and I daresay for good reason. Frank, you've violated the young man's trust. Violated it not just as a counselor but as a priest."

"Maybe so," Frank told him, finding it more and more difficult to remain at the table. He forced himself to stay seated. "But you're assuming that in my roles as counselor and priest, I should give this boy precisely what he wants. I should rubber-stamp his adolescent assumptions about God's actions in the world. Listen: this kid is under the influence of a fundamentalist roommate, the roommate being quite a wacko, to put it bluntly, and the counselee has picked up the roomie's notion that God is a celestial puppet master. Or, better yet, God is a coin-op vending machine stocked with eschatological fast food. You pop in some prayers, you push a few buttons, and out comes exactly what you've prayed for. Good grades. A cute girlfriend. Enough snow for a ski trip. A solution to the world's problems. The Second Advent, even."

Pete listened without interrupting but looked irritable.

Frank couldn't hold back. "You know why I pushed back? Here's the background. My most recent session with this kid followed a squad shift in which I witnessed the aftermath of an especially appalling incident. A six-year-old girl died of a gunshot wound. Why did the girl die of a gunshot wound? Apparently because her four-year-old brother found their dad's pistol, aimed it at his sister, and pulled the trigger. Of course everyone involved—notably her parents, as you might imagine—must now be wondering how this could happen, how God could possibly let an innocent child suffer such a fate?"

Pete raised his right forefinger like a student discreetly requesting permission to speak.

Ignoring him, Frank went on: "Good question! All I know is that we arrived at the house, we found the kid lying in a puddle of her own blood, the parents were both going ballistic—if you'll pardon the expression—and there wasn't much to be done. So if you're wondering why I remarked to the counselee how God sometimes comes off like an underachiever—"

"Frank, enough!" Pete said. "This is appalling."

Frank couldn't restrain a laugh. "Isn't that just the point? It's totally, utterly appalling. Beyond belief." He laughs again, this time at his own words. "Of course at the child's funeral the pastor will comfort the mourners. The girl's death may be incomprehensible, but it doesn't lack for meaning, right? The meaning is simply beyond our grasp. Beyond our ken. Rest assured, all ye who grieve: God has a plan we can't discern. His love is too deep for us to comprehend."

"Frank—"

"How, then, should we respond? With renewed faith."

"Frank, listen to me—"

"We must maintain our faith not despite this pointless, appalling loss but because of it."

Pete said, "That happens to be true. What's the alternative? Frank, there's nothing the least bit original in the doubts you're expressing. Need I remind you that greater minds than ours have wrestled with this issue—"

"Wrestled!" Frank exclaimed. "If you want to see wrestling, you should've seen the mom wrestle with her daughter's body. As if she could shake it back to life. She held the girl's body and shook it hard—hard enough, surely, to raise her daughter from the dead."

"I really don't have time for this." Pete stood suddenly, pushing his chair back.

"The mom said, 'Oh, God— No— No, no—oh, God, no! Please, God—no, no, no!'"

"Excuse me," Pete said. "I have some phone calls to make."

Very well, Frank told himself. Make your calls.

He could well imagine which calls those might be.

His own response was to decide *against* making a call of his own that he'd intended. He didn't phone the squad house to cancel yet another shift.

29

Padre."

"Tyler."

"Guess you're feeling better."

"Much better, thanks."

"Cool."

Frank, entering the squad's ready room a few days later, wasn't prepared for this civility . . . or for what counted as civility in Tyler. Laurie must have given him a talking-to. Where was she, anyway? Tyler sat alone on the sofa eating a burger and flipped through a catalogue.

EMERGENCY ESSENTIALS
Be Prepared For Anything!

The door to the bays swung open just then: Laurie. Carrying two cardboard boxes, she walked in and stopped short. Quick smile. "Hey."

"Hello." How awkward to see her again . . . and how delightful.

"Glad you're back."

"I've missed the place."

"Missed the *action?*" Tyler asked without even looking up.

Frank expected a lecture, even a tirade, probably doubling back on the incident of Frank's supposed chest pain. *You gonna carry your weight? Gonna make sure you don't make a tough job even tougher?* Tyler only gazed at him for a moment, then returned to his catalogue.

Laurie closed the door. She set down the boxes, pushed a chair away from the coffee table, and sat.

191

Frank seated himself nearby.

She asked, "Sure you're up for this?"

"The doctor says I'm fine. I feel fine. Let's give it a try."

"Fair enough."

Tyler ignored them.

"How's it been here lately?" Frank asked.

"Typical," Laurie said. "Weather-related fender-benders plus two bigger MVA's. People with flu. Old folks falling on the ice. The usual kid stuff—cuts, fevers, asthma, burns. A few teen OD's. Nothing to write home about."

"Sounds almost bearable."

"Almost. Staffing's been tight."

"All the more reason for me to get back here."

"If it works for you, it works for us."

Glancing up over the rim of his catalogue, Tyler said, "Did you know that freeze-dried foods have nearly indefinite shelf life? Ten, fifteen, twenty years. Stuff lasts damn near forever."

Frank hoped for a slow shift, slow enough to allow chat time with Laurie. Not because he wanted a heart-to-heart: too risky. But hanging out and catching up would do them good. Having Tyler in the background or even joining the conversation itself might work well, too. Anything that reset the dial. The situation felt auspicious. Unpacking supplies, sweeping the bays, doing paperwork—these tasks offered a good backdrop. Restocking the rigs, especially, would give Frank and Laurie a chance to talk with a modicum of privacy.

Frank carried clean towels and sheets to the ambulance, stepped up into the patient compartment, and placed the linens into their cabinets. Laurie followed with a box of non-rebreather masks and oxygen tubing.

"So."

"So."

"Once again I want to say—"

"*Don't.*"

"It was so awkward."

"Of *course* it was. Getting sick is awkward. It happens, though, doesn't it? I've noticed that over the years. I bet you have, too. Been through it myself. So: it happened, it's over, you're fine."

Frank watched her place some plastic packets into the proper drawers. "I know I didn't exactly commit a mortal sin that night, but I messed up the call. A terrible call."

"You weren't the only one who found it terrible."

"I'm sure."

"Imagine how Tyler felt, seeing a dead kid his son's age."

"All the more reason for me to feel ashamed for being so self-centered. I've blown my credibility."

"I'm not sure what you're saying."

"Should I continue volunteering here?"

"That depends."

"On?"

"Whether you want to."

"And whether you do."

"Nothing I can think of would disqualify you."

"Tyler may disagree."

"It's not Tyler's decision," she told him. "Not his alone, anyway. There's the Performance Review Committee."

Frank nodded.

"Just like every new volunteer, You're on probation—you have been from the start—but you're still in good standing."

"You've checked up on me?" He wasn't sure if he felt pleased or offended.

"I don't need to. I'm on the committee."

"I see."

"I'll be blunt," Laurie said. "If you want to keep volunteering, fine. If you're having second thoughts, that's fine too."

She stepped out of the rig, walked somewhere else within the ambulance bays—he could hear the footsteps but couldn't see her—and returned a minute later with another box.

Frank told himself to restrain his question but couldn't hold back: "Do you have any opinion on the matter?"

Laurie smiled in a way that made his groin tingle. "Give me a break."

30

Liftoff! Seated among the other astronauts, Frank grew alarmed as the engines roared and the rocket trembled. Laurie's presence in the next seat calmed him. That, and the Zapotec villagers seated throughout the cabin—the men in their white homespun shirts and trousers, the women in their heavily embroidered blouses and long skirts. Frank felt reassured, too, that the spacecraft looked like the inside of an provincial Mexican bus: rows of straight-backed seats, luggage racks crammed with bundles, cheap suitcases, even a crate full of live chickens. Up front, Father Mariano manned the controls. The craft gained altitude.

Then, abruptly, a violent jolt. Flashing lights! Blaring alarms! Cascading system failures! Explosions!

Frank now found himself outside and falling, the panorama of Earth spread out below. Instead of fear and panic, however, he felt initial puzzlement, then calm. Then delight: Laurie was falling beside him at the same rate of descent. Weightless, they reached out to touch. They kissed. Frank unbuttoned her blouse, removed it, let it blow away. Laurie took off Frank's shirt. Slacks followed. Frank's underwear. Laurie's brassiere and thong. Now she floated before him naked and beautiful, her long hair billowing like flames. Buoyant, blissful, they embraced and caressed.

He awoke clutching his pillow. Lay there. No shame or bafflement lingered in his body, mind, and soul . . . just longing.

31

No snow fell. There should have been snow. Late November already . . . but without snow. A few squalls had hit the higher peaks and left them glowing white each day, but on the plains, even in the foothills: nothing. In a few days, Thanksgiving. Frank could recall storms during his boyhood that had blanketed the city in October, even in September, and one year on September first. Not any more. The air grew cold and blustery but stayed empty of flakes. Blown leaves scurried like lemmings as they rushed off to find their cliff, but no snow fell.

Walking to the Center, Frank crossed the campus among the students, some in chatty clusters, others walking alone, many of them texting, checking e-mail, or talking on their phones. Interesting, how eagerly these young people encapsulated themselves in their electronic bubbles. Somehow they coped.

He walked into the Front Range Café to buy a cappuccino. Waiting in line, he noted with a mix of delight and puzzlement when a lovely young woman ahead of Frank in line turned three times to glance at him and smile. She was a buxom brunette attired in hiking shorts, T-shirt, and a light cotton hoodie despite the cold weather. What could have prompted this beauty's persistent attention? When he grasped her identity at last—Stacey from next door!—Frank felt embarrassed to realize that he could barely recognize this young woman with her clothes on.

They ended up side-by-side while waiting for their beverages.

"Frank! Here we are!" she exclaimed with a loud laugh.

"Here indeed."

"I've *missed* you! Where have you been? I hardly see you any more!"

Her half-shouted words amused and embarrassed him. Were people staring? He said, "Life's busy, isn't it?"

"Sure is!" Stacey reached up and took her coffee from the counter. "How's the EMT business?"

"Sometimes easy, sometimes hard. So many people have health problems."

"But you like helping people, right?—so it must just be great."

"I try." The barista handed Frank his cappuccino. He took it and turned to Stacey, who had lingered instead of leaving.

"I try, too!" she exclaimed. "That's why I'm majoring in fitness sciences—to help people. And guess what? I'm learning CPR."

"Good idea."

"It's a requirement for the major."

"A smart thing anyway, having that skill."

"Right!" she blurted out, giggling. "You never know when you might have to save a life. Though of course right now we're just practicing on the dummies." Stacey snickered. "Dummies! It must be weird to do it with a real person—" She guffawed as she spoke the words *do it,* then continued: "—if you know what I mean."

Speaking with her, Frank felt what he always felt during these awkward conversations—zingy and energized. Who needed cappuccino when he could chat with Stacey? "Perhaps I do."

"You have to be ready."

"Always true."

"Well! It's great bumping into you, Frank! See you soon! Have fun saving all those lives!"

"I'll try."

Sessions: the usual. The New Usual, anyway.

Mark was conspicuous by his absence. Just as well—Frank had lost patience with Mr. End-of-Days and his tedious anxieties. Whatever blowback came of their recent squabbles, he would cope. No doubt Pete would complain to someone within the Order. So be it. Frank would receive a phone call; he would explain his side of the incident; the situation would subside. Meanwhile, at least he wouldn't have to interact with that strident little twerp.

Mike the frat boy? He seemed to be making progress. Was considering a move from his fraternity to off-campus housing. Was contemplating a switch of majors from Business Administration to Psychology. How reassuring to watch him move in positive directions.

Zach and Mindy and their ongoing pre-nuptial fracas? T-minus two weeks till the wedding . . . but the couple still couldn't agree on much of anything. Frank's efforts to focus on their communication problems went nowhere. Zach seemed irritable but passive. Mindy continued to obsess on issues of décor, the gown, the bridesmaids' attire, the guest list, and the requisite splendor of her ceremony. She even referred to the occasion in solitary terms: "My ceremony."

And Celeste . . . Where was Celeste? She had skipped two sessions in a row. Frank left three messages on her voicemail but received nothing in return. He made a note to phone the resident advisor at Celeste's dorm and ask how she was doing.

Dinner that night at the local trattoria: Marissa, Janice, and Jenna. He couldn't imagine greater solace than sitting in this warm place and enjoying *soufflé al formaggio facile, ravioli al ragu d'Anatra,* and a well-aged *mate brunello di Montalcino* with his three colleagues.

Early phases of the conversation touched on the women's respective spouses. Marissa's husband, Jack, was back in town following a denominational conference on immigration issues. Jenna's husband, Jake, had just been appointed head of the medical center's thoracic surgery department. Janice's wife, Arielle, had learned recently that a prestigious art gallery in New York would start showing her tapestries. Comments, congratulations, and toasts ensued. Jokes and jollity. Then, as if to fill the interpersonal gap in Frank's life, Marissa asked:

"How's your girlfriend?"

Frank couldn't restrain his laugh. "Girlfriend! Don't I wish!"

"What's this?" Janice asked, suspending her fork's progress halfway from plate to mouth. "Have I missed something?"

Jenna said, "Frank met a young lady at the ambulance squad. The sparks flew. That's all we know."

"That's all you'll know because that's all there is," Frank said. "There's been some mutual interest, but so what? The young lady in question has a boyfriend. I have a collar 'round my neck and a leash stretching all the way to Rome. End of story."

Everyone fell silent. Frank noticed a few glances among the women but couldn't interpret them; they had shifted into female telepathic mode.

Then Marissa said, "Well, obviously we can't really venture an opinion on the matter. We certainly can't *encourage* you, can we? Even saying it's a damn shame—pardon the expression—would be inappropriate. Still—"

"It's a damn shame," Janice said.

"It's a damn shame," Jenna said.

"Look," Frank told them. "This isn't actually a problem. I know where I stand. I know what I have to do. I have enough on my plate without a side dish of romance, so to speak." He laughed at his phrasing, just once but loudly. "My confrere is still distressed over my involvement with the squad, and rightly so—"

"Not if it's on your time off," Marissa said.

"Right. In theory. But in practice— Let's just say there's been some . . . dissonance. The squad is engrossing and intense. The work here at the Center is— I don't need to tell you three what it's like. So, the question comes up yet again: how many engrossing, intense commitments can a pastor manage? How many batons, clubs, scimitars, and flaming torches can a minister, priest, or rabbi juggle before he or she starts fumbling?"

Janice said, "I can't imagine you fumbling."

"Pete can, I assure you."

"Surely he's open-minded about the situation, isn't he?" Marissa said. "Even you priests can have outside relationships.

Friendships, right? With women as well as men. Isn't he willing to discuss it?"

Frank laughed louder than he intended. "He is! In fact, he's quite happy to bring up the squad every other day or so. As well as my ability to fumble. He's quite happy, in fact, to express his concerns to the provincial."

"The *provincial?*" Jenna said quizzically.

"The head of our region for the order."

"He's blowing the whistle on you?" Janice inquired. "On what grounds?"

"I guess I'll find out. Inattention to pastoral responsibilities, perhaps? Lack of commitment to RMU's Catholic community? Neglect of duties at the Center?"

"That's ridiculous," said Marissa. "I sure as heck haven't seen you neglect any duties."

"Maybe he has," Frank responded. "Or thinks he has."

"We'll vouch for you," Janice said.

Frank felt touched by their supportiveness but grew more and more uneasy as the discussion continued. Any reminder of Pete made him irritable. "Enough about me!" he said abruptly. "Thanks, all of you. Truly. But let's switch the subject. I'm tired of myself, tired of Pete, tired of the squad. Tell me more about *you.*" He turned to Jenna. "How are you feeling?"

She smiled despite looking surprised by his question. "How am I feeling? I'm feeling how every woman feels at this stage of a pregnancy: *Get this kid out of me!*"

Everyone laughed. "Ain't it the truth," said Marissa.

"To answer your question, though," Jenna said, "I'm fine. The O.B. doc says everything's going well for both the baby and me, which is all that really matters. So, T-minus five weeks and counting."

Janice said, "And Jake? He must be thrilled and excited."

"Both of those—and nervous too."

Marissa looked surprised. "Nervous? He's a doctor."

"Jake is the world's best husband," Jenna told them, "and the world's best father. He's also a fearless surgeon. He can open a patient's chest and operate for hours on the most challenging problems you can imagine. Lungs, aorta, chest wall, you name it. But labor and delivery? Not his finest hour. When I was giving birth to Eliza, my husband the fearless surgeon nearly fainted."

Frank couldn't resist coming to the man's defense: "I'd faint, too, under the circumstances."

"You're a different kind of father, Father."

"True."

"So, yeah—Jake is thrilled," Jenna went on. "He's ready. He'll be fine."

"To your health," Frank said, raising his glass. "All three of you."

The women raised their glasses and echoed his toast.

32

The sense of dread. It made no sense, but he couldn't shake it. Big trouble was coming, trouble far beyond a phone call from the provincial. That too, but something else, something worse, something out of the ordinary. Or had he simply picked up the contagious bug, a case of the jitters so many people were feeling. From Mark the apocalyptic undergrad, perhaps? Hard to say. All Frank knew was that he struggled each day with a deep malaise, an ache of foreboding. He woke up at night feeling as he sometimes felt while driving in bad weather, suddenly aware of misjudging the conditions: the road was slicker than he'd thought, the car had lost traction, he was about to skid. When that unease hit him, he would lie awake fretting and wondering. Would examine his psyche, probe his consciousness, ransack the cluttered trunk of his soul to locate the source of his anxieties. Worries about his heart? Frank would take his pulse: seventy-six and regular, not bad for a man his age. No angina pectoris. Something else, then? Something neurological, perhaps. One of those strange neuromuscular diseases . . . ? Yet further consideration persuaded him that his own health wasn't what caused these nocturnal worries. What, then? He sized up the options as if considering a differential diagnosis. His obligations at the Center . . . Pete's criticisms . . . The squad . . . Laurie's presence in his life . . . Tyler off to one side, watching and glaring . . . Weren't these sufficient issues, any or all of them? Yet somehow he couldn't feel sure he'd found what he was looking for, hadn't dug deep enough into his being to identify what might be festering somewhere inside.

* * *

Liturgical responsibilities: the usual. Counseling sessions: the usual. Bureaucratic tasks: the usual.

Students arrived and departed like migrating birds, each with a burden of legitimate but too-familiar anxieties, frustrations, longings, and confusions. More interesting than the rest were Aisha, a Muslim exchange student struggling to decide whether she should convert to Catholicism; Jerry, a gay student eager for Frank's repeated reassurances that he was altogether welcome in the university congregation; and Martin, a sophomore transitioning from female to male. Some of the "frequent flyers," as Frank referred to them in private, showed up as well. Mike, the ethically tormented frat boy. Zach and Mindy, the soon-to-be-married, probably soon-to-be-divorced young couple. Celeste, the clinically depressed transfer student. Conspicuously absent was Mark, Mr. End Times. Conspicuously present was Gabriela Espinoza.

"I just don't know what to think," she told Frank in the first few minutes of her second session.

"Think in what sense?" Frank asked.

"About my husband."

"Figuring him out?"

A terse laugh: Heh! "Don't I wish! I gave up figuring him out long ago!" After a pause she said, "As far as I can tell, he's un-figure-out-able."

"Mr. Mystery."

"Mr. Powder Keg. He's the husband equivalent of Wile E. Coyote in those old Road Runner cartoons. He's holding this big, round, black bomb, and the wick is lit and sending off sparks. Wile E. will either keep holding it and get blown up, or he's gonna throw it and blow up someone else. Only with my husband, the bomb never explodes."

"Maybe some day?"

"Maybe—but so far, so good."

"Lucky for you."

"Lucky for everyone."

"You think your luck will hold?"

"I sure hope so! But I can tell you this: all those sparks are bad enough. All that energy really puts me on edge."

"I can imagine."

"You know what his pals call him? For a nickname?"

Frank felt a shiver of unease. "Nitro?"

"Dyne-o-Mite."

Frank felt the room grow hot and close. His back, neck, and face began to prickle. "You're kidding." How could he have been such an idiot! *Of course.*

She chuckled. *"So* appropriate!"

He forced himself to say: "If that's what his pals call him, maybe you aren't the only person who considers him a powder keg."

"True. But I'm the one who lived with him. Who tried to raise a son with him. Who has to cope with him now on the custody issues."

Tyler! Just what he needed, getting caught up in that man's marital drama. Then he realized that Gabriela had continued talking and that he'd lost track of her comments.

"No, it's something else," she went on. "Something weird. He's so unpredictable, so . . . *impulsive.*"

He tried to imagine how he could respond to this situation, given RMU's guidelines for ethical practices. How would he avoid potential conflicts of interest.

Now she was addressing him directly: " . . . or should I—how do I put it—take a different approach?"

He tried to cover his lapse of attention. "Let's step back to what you said a moment ago. You referred to your ex as impulsive. Do you mean *physically* impulsive? Are you concerned he'll lash out at you?" Frank faltered, then put the question more bluntly: "Concerned he'll abuse you?"

She gazed at him thoughtfully. "Tyler isn't violent. A lot of people think he would be, or could be—he's such an angry man—but he's not violent. Never has been. I doubt he ever will be."

"You feel confident you're not in danger?"

"He won't hurt me, if that's what you're thinking. He'll huff and puff, he'll stomp around, he'll rant and rave. That's all. But Father, I'm still worried. Tyler has some funny ideas. He's convinced a huge catastrophe is about to happen . . . maybe even the end of the world. He wants to take action. He has a plan. I have reason to believe he's getting ready to bail out and head for the hills."

"Let him bail, then," Frank said, forcing a laugh. He recalled Tyler perusing that catalogue of emergency supplies. "That would solve some of your problems, wouldn't it?"

"Not if he takes Jared with him."

He feigned ignorance. "Jared?"

"My eight-year-old."

The words hit him like a slap. "He would abduct your son?"

"That's what I'm wondering. What I'm dreading."

"Has he threatened to take the boy?"

"Not threatened, no, but I'm sure it's on his mind. Tyler loves Jared more than anyone or anything. He'll do anything to keep him safe. Which isn't to say that taking him and hiding in the mountains would be the right thing. Like I said, he has some funny ideas. I'll say this much, though: Tyler's intentions are good."

"I wouldn't call abducting your son so well-intentioned."

"Of course not."

"More to the point, he has no right to abduct the boy even if he believes the world will end next Tuesday."

"You don't have to convince *me* of that."

"So let me ask you: what prompts a concern that Tyler would take your son?"

"All I can tell you is—he seems to think a big disaster will happen soon. I know he's committed to Jared's safety and well-being. So, putting two and two together—" She made a quizzical gesture. "It's not an unreasonable concern."

"I wouldn't think so."

"Something else: he has this girlfriend."

Frank now listened with even greater focus. "And?"

"She's an EMT just like him. Not a bad person. Kind of a tough cookie, but that's his problem. My problem is: I don't trust her.

She's never had kids, she likes Jared, and she spends lots of time at Tyler apartment, so she's often there on visitation weekends. I wouldn't be surprised if she's egging Tyler on."

"She's encouraging him to abduct the boy?"

"Maybe not directly. Let's just say she's viewing Jared in the bigger picture."

"All three of them hiding up in the mountains?"

"Something like that."

They discussed the situation for another ten or twelve minutes but reached no conclusions. Frank wanted to continue but knew they were out of time. He made his standard comments to wind down the session. "These are important issues," he said, "and we'll explore them further next time. If there are major developments, please call me here at the Center."

33

Late that week, an uneventful but peculiar shift. Uneventful: no calls came in. Peculiar: two other events took place instead.

The first was the squad house cleanup. Foothills EMS crews took turns straightening up the place, and this week the task fell to Laurie, Tyler, and Frank. Routine housekeeping—no more, no less. Frank didn't mind the chores: surely preferable to just sitting in the ready room while his crewmembers watched sports on TV. He was surprised, however, when Tyler complained about this assignment.

"These supposedly organized EMTs live like pigs," he said, "then expect other folks to clean up after them."

Laurie snickered at these words. "You're not exactly Mr. Tidy yourself. Not if your apartment is any evidence."

"My apartment is my own business."

"Maybe so. But you know what? You'll lose points if Gabi sees your workplace is a pigsty."

Frank wasn't clear what this last remark meant—why would Tyler's ex-wife hold him responsible for his workplace?—but he grew alert and concerned to hear Gabi's name. Gabriela!

Tyler resisted at first, bitching every step of the way. Then, like an old car taking a while to warm up, he began to run more smoothly. Soon nothing would restrain him. While Frank and Laurie cleaned the kitchen, Tyler found some garbage bags and started throwing stuff out: trash, old magazines, fast-food bags and boxes, stale food from the fridge and the cupboards. The intensity of his efforts amazed Frank, almost shocked him. Vacuuming the meeting room, the dorm, and the ready room,

Tyler wielded the wand like a weapon, vanquishing dust and dirt as he bashed against the furniture and the baseboards. Tyler kept going even when Laurie told him to stop. Just as on a call, he revved up until the needle of his tachometer angled into the danger zone. Frank felt amused at first, then concerned, then almost frightened by the intensity, the ferocity, of what he witnessed. Watching Tyler, Frank couldn't help but wonder what drove the guy. Was he just trying to prove he wasn't a slob? Was he trying to one-up Frank in some way? Had he simply clicked into autopilot, shifted into EMT mode, and started treating the squad house as a busted-up patient in need of critical intervention?

Throughout his four-thousand-RPM effort, he regaled Frank with an intense commentary. "Laurie tells me, 'You'll lose points if your ex-wife sees this place.' Right! You want to know why? Padre, here's what it's like to be a father nowadays. Not a capital-F Father like you, but a *real* father. A down-to-earth father. A father who lost custody of his kid. Here's how the system works. You bust your ass, you work your fuckin' crock-of-shit job, you jump through every hoop like a fuckin' circus dog, you deposit your pathetic paycheck in the bank 'cause that's all you get—and then what? The State of Colorado garnishes your wages and walks off with sixty percent of your chickenfeed. Why? Because your ex-wife owns you. You're a slave. Even though you have the illusion of freedom—you don't live in a shack on her plantation, you've got your own apartment, right?—most of what you earn goes straight into her bank account. And all you can do is grin and say, *Yes, Ma'am, of course, Ma'am, whatever you want, Ma'am.* 'Cause if you don't—if you don't bow and scrape and do exactly what the bitch has sweet-talked the judge into doing—then you won't see your kid every other weekend, which is what the courts have decreed. In fact, you won't get to see your kid at all. That's the worst of it. You try to be a good father, you follow all the rules, you flush your own self-interest down the fuckin' toilet, but even then, after basically killing yourself to do what everybody tells you, you lose access to your own son. The social worker decides you're so stressed, depressed, repressed, and distressed that you're probably a risk to the kid's wellbeing. And here's the kicker: if you don't buff up your shabby workplace to the point that Martha Fuckin' Stewart would give you a gold star—well, the social worker will write a report saying you're a fuckin' psychopath, and then you may as well kiss the boy goodbye till he turns fourteen and has the legal right to come and see you of his own volition."

Doing his own chores, Frank let Tyler rant.

Soon they finished. Tyler looked weary yet also pleased with himself. "Okay, Ms. Happy Homemaker," he said, turning to Laurie. "Are you *satisfied?*"

"The place looks great."

"Damn right it does. I hope it meets your expectations, too, 'cause we wasted half the shift acting like Mexican domestics."

Only later did Frank understand why the cleanup mattered. Someone knocked on the door at five, Tyler got up to answer it, and Frank heard him speak with two people outside. The voices suggested a woman and a child. The visitors didn't come inside at first. Then, following a brief exchange, Tyler entered the squad house hand-in-hand with a small boy.

"Padre, this is my son," Tyler said. "Jared, this is Padre."

"Hi," said Jared.

Frank reached out and shook hands with the boy. Jared closely resembled his dad: the same stocky build, the same wavy black hair, the same serious gaze.

When Laurie walked into the room, Jared rushed over and gave her a long hug. She said, "Hey there, tiger."

"Hi! Hi! Hi!" The boy seemed unwilling to disengage.

"I've missed you."

"Me too!"

Then, turning to Frank, Laurie said, "Sometimes this great little guy hangs out with us."

Frank heard himself say words he should have held back: "What if there's a call?"

"What do you think?" Tyler snapped. "Jared drives the rig and renders aid while Laurie and I hang back and watch ESPN."

"All I meant—"

"Padre, relax. We have it all figured out."

Several minutes of awkward conversation followed. Frank noticed a few sharp glances between Laurie and Tyler. Gradually the situation began to ease.

"Okay—food." Laurie retreated to the kitchen. While the guys hung out in the ready room, she fixed hamburgers and fries. Then, after she served the meal, everyone sat in the meeting room to eat.

Soon they finished. Tyler said, "Okay, Bud, let's get to work." He removed three plastic bins from his locker, placed them on the ready room table, and set up his son to play with Legos. Tyler even joined the boy in his playtime. Frank, sitting on the sofa, pretended to read an issue of *Off Grid* magazine he'd found on the floor, but he kept glancing at the guys when he could do so undetected.

Tyler and his son sat facing each other at the table. Big flat plastic bins of Legos rested nearby on chairs to their right and left. Both males looked intent on their separate projects. Not just intent . . . transfixed. Father and son seemed unaware of Frank as he watched them. Maybe they weren't even aware of each other. Like toddlers: parallel play.

What Frank saw concerned him. The boy's face showed the same sadness as Tyler's—the mouth slack and cautious, as if not fully convinced that smiling was a good idea; the eyes glancing about slowly, warily, as if to say, *Okay, now what?* Depression? Hardly a shock, given what the kid was going through—his parents' divorce, the custody squabbles, his dad's touchiness and pent-up anger . . . Small wonder Jared was so withdrawn. What seemed different about the boy, however, was at least a sense of possibility. Frank could see that in his Lego project: an outlandish craft of some sort, a huge blue-red-black-white-yellow fuselage covered with windows and doors and sprouting six wings, three shark-like tail fins, and so many engines—propellers, turbo jets, rockets—that Frank couldn't even count them all. And Tyler? He was constructing a bunker of some sort, four inches square and built solely from black bricks.

"Hey, bud, whatcha got there?" Tyler asked his son.

"Nothing much."

"Sure looks like something to me."

No response. Jared shoved his hands into the bin at his right, churned the Legos, located the piece he wanted, and inserted it into his craft.

"What is that, anyway?"

Without looking up, the boy said, "It's this—thing."

"Oh yeah? What kind of thing?"

"Just a—thing."

"Must be some specific kind, don't you think? Far as I know there's no general kind of thing."

The boy kept building his invention.

"All I can say is—it sure looks pretty darn cool to me," Tyler went on. "Must be one of those super all-terrain vehicles, right? Multi-environment. Plane-sub-rocket-ATV. Am I right?"

Jared looked up for a moment and smiled. Frank thought, Good Lord, what a fine little boy. If Tyler could only see that smile for what it was, the perfect gift, perhaps he'd leave his son in peace.

He didn't. "A vehicle like that could be pretty darn useful. Yup, I'd say *more* than useful—*crucial.* 'Cause you know what, bud? With a vehicle like that you can survive anything. Floods, fires, tornadoes, hurricanes, riots, terrorist attacks, even nuclear war—"

Frank saw Laurie extend her right leg slowly from where she sat, giving Tyler a quick little kick in the butt. Tyler reached around and grabbed her ankle. That foxy stare: *I'll get you later.* At once she pulled away, amused but clearly annoyed, smiling abruptly at Frank in embarrassment. Jared didn't seem to notice.

"Yeah, you could survive anything," Tyler went on. "Which is important. You know why? 'Cause you never know what the world is gonna throw at you. Times are tough, bud. No telling what's gonna happen these days, so you have to be ready. Ready for anything. Ready to defend yourself, ready to protect what's yours, ready to protect the people you love."

Jared nodded.

"You know what I mean?"

Another nod.

"You know your dad would do that for you, don't you? Would defend you?"

No response.

"Jared."

Still no response.

"You know I'd do that for you, right?"

Frank felt more and more concerned as Tyler kept badgering the boy. At best his questions would disrupt the game. At worst he would trigger an argument with Laurie and make a shambles of Jared's visit. Frank felt relieved when Laurie said nothing, letting Tyler lecture his son even as the boy struggled to play in peace.

Then, looking more closely, he realized for the first time what Tyler had constructed: a cube-shaped bunker without any windows or a door, and inside it three Lego people—a man, a woman, and a kid.

Frank told himself to keep his thoughts to himself, but he didn't: "Looks like those folks are ready for the end of the world."

Tyler turned and stared at Frank with the unblinking gaze of a cat that, having cornered a mouse, is now calculating when to pounce. "Maybe they know something you don't."

"Or maybe the question should be: What does the *builder* know?"

"What *builder?*"

"The builder of the bunker."

For a moment Tyler didn't respond. Laurie watched the men but said nothing. Jared, engrossed in his project, ignored the grownups. Then Tyler said, "C'mere," and flicked his thumb toward the meeting room.

Frank held back. The last thing he wanted was a private conversation with Dyne-o-Mite. He said, "Of course," and got up.

The men left the ready room and crossed the meeting hall. Stopping near the staircase to the dorm, Tyler pivoted to face Frank and said, "What's your problem?"

"There's no problem."

"Coulda fooled me. Otherwise why the fuck are you intruding into my father-son time?"

"I just asked a question."

"A pointless, pushy, none-of-your-damn business question."

"All I meant was—"

"You meant, What's on this guy's brain when he builds what he's building. That bunker, as you call it. Well—if you really want to know, I'll tell you what I'm thinking. Time's running out. Some people know that. Some people don't."

"Let me guess," Frank said. "You're one of the few who's reached the crucial insight."

"If that's what you want to call it."

"An insight you reached at Ground Zero?"

"You might say that."

"I'm sure that was stressful."

Tyler laughed at Frank's words. "Don't give me your empathetic bullshit, okay? What I saw was nothing."

"Excuse me?"

"*Nothing* meaning—*nothing.* That's the whole point. Why? Maybe you should tell me, Padre. You're the man of the cloth. You're the shepherd looking after the flock. But you know what? I don't think you get it. What I saw at The Pile was a warning. We're at the brink of nothing. And you know who's warning us, too. Or you ought to."

Frank could guess where Tyler was heading—some sort of millennial premonition—but he said, "Clarify."

"Clarify," Tyler said with a huff. "Try Revelation twenty, verses one through—"

"Excuse me?"

"You, of all people, should catch the reference."

"The so-called hot verses? Fire and brimstone?"

"You got it."

"Interesting," Frank said. "As if the Nine Eleven attacks were a divine revelation rather than a just further evidence of human cruelty and stupidity."

"The writing's on the wall, Padre."

"And you, Tyler, can read what's written there."

"Look, things can't keep going like this. There's so much bad shit. Chaos. Wars. Plagues—"

"What if things do keep going?"

"They can't. Not like this. And you know it, too—or at least you oughtta."

"Just because I'm a priest doesn't mean I think the world's about to end."

"That's pretty lame. That's like saying, Just 'cause I'm a fire-fighter and I smell smoke all around me, and I see flames shooting out of every window in the house right ahead of me, and I see the family inside waving frantically at the windows, and I hear 'em screaming for help—none of that means the house is on fire."

Frank couldn't contain himself. "Ah, the great human hatred of uncertainty!" he exclaimed. "Things can't keep going like this. Time must have a stop."

He expected Tyler to rail against him—curse him, mock him, accuse him of being a stubborn Papist or a stupid intellectual. But Tyler just gazed at Frank, steady and hostile but without erupting into rage. Then he said, "That's just great. You're the pastor, the priest who's so close to God and eager to do God's will on earth. But you're not doing God's will—"

"What do *you* know about God's will?"

"Let me finish. You're not doing God's will on earth, and you don't even seem to care. So here we are in what sure as hell looks like the End Times—"

"To you it does."

"—and the signs are everywhere, and who knows how long we've got left—"

"Which is the whole point. Who knows? You?"

"—and you don't give a shit."

Losing his patience, Frank said, "I think I've had quite enough of this conversation." He couldn't decide what to do. Keeping this man's company was unbearable. He couldn't imagine how to tolerate him even through a single shift. "I understand that you have strong feelings on this topic," he said at last, forcing himself to sound calmer now. "I respect that. Obviously we disagree on some issues. But there's no reason you should accuse me of indifference."

Tyler huffed in amusement. "I didn't accuse you of indifference."

"No? I'd say that in a discussion of humanity's ultimate fate, telling a priest that he doesn't give a shit could be interpreted as an accusation of indifference."

Tyler didn't respond.

"I'd like you to apologize," Frank said.

He heard Laurie's voice from the ready room: "That's just so cool!"

He heard Jared's laughter.

Frank waited.

Tyler looked at his watch. "Let's go back before Laurie gets pissed off at us."

34

Advent. As if his schedule wasn't busy enough already, now the Christmas countdown started. The Center would begin hosting various interfaith events; numerous secular festivities would take place on campus; Pete and Frank would celebrate more than the usual weekly Masses. December would be a steeplechase. There would be all the fa-la-la as well, demanding even more time and energy. All Frank could do, really, was chip away at his tasks.

Then, late on a Saturday morning, when he had fled the rectory for the solitude of his on-campus office, he received a call from Pete: "Where are you?"

Seated at his desk, Frank said, "At the Center."

"Interesting."

"Why is it interesting?"

"Because I just heard from a certain bride and groom. They, their family, and a hundred guests are waiting for you at St. Cecilia's. They seem to be suffering from the delusion that you'll officiate at their wedding today."

Frank went cold. "Oh my God!"

"Frank, it's not impressive when the priest is the party who fails to show up at the altar."

He succeeded in racing over to St. Cecilia's, throwing on his vestments, and performing the ceremony without totally ruining the occasion. Frank apologized profusely to the bride, the groom, and their parents. Freezing rain had fallen over the past two hours—highly unusual that time of year—so he implied

219

that the weather had thrown him off schedule. The bride's mood made the ice feel lush by comparison. Zach, the groom, was a little more forgiving . . . or perhaps he simply deferred to Mindy on this point, as on all others. Best, then, for Frank to do his duty, linger briefly at the reception, and clear out.

How could he have forgotten? Frank wondered if his lapse had been a subconscious act of sabotage. He disliked the groom and loathed the bride. Small wonder that he nearly detonated a bomb under the ceremonial bridge that would carry them over to married life. Or had something else disrupted him? Of course: thoughts of Father Gregory's imminent arrival. Given Frank's state of flux and his confreres' frustrations, the standard protocol would've been a trip to Chicago, a discussion with the director of personnel, and a subsequent decision about how to proceed. Gregory happened to be in transit for a conference in California, however, thus could easily stop off in Denver en route to the West Coast. Visiting Frank at RMU would be convenient for both of them. Hardly a summons from the Inquisition . . . Still, Frank wasn't surprised that this impending event churn the depths of his psyche.

Laurie churned it too. Finishing a session at the Center two days later, Frank was surprised to hear Serena's voice on the intercom: "Ms. Anders to see you."

He stepped out of his office and found Laurie in the waiting room.

"I'm so sorry to interrupt," she said, walking over. "I just happened to be in the area."

He ignored the fib. "I'm glad you stopped by." He hoped that his matter-of-fact tone provided enough smoke to hide his delight from Serena. "I have a session coming up shortly, but we can probably fit you in later this afternoon." Did Laurie understand why he spoke like that here?

"Fine," she said.

"But I was just stepping out to get a coffee, so I suppose we could chat for a few minutes."

They walked out together. The Front Range Grill was sparsely populated with the mid-morning clientele. Laurie and Frank waited in line, bought coffee and pastries, and found a booth.

"You look tired," he said, concerned about her obvious fatigue.

"I am tired. Of course I'm tired. Who isn't tired?"

"I don't mean to sound critical."

"I was up all night with the squad. Then I worked my shift at the store."

"The store?"

"Walmart."

He couldn't restrain his surprise. "You work at *Walmart?*"

"Sure can't pay the bills on an EMT's salary."

"I apologize," he said. "That was rude of me. Worse than rude—presumptuous."

"No need to apologize, but it's not like here." She gestured at the students and faculty in the café. "Not like you guys—getting paid to sit around and talk." She must have noticed a change in his expression. "Sorry!" she said. "Now I've done it too!"

"Don't be silly."

"We're even."

"Let's not keep score."

"I guess we both do what we have to do."

He stirred his cappuccino, avoided her gaze, but couldn't stop thinking about her. This sudden visit . . .

After a long pause she said, "I hope I'm not putting you on the spot."

"I'm just a little surprised you're here."

"I know you're busy."

"I'm happy to see you, but in the future it's best if you make an appointment."

"I'm sure you know I'm not here for psychotherapy."

"In which case dropping by isn't the ideal situation for either of us."

"If you like," she said, "I can leave."

"I hope you believe what I said—I'm pleased to see you," Frank told her. "To be honest, I'm delighted. It's not your presence that's a problem. It's not even your presence here. It's the context."

"Context."

"I'm stuck with my role, my duties, my— What my friend Rabbi Miller would call my shtick. My song-and-dance, my act as a priest."

Laurie couldn't hold back from laughing. "Your *act!*"

"That's how it feels at the moment, but it's what I'm doing. What I have to do."

"I hear you. So, two things. One: like I said, I don't want to put you on the spot. And two: I have my own equivalent. Not a church breathing down my neck, of course, not a university, but certainly some other people. One in particular."

"I can imagine."

"So, yeah, I have my own song-and-dance."

"Your friend doesn't like me."

"Tyler doesn't like anyone. Or thinks he doesn't."

"Quite a bundle of nerves, that one."

"Never fear, Tyler's here!"

"He seems intent on further action," Frank said. "Hard to say what, exactly, but something."

"Something big."

"Any ideas? The End Times?"

"Maybe, maybe not."

"He seems to be making preparations of some sort."

"Tell me about it." When Frank didn't respond, Laurie said, "He's definitely bent out of shape about the future."

"A lot of people seem to be."

"Frank, what do *you* think will happen?"

"Depends on what you mean by *happen.*"

"To the world."

"*Happen* in the way Tyler is so keyed up about? Happen in a cataclysmic sense? Apocalyptic, even?"

She nodded.

He stirred the foam in his coffee cup. "You're thinking: Frank is a priest, so he'll say the last days are upon us."

Laurie watched him and waited.

"That's not what I'll say," told her. "First, because my particular faith tradition doesn't actually nudge me in that direction. Second—speaking personally now—because I don't believe we've reached the end of the line. The world is a sorry mess, but that doesn't mean God plans to pull the plug on the human experiment. No, we're stuck with the mess we've made. We'll be stuck for a long time to come. When I expressed that opinion to Tyler, he countered with anger and contempt."

"Here again, don't take it personally."

"I'm trying. It's not easy."

"Tyler has lots of opinions that have nothing to do with you."

"I'm sure. But some do. Let's face it—he doesn't like Mexicans. Or Catholics. Or men who get too friendly with his girlfriend."

"Three for three."

"Three for three."

"That's what's happening?" she asked with an amused smile. "You're getting too friendly with his girlfriend?"

"I couldn't say."

"Couldn't? Or can't? Or just won't?"

"Let's say simply that whatever's happening between us, Tyler will have a rather different opinion than you or I."

"Safe to say."

"I should also note that whatever's happening between you and me, our discussing it here," he said, gesturing at the cafeteria and at the people around them— "isn't the ideal option."

Laurie nodded. "I get it. Sorry."

He looked at his watch. "Here's the sad truth. I want to talk with you about . . . about what we're talking about. I'd certainly rather talk with you than do what I'm supposed to be doing. Unfortunately, I'm about to be late for my next session."

"Go, then."

"We should find a time."

"I'm sorry I've bothered you."

"Don't be. You haven't. But we need to talk some other time."

"Deal."

Frank took a last sip of his coffee, eased out of the booth, smiled, and walked out.

Gabriela Espinoza. How, Frank wondered, should he handle this situation? How, especially, given the possibility of Tyler's absconding with the boy? Frank tried to interpret the recent remarks and incident in case they shed light on the situation. He disliked Tyler, he didn't trust him, but Frank had no clear evidence of bad intentions. Building a Lego bunker and ranting about the Writing on the Wall didn't prove anything. Still, the recent squabble was disturbing. What, then, were Frank's obligations? To sleuth around further? To nudge Laurie? Or simply to tell Gabriela that, believe it or not, Frank already knew her ex, which raised some ethical concerns about his advising her?

Then, two days later, Pete's sudden comment right before breakfast: "That female student you've been counseling . . . ?"

At once Frank conjured a lovely image of Gabriela.

" . . . the undergraduate who's clinically depressed?" Pete continued. "The sophomore with curly blonde hair?"

"What about her?" Frank asked, now realizing that Pete was referring to Celeste.

"We just got a call that she's at the U. of Colorado Medical Center."

"What! When?"

"She got admitted through the E.R."

"Why? What happened?"

"Suicide attempt."

Frank felt dizzy with alarm. "My God—is she okay?"

"Depends on your definition of *okay*. She's alive, at least. Took pills. The doctors pumped her stomach. Obviously you'd better check up on her. More so than you've been checking in recent days, anyway."

35

After confirming with the hospital that Celeste's condition had stabilized, Frank showered, downed an espresso, and walked over to the campus. A professor-friend had loaned her office for the interview—for the *discussion,* or whatever it was—sparing Frank from needing to use the Center or the rectory. Better to have more privacy. To meet on neutral turf. Yet Frank's fatigue after several days of minimal sleep left him feeling low and apprehensive. The *discussion!*

He arrived first. The professor's office was small but attractive, with lovely Scandinavian furniture throughout, original art on the walls, warm lighting, and a view of the main campus. Wall-to-wall shelves full of books, of course. Particularly thoughtful touches: a carafe of fresh-brewed coffee and a plate of pastries.

A light rap on the door.

Frank turned to see a tall man waiting there. Gray-blond, bearded, and still handsome at seventy-five, he wore dark slacks, a fisherman's-knit sweater, and a tan wool blazer rather than a suit and Roman collar.

"Gregory."

"Frank."

The men embraced. "So good to see you."

"Please come in."

Father Gregory entered, commenting about the professor's fine taste in décor. They chatted briefly about the Order—who had retired, who was working overseas, who had been facing health problems. They sat.

Smiling, Gregory said, "You know I want to be as supportive as possible."

"Of course. I've never expected anything else," Frank told him. "That being said, I know you have a job to do, and I know that the job includes asking tough questions. Do what you must. I'll cooperate as fully as possible." Despite the calm tone of his own words, he felt dizzy, almost faint, as these first comments went back and forth. Badminton more than boxing, he decided. Still: some kind of duel.

"I appreciate that. I also appreciate how difficult this must be for you."

Frank gestured vaguely. "It's—what it is. Which, to be honest, isn't altogether clear to me."

"Understood. That's part of why I'm here."

Getting up to pour coffee for Gregory and himself, Frank returned to his chair with the cups. "So," he said, and they settled in for the long conversation.

The comments and questions were what Frank had expected. *It seems you're not altogether happy at the moment,* Gregory began. *Can you tell me a little about what's going on for you?* How should Frank respond? He wanted to say, *I love God and love my parishioners, but I'm tired of the work and weary of the Church. I'm tired of living like a eunuch.* "I seem to be experiencing some kind of burnout," Frank heard himself say. "What kind, exactly, still isn't clear to me."

"You've been a priest for a long time," Gregory said. "What, thirty years?"

"Thirty and change."

"That's a long time in any profession."

"*Change* in various senses of the word," Frank added.

"True for all of us. But can you be a little more specific about the burnout?"

Frank felt his mind flood with images, bits of conversation, shapeless emotions. A thought came to him: today wasn't really the right day for this discussion. He was too tired, too disorganized, too upset. Interacting even with someone as kind, thoughtful, and patient as Gregory wouldn't go well. Frank would ramble, babble, blurt out resentments and accusations, get upset. He couldn't possibly explain himself articulately, much less justify his concerns. Better to reschedule. Gregory would understand. Yet Frank wanted intensely to get the whole business over with—to make his case and back off—that he decided to proceed. *Basta!* Enough already!

He heard his own voice saying whatever it said, words about the repetitive nature of pastoral counseling, about chronic low-grade tensions with Pete, about feelings of restlessness and isolation. He heard Gregory responding in a calm voice, asking follow-up questions, sounding like and indeed being a gentle pastor shepherding a lost sheep. The Order would help Frank work through the situation . . . There might be some way of addressing Frank's dissatisfactions . . . Gregory would help ease Frank's concerns . . . Would work earnestly to provide a way for Frank to remain within the Order . . .

What are your issues with the Church? Gregory asked. *Do you believe that it's possible for you to remain a priest? To continue feeling you're part of the Order?*

Issues with the Church . . . Frank couldn't help noting one of his earliest memories—from age four, maybe even three—a memory of sitting in the parish church in west Denver and watching his grandmother pray. How calm she looked, how happy, as she whispered the Rosary and let her fingers work their way across the beads. He recalled how much he too wanted that calm, that happiness. How he too had found it for a long time.

He also recalled a trip to Italy during his early thirties. Frank had been a priest for how long at that point? Five or six years. He and three other priests from the Order had spent a week in Rome for a conference of Catholic pastoral counselors. Frank had no recollection now of the official events, though he had vivid memories of meals at local restaurants. *Minestra di broccoli e arzilla . . . Lumache alla romana . . . Fegato alla macellara . . . Pere cotte con le prugne . . .* Finished with his obligations, he had ventured off on his own, since the end of the trip coincided with a week of vacation time. Frank took the train north to Florence, found the city beautiful but much too crowded, then proceeded northeast to visit Venice and surrounding areas. Padova: that was the town he most enjoyed. The relative calm, the less-crowded restaurants, the frescoes present in the churches in such abundance. The visit overall? Unsettling. A number of his confreres had commented earlier that the trip was a pilgrimage. Not such a great leap of imagination: priests visiting Rome and touring churches, etc. But for Frank, at least, the pilgrimage turned out far different from what he had expected. A change, a shift. Some kind of slippage of his faith's tectonic plates deep within him? La Basilica di Sant'Antonio, burial place of the town's thirteenth-century patron saint. A major attraction: Anthony's jawbone. Frank wasn't drawn to religious relics, but he'd heard about this one and decided to have a look anyway. A hideous mandible encased in silver. Had he ever seen anything more grotesque? Medieval Catholics viewed relics as possessing miraculous properties, he knew that, and they believed that this bone beamed holiness outward like a radiation therapy device beaming curative ions into a cancer patient. Still: an appalling sight, a repulsive chunk of a long-dead priest. Frank left the church feeling physically ill.

"Frank?"

He looked up. Gregory. "Sorry."

"Are you all right?"

"I'm fine. Sorry—just under-rested. Kind of dazed."

"We can take a break."

"No, let's continue. I'm fine." He could see the concern in the Gregory's face, could hear it in his tone. Frank was intent on proceeding. Best to get this whole business over with . . .

"Very well," said Gregory. "Let's discuss the ambulance squad. Pete tells me you're involved with that. You're, what?—engrossed in that. Can you tell me why do you need this EMT work? And perhaps tell me how it fits with your responsibilities as a campus chaplain?"

The squad. Yes, the squad. Images surfaced in the pool of Frank's mind. Good calls, bad calls. Victims saved, victims lost. What Frank had learned from Laurie and Tyler, what he'd gotten right, what he'd gotten wrong. Above all, Laurie and Tyler themselves—one of them the most appealing person Frank had met in years, intelligent and vibrant in a rough-hewn way; the other intelligent and feral, even toxic.

"—and I'm wondering if there's also a more personal aspect of the situation," Gregory was saying. "Some kind of personal involvement?"

Laurie. He was asking about Laurie. How did he know about Laurie? From Pete, surely . . . yet how did Pete know? Frank felt a shiver of alarm as he grasped the situation. So now even Gregory, one of the kindest and most thoughtful of his confreres, someone Frank had known for decades, would zero in on Laurie. Or was Frank overreacting? Perhaps this was just one of the many issues that Gregory felt obliged to consider. Fair enough. Fair enough, too that Frank should explain the situation.

"By its very nature," he said, "working on the squad is personal. You can't do that work and not have it be personal. It's personal to enter people's homes when they're sick or even dying. It's personal to extricate them out of smashed-up cars. It's personal to work with a team where each member is dependent on the others—dependent in order to serve the victims properly, dependent to keep one another safe."

"You're sounding a little defensive."

He was aware that his voice had risen both in pitch and volume. "Sorry."

"I'm not accusing you of anything."

"No, but there's implicit judgment in your question."

"All I mean is that if a personal relationship has arisen and it's important to you, it's important to all of us too. I'm not saying you've done something wrong, but what you've done, or are doing, affects how we function as a community. You know that."

"I do."

"Hence my question."

An image of Laurie came to him, the sad eyes and the lustrous hair, the lovely figure and the deft, powerful hands, and with this image came a sense of longing. "There's an interesting woman

I work with," Frank began. He explained to Gregory how he'd felt drawn to Laurie, how he'd stepped carefully as he grew close to her, how he'd perceived his attraction yet held back, too, both to honor his commitment to his vows and to avoid igniting the tinderbox of Tyler's jealousy and rage. There was no physical relationship, he told Gregory, just the deepest magnetic pull he'd felt toward another human being since well before he became a seminarian. The uncertainty over what to do was both a millstone that dragged him down and a life raft that kept him on the surface. The surface of what? That too was unclear.

After a long time—Frank wasn't sure how long he'd been talking, or whether perhaps he'd already stopped—Gregory said, "Well—thank you. This is important, all of it. I understand that. I'm not finding fault with you. But what you've said will certainly help us all in figuring out what's next."

"Which is?" Frank asked.

"That depends on what you'd like to do."

"I'm still figuring that out."

A long pause. Gregory sat there looking calm and patient, his smile nearly imperceptible but clearly evident, his eyes watching Frank with unmistakable kindness.

Frank wanted to speak but didn't, or couldn't.

Gregory said, "Let me ask you— Is there more you'd like to discuss?"

"Not that I know of."

"Anything else on your mind?"

"Not really." He didn't want to discuss anything at all. He wanted to go back to the house and crawl into bed.

"All right, then. Can you suggest how much time you'll need to work through the current situation?"

"What are my options?"

"It's customary under these circumstances for the Order to allow a one-year leave-of-absence. By the end of that time, you'll need to indicate whether you'll stay or leave."

Frank just sat there.

"We can arrange suitable housing for you, of course, as well as spiritual direction. In short, we'll do everything possible to assist you in the process of discernment."

"Thank you." He couldn't figure out how to respond. He felt too tired, too addled, to find any more words.

"You're welcome," Gregory said. "I also welcome your contacting me at any time to discuss these matters further. I'm available."

Matters, Frank thought.

36

Having focused so intently on Gregory's visit, Frank almost spaced out his shift that same evening. He grabbed a quick supper and drove west to the squad house. He arrived late on account of the weather: a snowstorm had blown in over the Rockies at long last. Snow had been falling since noon, but highway crews hadn't caught up with the accumulation, so the drive took longer than usual.

Almost immediately the storm prompted the crew's first call: *Snow blower accident,* according to the dispatcher, *with possible amputations.*

"No possible about it," Tyler told Frank as Laurie drove the rig.

Frank, already anxious about the call, leaned forward from the compartment to hear Tyler up front.

"It's an old story," Tyler went on. "The white stuff comes down, guys wheel out their machinery, some joker reaches in to clear an obstruction, and *whoopsie-doodle!*—off come the digits. Here we go again."

What was the point in pushing back? Frank noticed that Laurie, too, didn't bother. Frank said, "Tell me what I should do."

"Me and Laurie will assess the victim and control the bleeding. You round up the wayward fingers. Remember the protocol?"

"Place them in a clean plastic bag, then put the first bag in a second bag filled with ice."

"You got it. Then we load and go."

They located the house and parked the rig. Inside they found a man—burly, bearded, and at least sixty years old—hunched over in the living room. A trail of blood stained the carpet from the door all the way to his chair. Having let in the EMTs, a much younger woman now returned to the chair and stood behind it. This lean, pretty redhead rested her hands on the victim's shoulders in a manner suggesting she was his wife rather than his daughter.

"I can't believe I *did* that," the man said. "I know the drill! You don't fuckin' reach into the blades! So what do I do? I reach into the fuckin' blades! Then the piston gives that one last kick—"

Frank was surprised when the guy broke down, sobbing like a child into the palm of his uninjured hand.

The right hand, tightly wrapped in a dishtowel, was already soaked with blood.

Laurie knelt beside the chair. "Don't beat yourself up. We'll take care of this."

"I mean, *really*—"

"We'll take care of it. Let's have a look."

The damage was so much worse than Frank had expected—not just two or three fingers but four—that he averted his gaze from the sight.

Tyler noticed his reaction. "Don't wimp out, Padre. Take the guy's vital signs, then do what we discussed."

In less than five minutes they had prepared the victim for transport; he lay on the gurney inside the rig; the EMTs and the patient drove off in the rig; and the wife followed in her SUV. Tyler, having already dressed the victim's hand with a large Quik-Clot, sat up front and drove. Laurie had started an IV and now monitored the man from the right-hand bench in the compartment. Frank sat in the tech chair and took the victim's blood pressure at frequent intervals—more frequent than necessary, perhaps, since keeping busy suppressed his nausea and dizziness.

"My wife is going to *kill* me," the man said. "Of all the stupid things for me to do! I know better, I really do. Now I'm—*fucked.*"

Laurie spoke to him in the calmest words Frank had ever

heard her speak. "I know you think I'm crazy, but you're gonna be fine."

"Yeah? How's that?" His eyes grew wild with sadness.

"'Cause the docs have ways of fixing fingers."

"Four of 'em!"

"No guarantees, but it can be done. Re-attachments. Done right there at Jeffco Med Center. We've already alerted the hospital we're in transit, and they'll have a team of surgeons available almost immediately."

"How will I make a living? I've always worked with my hands."

"I can't answer that," she said, "but I do believe it'll work out."

He fell silent for a while. Tears leaked from the sides of his eyes. Then his face contorted as he began to tremble and sob.

"We'll take good care of you." Laurie stroked his forehead.

The guy's voice squeaked out: *"My wife . . . "*

"What about your wife? She was right there with you, wasn't she?"

"Yeah, but for how long?" he asked. "She married a guy thirty years older than herself! A dumb old geezer who lops his fingers off!"

"Listen," Laurie told him. "You ain't no dumb old geezer. You look like a pretty cool dude to me. I bet she knows that. No, your wife won't be going anywhere any time soon."

"You think so?"

"I know so."

"How come?"

"'Cause she's got good taste in men."

Frank watched and listened, envious and admiring, as Laurie leaned forward and cradled the guy's head against her chest as he wept.

37

Just before getting ready for bed one evening, Frank heard loud knocks on the door. The noise crescendoed to pounding. He faltered for a moment, hoping that Pete would go deal with the racket, but apparently both of them had already gone to sleep. Frank left his room, crossed the living room, and pulled open the door.

Standing there, dressed only in pajamas and looking terrified, was Mr. Beach.

"*Kermith.*"

"Margaret's in a bad way!"

"What's wrong with her?"

"I don't know!"

At once Frank rushed out, following the old man to his house and finding Margaret sprawled on the kitchen floor. A shattered glass and some liquid lay spilled nearby. She appeared to be unconscious. Frank almost panicked at the sight before him. Now what! How could he cope without Laurie and Tyler guiding him? Without thinking he crouched, reached out to Margaret's neck, and tried to locate her carotid pulses. Nothing. "Call 911," he told Kermith.

"I did already."

"How long ago?"

"Just before I went to find you. They said they'll get here soon."

Which could mean anything. A busy night, bad calls—whatever else, some delays.

He tried to remember what to do. *ABC: Airway, Breathing, Circulation . . .* Just as he moved to reposition Mrs. Beach on the floor, a voice surprised him.

"What's going on?"

Frank turned to find Stacey standing in the doorway. Dressed in sweatpants and a T-shirt, she looked uneasy but alert. He told her, "You said you know CPR."

"Of course."

"Okay, let's do it."

He couldn't have felt more relieved when the local squad's abmulance arrived less than five minutes later. Three medics entered the house; Frank and Stacey backed off. Two medics took over doing CPR while a third assessed Margaret and readied the defibrillator. They shocked her several times between bouts of compressions and rescue breaths. Then, once they regained a pulse, one of the team brought a gurney from the ambulance, they loaded the patient, and they left. A police officer who had arrived on scene took Kermith to his squad car, which then drove away, following the ambulance. This left Frank and Stacey in the kitchen with ten or fifteen neighbors who had heard the commotion and, leaving their houses, now stood inside the Beach residence.

Among them was Pete, dressed in his pajamas and a bathrobe, looking tense and confused. He asked, "What was *that* all about?"

"Cardiac arrest," Frank said, "or so it seems."

"Good God—is she okay?"

"Unclear."

"May the Lord bless her and keep her."

Frank turned to Stacey, who, observing and listening, now abruptly put both hands to her face and started to cry. Frank watched her until he saw no recourse but to reach out.

She reached back and hugged him tightly. "Did I do okay?" she asked, sobbing. "I hope I did okay!"

"Better than *I* did, certainly," he told her.

"It's a lot different on a real person."

"Sure is."

"Do you think she'll—survive?"

"Hard to say. Let's hope so."

"I hope so too." Stacey clung to him for a long time as Pete, looking baffled and uneasy, monitored the situation.

<h1 style="text-align:center">38</h1>

Exhausted from lack of sleep—the damn post-CPR replay all night long!—Frank felt dazed and foggy when two phone calls came in the next morning.

The first was from Marissa.

"Frank—Jenna had her baby."

"That's wonderful!"

"A little girl."

"Splendid news. I assume they're okay, mother and child?"

"Jenna, yes. The child, probably."

"What do you mean, *probably?*"

"The situation isn't clear yet, but apparently there's concern about some significant birth defects."

"My God."

"The baby's in the neonatal unit for assessment and initial treatment. Beyond that, I don't have much information."

Frank couldn't imagine how to respond.

"Frank?"

"Sorry. I'm just trying to grasp what this means."

"Me too."

"Should I call them? Jenna and Jake?"

"Not yet. As you can imagine, they've got their hands full at the moment."

"Of course."

Kermith Beach reached Frank on the rectory's home line shortly after lunch. "Here's an update about Margaret."

"I'm relieved you've called. How is she?"

"Better. Not out of the woods, but better."

"What's the diagnosis?"

"Heart attack. Clogged arteries. She'll have a bypass operation."

"I hope that goes well."

"The doctors think she'll make a good recovery."

"Thank God. Pete and I will be praying for you both."

"Thank you, Frank." A pause. "And of course thanks for what you did the other night."

"No need for thanks. I'm just glad you came to find me."

Hanging up, he fought against the swell of anger that washed over him: anger that Jenna's baby should suffer a cruel fate while crabby old Mrs. Beach should survive unscathed.

That same afternoon, a third call. Father Gregory phoned Frank from Chicago "to follow up on the current situation," as he phrased it. He sounded cordial enough but quickly dispensed with small talk. "So, here's where things stand. We think you should take a leave of absence."

"*Leave of absence* . . . Meaning what, exactly?" Frank, standing by the desk in his room, heard the words well enough but couldn't make sense of them.

"Meaning—you should step back from your duties."

"For how long?"

"A while."

"How long a while?"

"Until there's some clarity."

He wanted to protest but didn't know what to say. This was all so vague, so remote. *We think you should take a leave of absence . . . Until there's some clarity . . .*

"I thought you said we'd have further discussions. A period of discernment."

"You'll have that, Frank. That's what we're providing."

"But starting already? I thought you said—"

"Frank, you weren't altogether forthcoming."

"I was! I answered your questions."

"Toward the end of our discussion I asked if you had anything else on your mind, and you said no."

"That was the case."

"Gabriela Espinoza?"

Frank felt an almost electric jolt of alarm. "What about her?"

"She's filed a complaint against you at the Center."

"A complaint! I've taken good care of her. I've responded to all her issues."

"Including your knowing her husband? Frank, that's a clear conflict of interest. You should've flagged that with her. You should've transitioned her to Pete."

"I was going to!" Frank exclaimed. "I just hadn't quite gotten there."

"You should've. Sorry, but this is a serious breach of our protocols. Along with the various other issues—"

"I can explain."

"Frank, you need to take a leave of absence."

"What about my clients?" Frank asked, starting to panic. "My parishioners?"

"They'll be in good hands with Pete."

"My counselees— I'm the one who has a relationship with them. Who knows what they're going through."

"Pete will be a good shepherd for the entire flock."

Frank couldn't believe that Gregory would resort to pastoral clichés. "Look," he said, restraining himself, "some of the sheep in question have been entrusted to this shepherd."

"True. And may be entrusted to you once again in the future. But as we discussed the other day, you're thinking through where you stand and where you're heading, and that puts your parishioners in a difficult position."

"You can trust me to step carefully while I figure things out."

"Frank, some of the steps haven't been altogether careful."

"That won't happen again."

Gregory ignored him. "Also," he said, "you need to relocate."

"Relocate to *where*? I live *here*."

"Frank— Under the circumstances, it's best for you to be somewhere else. The situation could get awkward otherwise. I'm sure you understand." He quickly added, "Please don't worry.

We'll make sure you have comfortable accommodations. We've already explored the options. For instance, you can stay at the novitiate in west Denver, if that suits you."

"Suit me for *what!*" Frank exclaimed.

"Please don't be upset."

"Why shouldn't I be upset? I work at the Center. I live at the campus ministry house. This place is my *home.*"

"Not if you're not fulfilling your duties as a full member of the community."

39

azed, dizzy, furious, and too sad to cry, Frank stood beside his desk long after the call had ended. He placed his phone on the desktop. He stared out the window at the back yard. What little snow had fallen so far this winter had half-thawed and refrozen several times until it compacted into a Styrofoam-like surface. A single gray squirrel now scratched at the gray-white ground, scampered over to another spot, scratched there too, scampered again, and kept scratching, baffled by the difficulty of reaching whatever he had buried. Then, abruptly, the critter shot away and disappeared into the Beaches' shrubbery.

Frank walked out of his room, put on his coat, grabbed his keys, left the house, and drove away.

Laurie was startled to see him but only said, "Oh!"

"I shouldn't just barge in like this."

"I'm glad you did. I'm just—surprised."

"I apologize for bothering you."

"Don't be ridiculous."

"I hope I'm not interrupting—"

"He's not here, if that's what you mean."

Frank stepped into her apartment, watched Laurie close the door, and simply stood there.

"What's the matter?" she asked. "Are you okay?"

"They've suspended me. The Order has. Sort of. Like a naughty schoolboy."

An odd expression eased onto her face, bafflement hinting at other emotions, too, maybe amusement or dismay. "You're not a priest any more?"

"Still a priest. I'm sidelined, I guess, not expelled. But I can't do my work at the university now. Can't live there. For a while, anyway."

"Frank."

"I had to tell you. I'm sorry."

"Don't be sorry."

"I should've called first." He didn't know what to think or do.

"This is awful." She gestured oddly with both hands. "Is it because of—me?"

"No—not you. Or— Yes, because of you. Or—yes and no. A chain of events, let's say. I think it would've occurred eventually no matter what. But maybe sooner now than I'd expected. Faster."

"What will happen?"

"I don't know yet."

"Will you . . . leave?" She gazed at him for a long time.

Frank wanted to reach out and embrace her, but he didn't. He wanted her to reach out and embrace him, but she didn't. They stood and stared at each other.

"Well," she said at last. "Come in and let's talk."

IV

MCI

40

He watched Laurie try to make him a cappuccino. "Sorry," she said, "but I don't have one of those little foamer gadgets."

"It doesn't matter," Frank told her.

"Are you hungry?"

"Not really."

"I can fix a sandwich."

"Coffee is all I need."

They stood in the kitchen while she puttered at the stove. She gazed at him now and then, smiling the kind smile she might have offered if Frank had just told her about receiving a scary medical diagnosis. He tried to give her some leeway by looking at the photos on the refrigerator. Laurie and Tyler posing next to an ambulance . . . Laurie and Tyler in hiking attire, the Rockies in the distance . . . Tyler and his son on a hunting trip—both males in camouflage jackets, Tyler cradling a hunting rifle . . . Jared on a different outdoor outing, this time showing off a trout he'd caught . . .

Laurie handed him a cup, took her own, and led Frank to the living room. They sat on the sofa. "So . . . what happens next?"

He set his coffee on the table without taking a sip. "Hard to say. I'll move out of the parish house. I'm supposed to withdraw from my normal activities—counseling and liturgy. Some kind of review process will take place. Then the Order will either ask me to leave or allow me to stay."

"Which would you prefer?"

"I'm not sure yet." He felt calmer now, being here with Laurie.

"If you could do anything you wanted," she asked, "what would it be?"

He couldn't help but smile—she was the counselor now—but he found the switch of roles somehow reassuring. "This will shock you."

"Go ahead, shock me."

"You're sure?"

She nodded.

"Eye surgery."

"Sorry?"

"When I lived in Oaxaca, the mission ran a rural health center. Routine medical care, mostly. Three nurses provided most of it, and a doctor rotated in once a week. They treated sick kids, cleaned up wounds, delivered babies, handed out medicine for flu and dysentery." An image came to him: the shabby whitewashed three-room building that parishioners had constructed for the benefit of everyone in their community. "Twice each year, a team showed up to do cataract operations. Two surgeons, two nurses, and two or three translators would arrive, set up a clinic, and treat dozens of patients who flocked in from the countryside. The team let me observe some of the procedures. I'd put on a gown, gloves, and mask and I'd watch. It's a tricky but amazingly elegant procedure. Out comes the bad lens; in goes the good lens. People show up blind and leave able to see. It's almost miraculous." His own words surprised him, but they came forth unbidden. If I could do anything I wanted, that would be what I'd choose."

"Why don't you, then?"

He laughed. "Right! I'll go to college two or three years for the prerequisites, attend medical school for another four, then do a long residency in ophthalmology. I'll be ready to practice by the time I hit seventy."

"No, silly. Not that way. Just get an O.R. tech certificate."

"Which is?"

"A diploma for assisting surgeons. It's a one-year program, two at most."

He didn't respond; maybe couldn't. He felt as uncomfortable as if Laurie had propositioned him.

"You could do it."

"At my age?"

Her expression suddenly turned to annoyance. "Don't give me that my-age bullshit! I know a guy who finished his RN degree at sixty-five. Took him seven years, but he did it, and he's still working at seventy-whatever. The O.R. tech program would be a snap. With your EMT background, you'd be a shoe-in at any program."

He mulled it over. "It sounds far fetched."

Another shift now: from annoyance to amusement. "Here's a thought," she said. "Let's *both* get O.R. tech diplomas. You and me. Then let's go to Mexico and help those doctors give people their sight back."

Fumbling for a moment, Frank said, "You can't be serious."

"Of *course* I'm serious. It's perfect. It'll get us both out of our crummy situations. Do something new."

"True."

"New and useful."

"What about Tyler?" Frank asked with growing unease.

"What about him?"

"He won't be—won't be exactly, what, *thrilled* by what you're suggesting."

"It's none of his damn business."

"He may think otherwise."

"Tyler thinks all kinds of things," Laurie said. "He can think whatever he wants, but he can't tell me what to do. Besides, I believe Tyler's about to make some changes in his own life shortly. Will be taking a little trip." She paused for a moment, weighing her options. "Besides, we've been on the skids for months now. It's only a matter of time. I'll head off in one direction, Tyler in another."

"Where is he going?" Frank asked, suddenly recalling Gabriela Espinoza's concerns. *Taking a little trip . . .*

"Who knows! With Tyler there's no telling. Always restless, that one."

"What *kind* of trip?"

"Frank," she said, her voice turning brittle, "you seem more interested in Tyler's plan than mine. "

"Not at all."

"Sure sounds like it. I mean, didn't I just suggest something that fits what you said you'd like to do? Eye surgery? And—not to put too fine a point on it—didn't I add myself into the bargain? 'Cause if I do say so myself, I think we've got something good. You and me. Something worth our time and attention."

"Laurie—"

"I'm not saying let's go spend the rest of our lives together, right? But it's been clear from the get-go that we're both real unhappy with our lives, we both need something better, and maybe we're each part of what the other needs. So what I'm suggesting—"

"I don't want to sound negative—"

"You do sound negative."

"I appreciate what you've suggested."

She laughed abruptly. "Appreciate!"

"I love what you've suggested. It's—thrilling." He wanted to reach out, wanted the solace of her embrace, but held back. "It's too much for me to think about. My head is swimming. That phone call from the Order— I feel like I just got shoved down a staircase."

"Of course," she told him, her tone calmer now. "Frank, I'm sorry. I've been ridiculous. Not because what I offered couldn't be good—'cause it could be. It would be. But I shouldn't throw everything at you all at once."

"Please don't apologize."

"No, I'm sorry. I'm really sorry."

"Don't be. It's fine."

"Thank you for your kindness," Frank said, and he got up from the sofa.

41

Two more nights at the parish house, both sleepless, and two days of packing. He felt at once relieved and dismayed by how little time and effort he expended to box up his possessions. Books, mostly. Some clothes. Three framed photos. Personal papers. Everything else would stay. When he sorted through his cooking equipment, Frank decided that taking pots, pans, and implements made no sense. He told Pete, "I'd like to leave this stuff here for now, okay?" Pete responded, "Oh, just clear it out." Frank couldn't help wondering what made the situation so urgent. This is just a leave of absence! He ignored Pete's remark and left his gear in the kitchen. Then, late on the second day, two movers showed up with a panel truck, they loaded Frank's five boxes, garment bag, and roll-aboard. The plan: Frank would relocate to the Order's novitiate west of downtown Denver. Just before setting out, however, he grasped that this transition would be unbearable. To settle in with the novices and clergy looking after them? *¡Ni modo!* He'd feel like a soldier stripped of his rank and drummed out of the corps.

"Where to?" asked one of the movers.

Frank gave him the novitiate's address. "Let me get something out of there first," he said, and he removed his rollaboard.

Then he made a phone call, slung his luggage into his car, and drove away.

The Marriott Residence Inn was just a half-mile south of the RMU campus but could have been anywhere. Buffalo, Des Moines, Baton Rouge, Portland, Pasadena . . . Frank had stayed at such places many times in the past and knew they were all

253

the same. Living room and adjacent kitchenette. Bedroom and adjacent bathroom. Light beige walls, burgundy-and-gold trim. White quilt and four pillows on the bed. Framed art in the two bigger rooms: generic paintings of the Maroon Bells, the Boulder Flatirons, and a skier on a slope. The picture window offered a view of the hotel parking lot and, beyond it, a primly landscaped low-rise office complex.

Very well, he thought. *If this is where you want me to be, this is where I'll be.*

Frank knew he shouldn't spend time on campus. He had a right to be there, of course, but showing up would be fraught. There would be questions and exploratory comments: *Father, I haven't see you lately . . .* Other than stopping by the Center to retrieve his appointment book and a few other items, he stayed clear. But staying clear didn't oblige him to live like a hermit. He needn't withdraw from the world. If nothing else, he would keep in touch with friends who lived and worked beyond the Order's reach.

He met with Janice at the place she suggested: a wine bar. He noted with amusement that she ordered a glass of *pinot grigio*. He asked, "Wine is—how to put it—not an issue for a Zen priest?"

"The Buddhist precepts prohibit intoxicants, and most lineages would ban what I'm doing right now." She raised her glass to toast him. "Fortunately, there's some wiggle room within the Zen tradition."

"Very well," Frank said, raising his *nero d'Avola*. "To wiggle room." They clinked glasses.

"To wiggle room. I hope your order has the good sense to allow you some."

"I guess I'll find out."

"You have a right to be happy."

"I just wish I knew what that meant."

"Don't we all."

* * *

Frank visited Jenna the next morning. Sitting with her in the Millers' silent living room, he told her, "I don't know what to say."

"You and I both know that sometimes there's nothing to be said."

"Still."

"Please don't worry."

"I can't help but worry."

"Of course. I appreciate that, we're getting the problems under control. Jake has so many contacts throughout the medical community—he's the perfect person to ask the right questions, figure out what to do, and work the system. We'll find the best specialists available."

"Is the child in danger?"

"Not in danger of dying, if that's what you mean. She faces lots of issues. There will be corrective surgeries."

"God, it's so unfair."

"It's not a question of fairness. Nobody *did* anything. Nobody caused this problem. It's just what happened. It is what it is. As far as fairness, I'd say what you face is truly unfair."

Frank sensed her need to change the subject, so he let her do so. "What I face is nothing by comparison," he replied, "and maybe it's nothing at all. But thank you anyway."

"I wish I could do something."

"There's nothing to be done."

"I imagine that the Church wouldn't be too interested in a female rabbi's opinion."

"Probably not, but that's just as well. At least for you. Why get caught up in the Catholic machinery?"

A day later, lunch with Marissa.

"I'm worried about my clients," he told her. "Some are really struggling."

"Pete will surely take good care of them."

"True—but he doesn't understand the nuances of what these particular people are going through. So much of the process is about the *relationship*, right? Pete doesn't have that with them."

Marissa seemed to focus on her salad.

Watching her, Frank noted how she looked up occasionally, then returned her attention to the greens and grilled chicken. "Let me ask you outright," he said. "Have I totally screwed up?"

"I'm not the right person to answer that question." She seemed to be withholding any but occasional eye contact.

"Which means you'd say Yes."

At last she met his gaze. "Frank, we all screw up. We're always screwing up, all of us. It's the nature of being human."

"I've tried to make sense of things. I've tried to do what's right."

"Of course. You're in a difficult position. You have several—what shall we call them? *constraints*—that complicate the situation. Maybe those constraints tripped you up."

"I'm aware that I haven't handled some issues altogether well."

"What happens next?" she asked abruptly.

"What happens is—I twist in the wind. For how long? Unclear. Then the Order will pass judgment on me, or else I'll pass judgment on the Order. Both, maybe. I'll either stay or I'll leave."

"I hope you'll believe me when I say I hope you'll stay."

He felt too glum to respond; then he decided to press the point. "I need your opinion on something. A matter of protocol."

Marissa waited.

"Ordinarily I would use the standard channels, of course, but I'm no longer privy to them, so I'm not sure what to do. Here's the issue. A student I've been counseling is worried that her ex-husband may be planning to abduct their eight-year-old son. I have no evidence that her concerns are either well founded or unfounded. Just as she and I were starting to explore the situation more deeply, the Order yanked the carpet out from under me. I no longer have access to her."

"Have you told all this to Pete?"

"This student complained to Pete about aspects of my counseling her, so I assumed they've discussed this specific issue."

"But you don't know for sure."

"For sure? No."

"Then I urge you to clarify the situation. Then Pete can counsel her—which I imagine will include advising her to inform the authorities. Inform at least the child's guardian ad litem and maybe the police as well."

"Maybe so." After a long pause he added: "There's a complicating factor."

She nodded.

"I happen to know the ex-husband."

"Wow. Definitely a complicating factor!" she said, laughing uneasily. "Do you think he'll do what your client fears he will?"

"I wouldn't rule it out."

"I see. Well, then—yes, you'd better let Pete know ASAP."

42

Sleep grew more difficult. He tossed and turned for hours. When he managed to sleep at all, dreams assaulted him like drunken patients.

One night he dreamed that Jesus appeared to him and said: *"In my father's house there are many munchkins."*

"Excuse me?" Frank asked. *"Munchkins?"*

Raising his right hand, the index finger pointing upward, while touching his left hand to his heart, Jesus said: *"In my father's house there are many Myshkins."*

Frank said, *"Myshkins?* Lord, I'm not sure I understand you."

"In my father's house there are many Mansons."

"You must be joking."

And Jesus said: *"You know—Charles, Marilyn, Shirley . . . "*

Then Frank woke up.

Another night he dreamed of his years in Oaxaca, of the rural parish he had helped to run, of people he had known there. He dreamed of Father Mariano, the parish priest, who used his own meager salary to feed patients at the local health clinic. He dreamed of Justina, a young mother who, having lost two premature babies two days earlier, shrugged off her loss with a smile: "It must be God's will." He dreamed of Graciela, a seventeen-year-old dying of leukemia, for whom Frank had donated blood repeatedly, and about whom he had marveled when he thought of his own cells, millions of them, coursing through the girl's body to fight for her life. *"Gracias, Padrecito,"* she told him after receiving each transfusion, her tone as matter-of-fact as if Frank had shared half of a sandwich with her, the girl's eyes full of delight.

This recollection, too: not of a dream but of a nighttime memory of a dreamlike state at Christmastime many decades earlier. Frank had been ten years old at the time. A flu epidemic was raging throughout the country. Catching the bug like most of his classmates, Frank took ill for more than a week. He wasn't sick enough to be hospitalized, but he experienced all the predictable miseries of influenza. Sleeping was an ordeal each night. Mami took good care of him and even dozed on a cot in Frank's room for two nights to be more readily available. Little by little he recovered. But one night halfway through the illness, Frank spiked a fever high enough to make him delirious, and during those hours of disorientation he descended into misery and fear.

No story, no drama, just an appalling state of— Of what? Frank perceived himself as a planet orbiting the sun, but something had gone wrong with his orbit. Rather than circling the source of all warmth and wellbeing, he was curving outward into space on a course that would take him farther and farther away from everything, deeper and deeper into nothing. He was alone. He was drifting away and would keep drifting until he left the solar system. The solitude he felt was complete. It filled him with despair. Nothing he could imagine doing, nothing he attempted to do, could reversed his outward drift.

He endured the night. The fever broke. He awoke relieved to find himself back in his own bed, Mami curled up on the nearby cot. Two days later, he started to recover. He shook the bug. His family's Christmastime celebrations—the gatherings with relatives, the sequence of feasts, Mass on Christmas Eve, and gifts on el Día de los Reyes—went ahead as planned. But for the rest of his life, what suffused Christmas more than any other feeling was recalling a sense of total emptiness that lingered long after his fever broke.

Frank slept at the Marriott but couldn't stand the place and wanted to be almost anywhere else. RMU was just a few blocks away. He felt the campus exert its magnetic pull. He struggled against the temptation to go back. Would it be so terrible if he just sat in the library and read? Probably not. Yet even going there could get . . . uncomfortable. Who knows who he might bump into? Zach and Mindy the fractious newlyweds. Mark the Last Days worrywart. Celeste the depressive. Gabriela— As each of his former counselees came to mind, Frank couldn't help but wonder how they were coping, what would become of them, what he might have done on their behalf if only circumstances had allowed for involvement in their lives. He caught himself glancing at his phone on the table. No, he shouldn't contact them. Should keep his distance.

He couldn't help wondering what he might have done differently. Whether he should've stayed clear of the whole EMT Thing. Should've held off getting drawn into Laurie and Tyler's world. He couldn't begin to guess where *that* was heading. *Eye surgery!* The truth was that even as Frank's pastoral duties evaporated, that other set of connections, that other realm of experience, felt more and more substantial.

If I can't be a priest, he decided, I can at least be an EMT.

43

"Are you available?"

"Of course," Frank said, delighted but puzzled when Laurie phoned him. Today was Monday, not Thursday, and only nine-ten in the morning. "What's going on?"

"Big MCI on I-70."

"MCI?"

"Mass Casualty Incident. Looks like a multi-car pileup in this case."

"How many cars?"

"Unclear. Must be bad, though—otherwise OEMS wouldn't be calling all hands on deck."

"I'll be right there."

Forty minutes later he parked at the squad house. He would have arrived sooner, but swirling wet snowfall, flakes big as moths, reduced visibility to a few car lengths and slowed his progress.

Laurie didn't even greet him as he entered the ambulance bay. Frank noticed that the two other Foothills rigs were already gone. Tyler sat waiting in the third truck's driver's seat.

Laurie stowed some equipment in the patient compartment, closed the double doors, and walked around to the front passenger side. "Let's go."

Frank climbed into the patient compartment and took his place in the tech seat. He turned to speak with Laurie and Tyler through the passage to the front. "What's the plan?"

"The plan," Tyler said, "is that we go do whatever has to be done."

"Any idea what happened?"

"What do *you* think? Bad weather, slick pavement, collisions."

Visibility grew even worse. Frank had no idea where they were. US 6? I-470? Other than two red taillights right ahead, he couldn't see anything beyond a grainy wall of snowfall.

"Shit!" Tyler swerved as the rig nearly hit a stalled panel truck. The ambulance shuddered for a moment, then stabilized.

"Slow down," Laurie said.

"If I go any slower," Tyler said, "we'll be the ones who get rear-ended."

They drove in silence.

Frank started to sense an uphill grade. The rig shimmied.

"We should've chained up," Laurie said.

"Too late now," Tyler said.

The windshield wipers ticked off the seconds, but the seconds didn't add up. Frank had no idea how long they drove. Other than the click-clack of the wipers, he heard only the engine's thrum. Seated back in the compartment, he had few sights to go by. Some faint headlights visible through the back-door windows . . . The swarming snow . . .

"Okay."

Hearing Tyler's voice, Frank craned his neck again and peered through the passageway. He couldn't see vehicles, exactly, just the strobing of red-white-blue flashers illuminating the snowfall. A few moments passed before Frank realized that the ambulance had stopped.

Laurie unhitched her belt and turned to Frank. "Scene safety, right?"

Tyler snorted when he heard this comment. "Yeah, right!"

They got out. Frank tried to get his bearings. The chaos of flashing lights . . . Felt like the inside a Fourth of July fireworks display . . . Wet snow slapped him in the face. Noises nearby: engines idling, voices shouting.

"Stay close till we figure out where we are."

He fought a hollow feeling in his gut. How could they help anyone if they couldn't see anyone to help?

Frank felt relieved when he saw two highway troopers approach. "Which squad?" one of them asked.

"Foothills," Tyler said.

The second trooper spoke into his walkie-talkie, words Frank couldn't follow, and the response, too, was incomprehensible.

"Proceed up the downhill lane, then check in at Sector One," said the first trooper. "Personnel there will advise you."

"Sector One," Laurie said, her voice sounding tense. "How many sectors?"

"Four so far."

"That bad?"

"That bad."

Laurie, Frank, and Tyler retreated to the rig. Although Frank felt a growing sense of alarm, he found reassurance in the signs of an organized response.

Tyler angled off the uphill lanes onto the other side as troopers with orange signal wands guided them through a gap in the guardrail. The rig ascended almost silently up the snow-covered highway. Then, noticing more officers wielding signal wands, Tyler slowed, pulled the rig to one side, and parked.

The EMTs got out.

"Foothills Three reporting for duty," Tyler told the officers.

"You can proceed and start triage," came the reply.

The snowfall eased for a few moments and gave Frank a glimpse of what lay before them. A parking lot? Worse: a junkyard. Cars, SUVs, and trucks jammed against one another from left to right. Some vehicles pointed downhill. Others had been shoved sideways. Still others faced backwards. A panel truck rested on its right side, exposing the undercarriage and the tires. A few cars angled upward against other vehicles, tilting like ice flows in an arctic river. Still more appalling than the vehicles were the people inside: men, women, and children peering out through the windows as they tried to make sense of their dilemma and decide how to escape.

A jumble of noises reached him: blaring horns . . . wailing car alarms . . . and a sudden, terrifying noise up ahead, wild and recurrent, that combined a crunch and a squeal. Once. Twice. A third time. Over and over. Frank realized that he wouldn't stop hearing this hellish sound until the collisions causing it started happening farther up the highway, far enough away that his ears couldn't detect them.

"Now you see why it's called a clusterfuck," Tyler said.

Frank recoiled from this comment but couldn't help noticing that many of these cars were mounted, each shoved against the next in a bizarre automotive daisy chain.

"What do we—do?" Frank asked with growing alarm.

"We get started," Tyler said. "Being the trauma bag and the triage kit."

By now other emergency vehicles had started arriving. Frank couldn't see them well, boxy shapes and flashing lights half-visible through the snowfall, but he heard a crescendo of sirens, diesel engines, slamming truck doors, and service radios. The din grew overwhelming. Frank felt relieved to hear it, almost delighted, despite the noise—he wouldn't be facing this mess alone with Laurie and Tyler. Yet he couldn't hold back from saying what welled up from his mind: "I don't see how we'll cope."

"OEMS has already set up a command center," Laurie said.

"Who?"

"The Office of Emergency Management. They have plans for these MCI's. They've established a command post and are delegating tasks."

At that moment, a car visible on their left started making a stuttery noise. The front driver-side door opened with an abrupt crunch. A middle-aged man shoved his way out and emerged near the guardrail.

Tyler said, "Are we gonna stand here yakking all day or shall we actually help these folks?" He walked the few feet to the rail, climbed over it, strode up to the man, and started assisting him as he stumbled forward.

"Tyler's right," Laurie said. "Get a trauma bag and a bunch of C-collars."

Frank obeyed her. He went back to the rig, grabbed what she had requested, and returned to the guardrail.

"You remember what to do?" Laurie asked.

"I think so."

"Run through the sequence for me."

"We do the triage assessments. Sixty seconds per victim. Tag them at the appropriate level of priority. Then move on to assess and tag the next victim."

"You got it."

"Words of wisdom?"

"Just the obvious—keep your focus and be careful."

"You too."

"Okay, good luck." She turned as if to walk away.

"We aren't working together?" he asked, shaking off a twinge of panic.

"Frank, there's too many folks. That's why we do triage. We'll size up everyone first. Let's get started." Giving him a handful of tags, she turned, picked up her trauma bag, and stepped over the rail.

Frank faltered, then walked a short distance up the highway. The pavement was so slick that he struggled to stay on his feet. He went ahead anyway. Right off he found two women in a mangled car. The driver, forty-something and dark-haired, saw him approach and immediately started shouting and slapping the driver-side window with her palms. Her face contorted with panic. The passenger, an old lady, was clearly unconscious—slumped over in the passenger seat. Frank grabbed the door handle and pulled. Nothing budged. Tried again: no luck. He shouted, "Unlock the door!"

"I did!" the younger woman cried out.

"Push hard!"

"I *am!*"

Increasingly alarmed, he couldn't figure out what to do. He tugged again. The door might as well have been welded shut. Same with the left-side passenger door. Damage to the auto body must've jammed the locks. Frank considered going around to the other side, but an SUV had lodged against the car, blocking his access.

"Get us out!" the driver yelled, her voice cracking.

"I'm trying," Frank said, but after two more tugs, both pointless, he gave up. He simply stood there.

Looking over the car's roof, he saw the SUV next to it and, inside the vehicle, a young bearded man in the driver's seat. He too gestured and called out. Frank already knew that he wouldn't be able to get over there: the SUV was shoved tight against the car on its left. He turned to look behind these two vehicles. The toppled panel truck he'd noticed earlier lay on its side. Behind that, a Toyota rested against the rail. Behind that, a pickup truck rested sideways against the Toyota's rear end. Behind that—

Frank eased backwards. Slowly at first, then faster, he stepped away. He told himself not to leave, but he left. He turned, skidding and stumbling through the snow, fell twice, force himself up, and only by luck found his way back to the Foothills rig. Trembling, he stood there. "Lord," he prayed aloud, "tell me what to do."

The commotion everywhere left him feeling swamped, flooded, drowned. Engine noises. Sirens. Shouts. Intricate, arrhythmic flashing lights.

Then, without warning, Tyler materialized out of the snow. A young man, his arm slung over Tyler's shoulder, walked alongside. "What's going on?" Tyler asked when he noticed Frank.

"I don't know."

"What d'you mean, *I don't know?*" Tyler's face tightened into an expression worse than contempt. "Get back out there and fuckin' *do your job!*"

Frank couldn't move.

"Shit!" Turning abruptly, Tyler opened the rig's side door, helped the young man up the steps, and followed him inside.

Frank stood outside alone. Wet snow plastered his face.

Tyler stepped out again a minute or two later. "All right. If you're not doing triage, at least look after this guy."

"I will. I shall."

"You sure? You're not just gonna stand here till you turn into Frosty the Snowman?"

"I'll check out the victim."

"Damn right you will." Without further comment, Tyler retreated into the storm.

Frank lingered a moment; then, reluctantly, he climbed into the rig with the young victim.

"Oh! Thank you!" the guy said. I'm just so glad you're here!"

"Tell me what happened," Frank said.

"I was just driving along and suddenly I saw so many cars in the road! I tried to stop, but—no way!"

"Are you injured?"

"I don't know."

"Let's check you out," Frank told him, relieved to have just one person in his care.

Before he could even start his assessments, the side door opened. Laurie stood there with a woman and a teenage girl. "Why are you here?" Laurie asked Frank, her face showing puzzlement or annoyance.

"I don't know," he said. He got up from the bench and helped Laurie ease the two new victims into the ambulance.

The girl trembled and wept but was altogether silent. The woman said, "Oh my God, thank you! Thank you! I'm so glad we're out of there!"

Laurie asked Frank, "Did Tyler assign you here?"

"Sort of."

"Well, then— Okay, do that. Check out this woman and her daughter. The airbags deployed, but I'm worried about the girl. Don't assume she's fine just because she's so quiet." Then, once the woman and the girl were seated on the gurney and the bench, Laurie stepped out through the side doorway and closed the door.

Frank had no idea what to do. No idea where to start. He had never felt so scared in his life, so aware that nothing he could do would be right, that nothing would be enough. Being here at all was a mistake, a failure.

* * *

He wasn't sure how much time had passed when Tyler showed up again, this time with another EMT, a burly male, someone Frank had never seen before. "Padre. Follow me."

Frank felt more relieved to see him than he would have thought possible. "What's happening?"

"This guy will take charge of the rig. Now follow me."

All Frank could do was obey. He struggled to keep up with Tyler as they left the ambulance and pushed through the storm. Working his way around all the emergency vehicles grew difficult. Then, abruptly, he saw two school buses up ahead. School buses! Ordinary, bright yellow school buses: engines running, lights on inside. Tyler led Frank over to one of them. A big square of plastic taped near the door read PRIORITY GREEN. As they approached, Tyler spoke to a state trooper standing near the bus. "This is Frank. Incident command radioed to assign him here."

The trooper nodded, then waved them on.

Frank followed Tyler into the bus. There they found themselves among twelve or fifteen people—men and women, mostly, but several kids as well. Some sat alone on their seats; others huddled together. All were clearly victims who, having been extricated from the pileup, had been brought to this relatively safe place. Most were clearly injured, a few with bloody faces, others holding cold packs to their heads or faces. Some moaned or wept.

Tyler said, "Here's your assignment: look after these folks."

"How?"

"What do you mean, how?"

"What should I do?"

"What do you think? Number one, don't let nobody leave. Number two, keep doing your assessments. These folks are all Priority Green, so they're the least-injured victims. But don't assume everything's just hunky-dory. Some will have suffered whiplash or contusions. Maybe worse stuff, too. If anyone starts to crash, radio out and request ALS. Tell 'em you're at Staging Area Two. Got that? *Staging Area Two.* Number three, monitor who's the worst hurt and who's doing okay. Number four, give 'em a little TLC. Do whatever you can. Squads will be arriving ASAP to start transport to area hospitals."

"I'll be doing this *alone?*"

Tyler looked at him blankly. "No, of course not—we'll send a rock band and a dozen Playboy bunnies to help you entertain the troops."

"All I meant—"

"Yes, you're here alone."

"I should be out there helping you and Laurie."

Tyler snorted with amusement or contempt. "Padre, we can't fuckin' afford your help. Stay here and do as I say. If you're not gonna help us solve this problem, at least don't make it any worse."

Frank would've responded, but at that moment a woman walked down the aisle and, approaching him, started asking questions. "Can you tell me when we'll be able to leave? I've been here at least half an hour already. How long will this go on?"

A middle-aged man walked over, too, and said, "Right—we've been stuck here quite a while."

Before Frank could start to reply, Tyler took advantage of the interruptions, stepped away, and left the bus. Frank saw no way to avoid the people demanding his attention now. "Listen to me," he said, raising his voice and addressing not just the man and the woman before him but everyone present. "My name is Frank Ochoa. I'm an EMT, and I'm here to help you. I know this is a terrible situation, but you're safe here, and I'll help you in any way possible. We'll get you out of here ASAP."

At once the questions erupted:

"How long will we be here?"

"Can you get me to the hospital?"

"Can I use your cell phone?"

He saw no alternative to interacting with these people, to doing what he could to treat them. As he soon realized, most were just minimally hurt or not at all. The triage teams had already tagged them, and all of their tags showed the lowest priority—Green. This being the morning rush, most of the victims were adults en route to work in Denver and the suburbs. Some were kids on their way to school. Many had been jolted or banged up in the collisions, but air bags had spared them more serious injuries. Some showed signs of the contusions and whiplash that Tyler had predicted. Almost all seemed to be anxious and alarmed— fair enough, given such a sudden, bizarre, terrifying experience. Frank scarcely knew where to begin as he tried to offer solace. Fortunately, two EMTs entered the bus carrying boxes of supplies. Frank now had a least a few items to give these people. Instant cold packs. Bandages and band-aids. Space blankets. Assessing each person as quickly as possible, Frank provided whatever he thought might ease pain, offer comfort, and calm anxieties. Little by little he made progress. He himself found comfort himself in how readily these folks helped one another—not just family members assisting relatives or friends helping friends but total strangers offering mutual assistance.

He started to feel less alarmed. He would get this situation under control.

Yet even as he grew calmer, something else disturbed him: a realization of his failure during the incident's early phase. He had let down Laurie and Tyler, had flunked an important test. Tyler had responded by yanking him out of the main action and shoving him onto the sidelines. Frank was doing the easiest, most rudimentary, least risky job possible.

The situation dragged on longer than he thought possible. Victims kept arriving: shaking, weeping, moaning men, women, and children. Frank had expected that EMS crews would show up to transport at least some of the people here, and at some point that began to happen. The door would open. An EMT or trooper would step inside. Frank would hear the request: "I've got room for three victims" or "I can transport two vics." Then Frank would decide who had priority: "Okay—you and you," or

"They'll take you and your son now." But more people arrived than left. The bus grew more crowded, not less so. The early arrivals grew resentful of the newcomers. Arguments flared up in the tightly packed rows. The wind intensified, shaking the bus and shoving in snow through a stuck window that nobody seemed able to close. The noise increased, too—the rattle of diesel engines, the yammer of service radios and walkie-talkies, the shriek of sirens as rigs pulled in and out. The air grew foul with exhaust. The wind, the snow, the noise, the fumes, and the tight quarters combined to intensify everyone's discomfort. What little order Frank had established, what little comfort he had provided, began to deteriorate.

He found his growing anxiety distracted by a scene right in front of him. A girl and her mother sat together in the second row on his left. The thirty-something mother sat cross-legged on her bench. The girl, perhaps six or seven years old, sat back, using her mom as an armchair, the woman's arms hugging her daughter to give warmth and solace. Frank needed a moment to realize that the girl was singing. Despite the anxious expression on the kid's face, the song was "Winter Wonderland."

His initial reaction was amazement verging on contempt. Winter wonderland! Then he thought: why not?

"Hey there," he said, crouching to address the girl directly. "Can you sing louder?"

Her face showed surprise at first, then amusement. *"Sleigh bells ring, are you listening?"* she sang. *"In the lane, snow is glistening."*

The mother, smiling at Frank, joined her daughter: *"A beautiful sight, oh we're happy tonight, walking in a winter wonderland."*

A few people nearby stopped talking and listened to the mother-daughter duet. Some of them joined in. Others listened and watched. A few appeared to be puzzled or annoyed. "Winter Wonderland"—the perfect soundtrack for a massive highway accident in the snow! No one protested, however, and a few more people started singing. Soon Frank saw what he'd hoped might happen but never could have predicted: the gradual spread of song throughout the group.

* * *

Once started, the singing wouldn't stop. It happened mostly on its own, as spontaneous as water welling up from a spring. How odd, he thought: to find himself officiating in a bizarre chapel, the victims seated like congregants on their pews as they lifted their voices in song. When the flow diminished, Frank drew it forth. He himself started singing whenever the group fell silent. The kids present were his best allies—unabashed about singing trite lyrics and perky tunes in such a bleak setting. He tried to stick with the secular songs—"Deck the Halls," "White Christmas," and "Jingle Bells." He even resorted to "Let It Snow," "Frosty the Snowman," and "Jingle Bell Rock," all songs he loathed. Some of these people sang and kept singing, and he didn't feel right to disrupt what happened so easily on its own. If they found solace in singing, let them sing. They sang "Away in a Manger," "O Holy Night," and "We Three Kings." They sang "Little Drum-mer Boy" and "Angels We Have Heard on High." They sang "O Come All Ye Faithful."

O come all ye faithful, joyful and triumphant,
Come ye, O come ye, to Bethlehem!

44

Frank lost track of time. The air grew brighter, then dimmer. His energy slumped as the situation stabilized, then perked up whenever a crisis occurred, such as the arrival of a more seriously hurt victim or a downturn among those already present; and then, once the crisis eased, his energy slumped again. He was too busy to think about anything but whatever happened at a particular moment. Victims needed ice packs or space blankets. People asked questions or made demands. *When will I get transported to the hospital? Why aren't more people here providing treatment? Can you bring us some food?* Fortunately, EMTs showed up every ten or twenty minutes to transport a few victims; but as the process of extrications accelerated, more victims showed up, too. Frank stayed busy without letup. Only when daylight faded did he begin to grasp the passage of time. Six-twelve. He had arrived on scene almost ten hours earlier—so long that he almost wondered if he'd always been here; if he'd ever done anything but look after these cold, hungry, aching people; if he'd remain here forever in this snow-blown Purgatory.

Local squads, assisted by EMS personnel from outlying towns, started arriving to transport the less-seriously injured victims. The process went on for a long time. Rigs and minivans parked near the school bus, loaded victims, and pulled away. All of the EMTs arriving were people Frank had never met. He didn't even recognize some of the towns whose names he read on their uniforms. He kept expecting Laurie and Tyler to show up, but they didn't. Which made sense: as experienced EMTs, they would attend to the more seriously injured victims. He wouldn't see them again until the MCI fully stabilized.

Around eight, a tall woman in a firefighter's turnout coat entered the tent and approached Frank. "Your name, please?"

"Frank Ochoa."

"Okay, good. I'm Jen Castelli, lieutenant incident commander for Jefferson County. We have more folks on scene now, and a relief crew will show up here shortly. Once they arrive, you can sign off."

"I'll stay longer if you wish."

"The situation is under control."

He didn't argue with her. The thought of leaving was too delightful to resist. "Very well, then."

"A crew is heading down to Jeffco General in a few minutes, so you can hitch a ride with them. They'll drop you off at your squad house en route."

"Many thanks."

She seemed to be done speaking but lingered anyway. Frank found her expression puzzling: a worrisome gaze.

"Is there more we should discuss?" he asked.

"You don't know, do you?"

"Know about what?"

"Two of your squad buddies had an accident earlier today. Skidded off the highway on their way down."

"My God— When?"

"Couple of hours ago."

"Who are they?" Frank felt a wave of nausea wash through him.

She leafed through some papers on a clipboard. "I would've told you earlier, of course, if I'd known you were here. It's been such a mess of a day— I haven't always known exactly who's on duty—" She cut herself short to scrutinize the clipboard. "Okay. I don't have the first names, but the last names— Anders and van Dyne."

He considered going to the squad house first. EMTs would undoubtedly be present, so he could find out what had happened and where to find Tyler and Laurie. Almost at once he ruled out that detour. Jeffco Med was the nearest hospital and the county trauma center, too, so surely that would surely be where Laurie and Tyler would've ended up. Frank would take his chances. Never mind that his uniform was messy with with blood. All the better to present his bona fides as a participant in the current crisis and thus gain entry into the hospital.

So, riding up front when an EMT from the Salida Rescue Squad drove Frank, a second EMT, and two lightly injured patients down from the foothills, Frank pondered the situation with deepening alarm. His mouth and throat felt so dry that he could scarcely talk. "You know anything about the EMTs who had an accident?" he managed to ask the driver.

"Say what?" She was a fortyish brunette who looked as tired as Frank felt.

"Two EMTs from a local squad slid off the road earlier today."

"Damn. Hadn't heard that."

"They're from my squad."

"Oh my God. I'm so sorry. How bad are they hurt?"

"Unclear."

"They're at Jeffco?"

"I assume so."

"Well—let's get you there pronto."

Dear Jesus, Let her not be dead, Frank prayed. *Let her not be injured.* And Tyler? *Thy will be done.* Tyler was negotiable.

The medical center was in upheaval. Eight or ten EMS rigs waited in line simply to approach the Emergency Department entrance. Frank took advantage of the gridlock to make his exit from the Salida squad's ambulance. "You need help unloading your victims?" he asked the driver.

"We'll be fine."

He thanked her, climbed out, and walked a hundred yards to the E.D. entrance.

Inside he found dozens of injured patients in the waiting area along with a scattering of EMTs and some scrubsuit-clad nurses. He approached the counter. "Frank Ochoa," he told the clerk. "Foothills EMS. I'm here to check up on someone."

"Patient or squad member?"

"Both. Laurie Anders and Tyler Van Dyne."

The clerk typed some info into her computer. "Anders got transferred up to Three West."

On the ward, Frank found Laurie's room without difficulty. Two EMTs from Foothills stood inside near the bed; two more waited outside. He recognized both from squad meetings, a woman and a man whose names he couldn't recall. "I'm Frank Ochoa from Laurie and Tyler's crew."

They shook hands warmly.

"How bad?"

"Not terrible, not great," said the man—fortyish, lean, bearded. "Could've been much worse, all considered."

"But how bad?"

The woman, a stocky redhead, said, "Concussion and whiplash. She's pretty banged up."

"I heard they went off the road."

"Hit a bad patch, skidded, rolled the rig. It's amazing they weren't both killed."

"What about Tyler?"

The man smiled a smile that could have meant almost anything—sadness, confusion, astonishment. "Poor brave, crazy Tyler. Saved victims all day long but wouldn't even wear his own seatbelt."

"He died?"

A nod.

"Damn."

The woman said, "Laurie was seated in the tech seat in back with two victims. Got tumbled up and slammed against the side of the compartment, but at least she was belted."

"Can I see her?"

"Of course, but keep in mind she's been sedated."

If he hadn't already known who she was, Frank wouldn't have guessed this person was Laurie. An area on the right side of her head had been shaved, and a clear dressing revealed a three-inch line of stitches on her scalp. A plastic collar encircled her neck. Her right arm lay encased in a plastic cast. Contusions and discolorations made her face almost unrecognizable.

Approaching the bed, Frank couldn't speak. The two EMTs present, both women, looked at him and smiled but said nothing. Then one of them nudged the other and they left the room. Frank realized at once: *they know.*

Alone with her now, he stood by the bed for a long time. "Laurie."

No response.

"Laurie. Frank here."

She opened her eyes, looked at him, and struggled to make sense of whatever she could hear and see. Her gaze examined his face. *"Mmmm."*

"I'm here."

Did she smile? He couldn't tell. Laurie stared at him for a while; then her eyes dimmed and the lids closed.

Frank reached out, pressed two fingertips against her wrist, and took her radial pulse. Strong and regular. A relief: she had simply dozed off.

He rested his hand on her forearm. He didn't know what to think. He felt sick to see her so battered, so *reduced,* yet a surge of delight coursed through his body to find her alive and no more severely hurt.

Frank lingered until he realized that staying made no sense. Leaving her bedside, he walked out of the room and stood with the four other squad members in the hallway. "Does she know about Tyler?"

The oldest person present, a muscular woman with nearly pure-white waist-length hair, said, "We told her this afternoon. She was upset, of course, but she's said nothing since then. She's not tracking much at the moment. Probably the sedation."

"Fair enough."

45

Frank considered staying at the hospital but decided against it. According to the EMTs and the ward nurses, Laurie's condition was stable. "Visiting hours will be over soon anyway," one of the nurses noted. Frank realized, too, that he had nothing to offer at the moment. He was so exhausted that the room kept lurching. A headache sprouted in his left temple and sent tendrils crawling through his brain. Better, then, to go home and get some rest. He would come back in the morning.

Calling a cab from the hospital lobby, he rode back to the squad house. The parking lot was full of cars. He could see enough through the windows to confirm that some squad members were present even if most remained at the scene on I-70. Going inside didn't make sense, he decided; he would just get caught up in the post-MCI debriefing and wouldn't break away for hours. He got into his car and drove back to the Marriott.

Frank closed the door to his room and stood motionless in the dark. Even with his eyes open he saw a thousand specks of light. Snowflakes. A blizzard.

He flicked on the overhead. Walking into the bathroom, he stripped off his uniform, shoved the reeking garments into a corner, turned the shower on full blast, and stepped into the stall.

For a long time he let the spray drench him. He couldn't get the image of Laurie out of his mind: battered, swollen, trussed in plastic and Velcro. Sadness drenched him like freezing rain.

And what would *she* be thinking? She would be thinking about Tyler.

At the moment of recalling that name, Frank felt a tangle of—

Of what? Of relief? Of delight, even? Tyler was dead. Gone. Frank would never again have to tolerate his insults and his mockery. *If you're not going to help us solve this problem, at least don't make it any worse.* And: *We just can't fuckin' afford your help.* The man treated Frank like a child—a problem child, yet—to the very end. At once a second thought crossed his mind: if Tyler hadn't sidelined Frank from the main action, Frank would probably have joined him and Laurie for that final drive to Jeffco General. Would have slid with them off the Interstate. It wasn't hard to grasp that Tyler had saved his life. Frank was aware, too, the Tyler had bestowed another gift on him: Laurie. Yet Tyler had also pulled off a remarkable victory. Had outwitted Frank. Had won the duel between them. How could Frank even begin to counter this brilliant final gambit? Laurie's last memory of Tyler would always be his valiant effort to find their way out of the storm.

Frank slept from eleven that night until past ten the next morning. He awoke exhausted, achy all over, dazed, and hungry. Forcing himself up, he sat on the mattress and waited for the room to stop tilting. He got out of bed, walked over to the window, and shoved open the curtains. The view, the view: one of those brilliant Colorado days that mock the human species following a storm. The sky was a cloudless blue, the Front Range peaks pure white. Little more than two inches of snow lay on the Marriott's grounds and parking lot. Even that thin blanket already appeared to be melting.

Frank pulled back from the window and fixed himself coffee in the Keurig. When he switched on the TV, he found what he expected: every local station focusing on the MCI. "One of the worst multi-car accidents in Colorado history," one newscaster called it. "An almost unprecedented chain-reaction pileup," said another. Footage taken from a helicopter showed a panorama of jammed-together cars and trucks, the Interstate's eastbound lane packed solid for hundreds of yards. Frank found it hard to believe that anyone had escaped that mess alive. Other video clips showed footage of EMTs extricating victims and loading them onto ambulances. A reporter interviewed two victims. One ranted about the responders' competence: "I can't believe how long it took those people to get me out of there! Incredible! I must've been stuck two or three hours before anyone even showed up!" The second, clearly shaken but somehow able to laugh, said, "I'm just glad to be here." Remarkably, the death toll was far lower than what Frank had anticipated and feared: only six motorists. At least eighty other people had been hurt, however, more than two dozen badly enough to require hospitalization.

Then this sidebar story about the Jeffco squad's accident: "Among those killed was Tyler van Dyne, an EMT on duty at the scene last night. Returning to Lakewood with two accident victims, the ambulance driven by van Dyne skidded and left the pavement near the Red Rocks exit. Van Dyne was pronounced dead at the scene. Also on board were Laurie Anders, van Dyne's partner on the squad, as well as two patients the EMTs were transporting. All three suffered injuries but are expected to re-cover."

Frank switched off the TV and sat on the bed for a long time. *Van Dyne's partner . . .*

His first impulse: return at once to Jefferson County Medical Center. No, not a good idea. Frank hadn't eaten in more than twenty-four hours, so it seemed wise to get some food. Heading downstairs, he treated himself to breakfast at the hotel restaurant. Then, while eating, he decided to stop by the rectory. He wanted to be in uniform when he went to the med center, but he'd left his spare EMT shirt and slacks back at the house. Once finished at the restaurant, he drove to the RMU neighborhood and parked in front of the Newman Center.

"What a surprise," Pete said as Frank entered.

"Just a pit stop," Frank said. "I'm here to get some clothes." He crossed the living room and walked into his room.

"You seem rather in a rush."

"Sorry. I *am* rushed."

Watching Frank rummage through his closet, Pete said, "Everything okay?"

"More or less."

"Quite a hellacious accident up there in the foothills."

"Quite."

"You hear about it from your squad pals?"

"I didn't need to hear. I was on scene with them."

"What!" Pete exclaimed. "Yesterday wasn't a Thursday."

"True enough. But I haven't had much to do lately, so I thought: What the hell, might be fun to go extricate people from car wrecks." Frank found his slacks and EMT shirt, slung the garments over his left arm, and shut the closet door.

Pete lingered in the bedroom doorway, blocking Frank's way out. "Good Lord—I had no idea. It must've been awful."

"It was."

"Are you okay?"

"Okay enough."

"Your friends? Your—partners?"

"I assume you watched the news."

"All evening."

"Then you probably know about the EMTs who went off the road."

Pete's expression of concern now deepened. "That was *your* squad?"

"My own crew members."

"Frank— Jesus, why didn't you just say so? What happened?"

"Laurie and Tyler told me to stay at the accident scene, so I did. I looked after victims awaiting transport. Laurie and Tyler drove away with some of the worse-hurt victims. That's why I wasn't in the ambulance."

"Thank God. But— Good God, Frank, I'm so sorry."

46

Arriving at the medical center, Frank found a scene similar to the previous evening's: Laurie in her room, two squad members sitting beside the bed, two more waiting in the hallway. The EMTs weren't the same ones visiting earlier. Frank recognized the two outside but didn't know their names.

They introduced themselves and shook hands with him.

"How's she doing?"

"See for yourself," said a middle-aged blonde.

Inside the room he found Laurie awake and chatting with the other visitors. Her face looked worse than yesterday, puffy and blotched reddish-purple across the right cheek and brow, but even from the doorway he could tell that she looked far more alert. He stepped inside. When the other squad members noticed him, they smiled, greeted him, and then muttered excuses as they left the room.

Frank walked over and stood next to the bed. Only her wheat-colored hair and her deep green eyes looked familiar.

He couldn't hold back from reaching out to stroke her left cheek and forehead.

Gazing at him, she let her eyes rim with tears.

"Go ahead," he told her.

"I don't want to."

"No reason to hold back."

She shook her head almost imperceptibly.

"I'm so sorry," Frank said.

"Me too." She stayed silent for a long time. He could see her clenching and unclenching her jaw. "Tyler was such a fuckhead. You'd think that after all the MVAs he'd seen, after all the people he'd extricated, the guy would at least have the sense to buckle his fuckin' seat belt. But no. Not Mr. Indestructible. Not Mr. The Laws of Physics Don't Apply to Me." She felt silent again. "On the plus side, he got what he always wanted."

Frank held back from commenting.

"Got to die a hero's death," she said.

"He certainly had a tendency—" Once again Frank held off from speaking his mind: *—a tendency toward martyrdom.* "Tyler had a tendency to put his life on the line."

"He liked saving people. He was good at it."

"Laurie— I'm so glad you're safe."

"Me too."

"What can I do for you?"

"Nothing."

"There must be something."

"I need a few days to get my head on straight, that's all."

"I feel helpless to make a difference."

"You don't need to make a difference. In a few days I'll be home."

"The squad folks tell me you're coming along really well."

"So I hear."

"I'm sure you know we're here for you. All of us. Me included. Me especially."

"I do know that."

47

He felt so exhausted and sore that he napped off and on at the Marriott, got up only to have dinner, then returned to bed an hour later. He woke at nine the next morning, soaked in the tub for a long time, and, on leaving the room, lingered downstairs over breakfast. Once finished eating, he went back to his room and took another nap. He woke with a start from a dream about twisted cars and trapped passengers.

Frank phoned the Jeffco Med Center and spoke with Laurie.

"I'm okay," she said. "The headaches are still an issue but seem to be easing. My neck is the main concern. The spine specialist wants to do another MRI. If she doesn't spot anything worrisome, I might get discharged tomorrow."

"That's great news."

"I'm going stir-crazy."

"Care for a little company?"

A long silence.

Frank waited.

"I think I'll just get some rest today," Laurie said. "I'm fine—I just need some space."

"Fair enough. Call me if you change your mind."

"I'll do that." After another pause she said, "Oh: on Saturday the squad will be hosting a memorial service for Tyler."

Restless, Frank phoned Jenna to see if he might visit her. She already knew from Pete about Frank's experiences of two days earlier. "Of course," she said. "But maybe you'd like to see Janice and Marissa too?"

"You're all so busy. Please don't disrupt your schedules."

287

"We'll work it out."

The four of them met for a late lunch at La Toscana. The women were almost comically solicitous, asking about his health, his state of mind, his plans.

"I'm fine," he told them. "Truly. Just tired and a little shook up."

"I can't even start to imagine what that must've been like," said Marissa. "All those trapped, hurt people."

"Frank, how did you—cope?" Jenna asked.

"I have no idea. Must've been divine guidance. Seriously. I had no idea what I was doing."

"Somehow you managed."

"It was—difficult. But it's over now, so I'll put it behind me."

"Your friend," Janice said. "How's she doing?"

"Not too bad. Still in the hospital but coming along. There will be further tests. She may get released soon."

"What a relief," Jenna said. Then, cautiously: "And after that?"

"Hard to say. She's clearly still in shock. The accident, her injuries . . . and of course her boyfriend's death. They had a conflicted relationship, to say the least, but she's clearly grieving him."

"Maybe all the more so because of the conflicts."

Everyone fell silent for a while. Then Janice asked, "And you?"

"I'm thinking things through."

"Best to take it slow."

"Give yourself time," said Marissa.

They ate in silence for several minutes. "I have a confession to make," Frank said at last.

Jenna said, "We forgive you, Father, though you have sinned."

"Not so fast. Hear me out. You'll be shocked."

"We're all ears," Marissa said.

"At the accident scene," he told them, "when I was looking after lots of hurt, scared victims, I encouraged them to sing Christmas carols."

The women waited. Janice spoke first: "And?"

"That was insensitive of me. There may well have been Jews among the injured—not to mention Buddhists, Muslims, or folks who are non-religious. Afterwards, I realized how thoughtless I'd been."

"Did anyone object?" Jenna asked.

"Not that I know of."

"Did people—*participate?*"

"They really got into it. A lot of them, anyway."

"And if any Jews or other non-Christians were present, is it possible that they had concerns beyond whether your holiday playlist was sufficiently P.C.?"

"Of course."

"Then I say don't worry about it," Jenna told him.

"Ditto," Janice said.

"Frank, you got those people through the emergency," Marissa said. "As clergy, we all know it's important to offer solace. To give people hope. You did that. You did that under almost impossible circumstances."

"Still—"

"Frank, we forgive you," Jenna told him. "Now say ten Hail Marys, go forth, and sin no more."

"Fat chance," Frank said.

After lunch he drove away from the RMU neighborhood, got on I-25, and headed north. He planned to take 70 West and stop off at the squad house. Instead, acting on impulse, he took the exit for downtown Denver. He drove east on Colfax Avenue and, without planning his moves, ended up parking near the cathedral. Frank walked into the church and stood near the back of the sanctuary for a long time. Then, checking his watch and confirming that he'd arrived at the proper time, he walked over to one of the confessional booths and entered one of them.

He sat there in silence for a while, inhaling the scent of old wood. "Bless me, Father, for I have sinned." He tried to say more but found that he couldn't speak.

"Yes, my son?" said a soft voice.

Frank sat there in silence. Images arose at once. The first car he had encountered on scene . . . The woman inside banging on the window and imploring him: *Can't you get us out? Please? Please!* Then Celeste's face. Then Mark's, Mr. End of Days. Then Stacey's. Then Tyler's, the derisive mouth saying: *We can't fuckin' afford your help.*

The priest's voice: "Please go on."

Frank faltered.

"Will you speak, please?"

After a long pause Frank managed to say, "I think I'll take a rain check."

"Excuse me?"

"I'll have to get back to you."

He left the booth and walked away.

48

Leaving the rectory after a brief stop to pick up more clothes, he heard someone call out: "Frank!"

Stacey, having just stepped out of her car, now strode up the snowy sidewalk to her house. Good Lord, he thought. Even in a down jacket she's all curves.

"Where have you been? I never see you any more."

Frank hesitated to say more but couldn't restrain himself. "I had to move out. I got pink-slipped."

Stacey cupped a hand to her mouth. "What! A priest can get *fired?*"

"Let's just say I'm off-duty for a while."

"But *why?* What have you *done?*"

"It's a long story."

"Frank, that's terrible! I'm so sorry! No, not just sorry. I shouldn't say this, but I'm really, really pissed—pardon my French! Nobody should do that to you. Was it Pete?"

"Not really."

"Well, that's a darn good thing, 'cause you know what? If it was him, I'd go right over and give that guy a real talking-to."

"I'm sure you would."

"Who was it? I mean, it's none of my business. But *why?* Frank, you're so *nice.* Why would anyone want you to leave? People need you here."

"It's complicated. Don't worry, I'm fine. It is what it is."

"I don't *like* what it is. Frank, don't go!" She sounded as whiny as a tired five-year-old. Then, as if playing her trump card, she asked, "What about your garden? Who's gonna raise the veggies?"

"I will," he told her. "Just not here." Glancing toward the house, he noticed Pete half-visible through the picture window—standing a few paces back but clearly watching him. A twinge of paranoia prompted him to look toward the Beaches' house. There she was too: Margaret peering past the lace curtains.

"Stacey," Frank said impulsively, "can I ask you a favor?"

"Sure."

"May I hug you goodbye?"

Looking surprised at first, then amused, she flashed a smile that startled him with its gleefulness.

They crossed the snowy lawn between the two walkways. Frank was startled but thrilled when Stacey not only embraced him but kissed him on the mouth. "Good!" she said gleefully. "Now I can tell people I've kissed a priest."

"Goodbye," Frank said.

"Bye, Frank. I'll miss you."

He didn't look back toward the rectory or the Beaches' house as he walked to his car.

49

Jeffco Three held the memorial service that weekend. So many people had expressed their interest in advance that the squad had relocated this event to the Lakewood Community Center's auditorium. Frank was stunned by the turnout. Almost all of the Jeffco Three's thirty-eight members attended; dozens of EMTs from other squads showed up; a surprising number of local firefighters and police officers turned out as well; and so did dozens of ordinary citizens. The EMTs, firefighters, and cops all arrived in uniform. A striking sight: all these personnel in their navy blue, black, or white attire. More impressive still was the sheer variety of people: as many women as men; folks in their fifties and sixties as well as younger ones; white, black, Asian, and Latino—far more interesting, Frank noted, than the endless rows of gray-haired men in monkish robes that he had observed over the years at the Order's meetings.

Much of the service resembled what Frank had seen when attending funerals for cops or firefighters. The squad captain spoke first, making generic remarks about honoring a member killed in the line of duty. A minister offered an invocation and a prayer. A bagpiper from the Lakewood Fire Department—a massive, bearded Irish American decked out in kilt and Celtic regalia—played "Amazing Grace." Then three speakers took turns offering their reminiscences. One made comments about the hazards of EMT work. The second told specific stories about the many occasions in which Tyler had gone above and beyond the call of duty throughout his almost fifteen years of service. The third offered a summary of Tyler's background—his boyhood in small-town eastern Colorado, his "imaginative employment history," as the speaker phrased it, and his complex personality. Each of the speakers made jokes, some surprisingly blunt, about the guy they all knew as "Dyne-o-Mite." Frank could sense that these people simultaneously found Tyler frustrating, even infuriating, yet valued his contribution to the squad's activities.

Listening to the speakers, Frank couldn't help but wonder if Tyler's presence in the world was God's idea of a joke. Could Tyler have been some sort of bizarre angel of mercy? The man had been smug, hostile, impatient, derisive, arrogant, short-tempered abrasive, foul-mouthed, and bigoted. He had surely inflicted abundant damage on other people throughout the course of his lifetime. Yet somehow Tyler had counterbalanced these negative attributes with some that were unquestionably positive. All of the eulogists highlighted Tyler's ability to snatch the sick and the injured from the jaws of death. What did a less than delightful personality matter, really, in terms of EMS? If you suffer cardiac arrest, you don't really care about the virtues or vices of the person who arrives to deliver CPR. You just want the EMT to jump-start your faltering heart. If you're trapped inside a smoldering car, the EMT's personality won't interest you. You simply want someone to pull you out.

Was it possible that Tyler's unpleasant, even repugnant attributes obscured but didn't contradict a far different nature? Was it possible that within the billowing, acrid pall of Tyler's hostility, abrasiveness, profanity, rudeness, machismo, and fuck-you attitude burned a refining fire? Tyler was foul-mouthed, foul-tempered, foul-minded, but he wasn't *only* foul. Some aspect of his nature went far beyond foulness to an altogether different state of being. The truth was, Tyler had probably done far more good throughout the course of his lifetime than most people. How many lives had he saved so far? Past conversations, as well as the eulogies now under way, suggested a list numbering in the hundreds. And among the victims who weren't necessarily in mortal danger, how many had Tyler spared from more severe consequences of injury or illness? From acute pain? From fear, anxiety, and terror in the midst of their crises? How many people had he reassured with his I'm-in-Charge attitude as their emergencies unfolded? No matter how tempting it might be to typecast Tyler solely as a destructive human being—Dyne-o-Mite!—Frank found that he couldn't. Wanted to, but couldn't. On the contrary, he realized reluctantly that in any assessment of which man had brought more good into the world, Tyler would come out far ahead of Frank.

To his surprise, Laurie now stood and walked over to the podium. He felt moved partly by her willingness to speak at all and partly because her slow, cautious motions made the intensity of her discomfort so vivid. Knowing what he did about her, Frank assumed that she felt even worse than she was letting on. He also couldn't imagine the stress she must be feeling to make her remarks in public.

"So." She simply stood there.

The audience waited in silence.

"Tyler, Tyler . . . What can I say about Tyler?"

Another long silence.

"Look—you guys have described what that matters most," Laurie said, nodding toward the EMTs who preceded her at the podium. "There's not much more I can say that you haven't said already."

Frank felt unnerved by her composure. Unnerved . . . and baffled. Except for a slight quaver in her voice at one point, she sounded calm, resolute, almost serene. Was that peacefulness a result of denial? Of lingering shock? Of strong pain medications? Or was she now at ease, perhaps even relieved, that Tyler had made his exit from the world?

"—and I'll tell you this," she was saying. "Tyler had his charms. I'll spare you the details!" She guffawed suddenly, just once.

As if to say, *Uh-huh,* a few members of the audience echoed her laugh.

"One of them was: he kept saving my butt. You guys know how we met?" A brief pause. "It was before the squad. Before I was on the squad, anyway. I was working for a different service. Tyler was with Jeffco Three but also moonlighted at a gas station. So, one night I just happen to pull into that station. I pump the gas, then go inside the office—this was before you could pay at the pump. Tyler's the guy on duty that night. He takes my card and runs the charge. He flirts with me the whole time. I can see plain as day he's real handsome, but I also see that he's, uh—*interested*. *Too* interested! Soon enough he starts giving me the creeps. All I want is to get out of there. But running the charge takes a while, and I need to use the ladies room real bad, so I decide to step away while the charge goes through. Tyler gives me the card afterward and he's like: 'You have yourself a real good evening.' I go back to my car. Just as I shut the door, though, there's Tyler at the window. He's like: 'Miss, there's a problem with your card.' And I'm like: 'What d'you mean, problem?' He says, 'The charge didn't go through.' 'But you said it did. I signed the slip.' He's insistent: 'Well, there's a problem.' This sounds fishy to me, to say the least. A transparent setup. The last thing I want is to go back into the office with this sleazy guy. But there's something kind of—I don't know, something *persuasive*—so I decide, Shit, let's hope for the best. I get out of the car and go back into the station with him. I'm not thrilled. I'm ready for anything. And you know what he says? Tyler says, 'Sorry I lied, but I had to. There's nothing wrong with your card. Here's the problem: I saw a man slip into your back seat just before you walked over to the car. I had to get you outta there.' Then he calls the cops, the cops show up right away, and yup: there's this dude hiding on the floor in the back. The cops order him out. He's armed with a knife. Who knows what he was intending, but it probably wasn't taking me out for dinner and a movie."

A ripple of laughter moved through the audience.

"That first experience was Tyler to a T. To lay it on the line, he was basically an impossible human being, but he was more than that. Lots more. I could tell you stories and stories about Tyler. About working with him. About living with him. About trying to make sense of him. But you get the idea." She faltered. Laurie didn't look upset, simply . . . blank. She stood there for a long time.

The audience waited in silence.
"That's what I have to say."

50

A reception followed the service. Most of the mourners straggled out of the auditorium and into the community center's cafeteria. Serving counters displayed sandwiches, salads, pizza, and beverages. People sat at tables or stood in clusters as they ate and talked. Frank stood in line and filled a plate, then chatted with fellow members from Foothills EMS and other squads. Most of these people made predictable, canned comments about Tyler. *The best damn EMT ever . . . One of the greats . . . We should all be so lucky if someone like Tyler shows up in our time of need . . .* A few comments were more blunt, even ribald. *I kept having to tell him: Buddy, you just can't friggin' use the rig to go cruisin' for chicks!* Frank overheard a few remarks that suggested even darker opinions: *—to be honest, I'm rather relieved—* As he listened, Frank kept trying to track Laurie. There: near the cafeteria's entrance at the moment, chatting with well-wishers.

Then someone else caught his eye, a lovely brunette standing off to the right. Gabriela Espinoza. Somehow he hadn't noticed her until now. She stood there with a small boy at her side. Frank excused himself, left the cluster of EMTs at his table, and approached her.

For a moment she simply stared, her expression not so much angry as *focused*, though perhaps her eyes revealed the focus of a cat deciding whether to pounce or not. "Father Ochoa."

"Please call me Frank."

"You should have told me." She gestured at his EMT uniform. "Of course."

Another silence. "Then why—?" Cutting herself short, she glanced at her son, who had been staring at Frank in silence throughout this exchange.

Frank said, "Hey there."

"Hi," said the boy almost inaudibly.

"I'm really sorry about your dad."

Jared nodded but didn't speak.

"He was a great EMT. The best."

Another nod.

Gabriela told Jared, "Go to Tía Ana for a moment," and she gestured toward another dark-haired woman standing nearby.

"This is awkward," Frank said once the boy had walked away. "I owe you an apology."

"That would appear to be true."

"When you first came to me for counseling, I had no idea who your husband was. I would've explained my connection if I'd known he was Tyler. By coincidence, I'd joined the same squad a few months earlier, and I was a member of his crew."

She looked at him intently, her expression opaque.

"You mentioned his nickname at some point," he went on. "Definitely one-of-a-kind, just like Tyler. I was going to say something so we could discuss how to proceed. Soon after that I went on a leave of absence."

"Father Pete told me. But you should've told me first."

"I'm aware of that. My intentions were good, I assure you, but I didn't move fast enough. There was a lot going on—"

"That's so lame," she said. "You should've contact me right away. I trusted you with the whole mess of what Tyler and I have gone through. I trusted your objectivity and your fairness. But the whole time I trusted you, you already knew Tyler. Had a working relationship."

Frank said, "I assure you that nothing about my relationship with Tyler would bias me in his favor."

"That's not the point."

"Of course not. And I apologize."

Gabriela stood there and gazed at him with no expression that Frank could fathom. Maybe that was what she intended.

"I'm terribly sorry about your husband," Frank said.

"Ex," she said. "But thank you."

"He was a remarkable man in his own way."

"Something like that."

"I deeply regret what happened."

"It was—inevitable. It's amazing this didn't happen sooner."

"He was very brave."

"Brave, yes. Among other things." She held his gaze.

"Please accept my condolences."

"Thank you."

"I also need to tell you— I won't be working at the university for a while."

"That's what Father Pete said."

"You'll be in good hands at the Center."

She gazed at him but didn't speak. Frank couldn't read her expression. Annoyance? Restrained anger? Something even more negative?

"Pete will be supportive."

"I'm sure he will."

"Again—I'm so sorry about Tyler."

People started to leave. Laurie lingered near the exit with eight or ten people clustering around her. Frank felt both impressed and troubled by her composure. He could hear her laughing. No problem with that—but what was she holding back? Was she perhaps not particularly upset about Tyler's death? Or was she so upset that composure was her only option?

Frank decided he should leave Laurie alone, both to give her some privacy and to avoid gossip within the squad. When he approached to signal her, however, she said, "Hang on a sec" and broke away from the people speaking with her. "Don't go yet."

"You have your hands full."

"I'm winding down. Burning out, actually. Please wait."

"You're positive?"

"I need you to take me somewhere."

Stepping out of the cafeteria, Frank waited near the walkway. Laurie emerged a few minutes later.

They walked to his car in silence. She looked uncomfortable—slow, awkward, at times unstable. Frank helped her into the passenger seat.

Once seated, he backed the car out, left the parking lot, and headed down the road. She gave him precise directions: *Go north on Kipling for a mile . . . Turn left onto West Florida . . . Go straight for eight or ten blocks . . . Then take a right onto South Union. I'll tell you when to turn.* They drove for a few minutes.

"Where are we going?"

"You'll see."

He didn't press for details. They weren't heading off to a restaurant, that much was clear: the neighborhoods became less and less residential, more and more industrial. Frank saw warehouses, a plant nursery, a used car lot. Soon Laurie told him to turn right. After driving just a block, they reached a self-storage center. She indicated a couple of turns among the blocky shed, then told him to stop at one of the units. Frank parked. Laurie sat there a few moments before opening her door.

"Need some help?"

"I wouldn't mind."

Walking around the car, he was startled by how unsteady she was, wobbly and slow, as if she had aged forty years in a week.

"This one." She gestured to the large corrugated steel door sealing a unit.

They walked over to it. She handed him a key. Frank unlocked the unit and noisily raised the door.

Laurie made a one-handed gesture at the pile of stuff inside.

The unit was filled with boxes and boxes, all neatly stacked boxes and containers. Many showed large, tidy black markings: DEHYDRTD or FRZ-DRD. Frank saw white plastic drums, too, each with a neat label: WHEAT or OATS or RICE. Hand tools propped against the front row: two axes, a splitting maul, a pickaxe, two shovels. Three big duffel bags. Two long aluminum gun cases. Five or six red gasoline cans.

Frank said, "Tyler's?"

"His exit strategy. Or at least the supplies to execute his strategy. He was a-headin' for the hills."

"Because of the Apocalypse? The Tribulation?"

"That's what he said, but I doubt it."

"He'd told you about this?"

"Of course. He wanted me to go up with him. *Up* meaning a place he already knew about. Every summer we went hiking and camping together, and year after year we camped for a week or two in a valley west of Minturn. Beautiful place. Lovely winding river. Big peaks on all sides. Tyler's favorite place on earth."

"He was retreating."

"He planned to ride out the hard times in safety."

"With you along for the ride."

"Tyler was always trying to rescue me. What would be better than rescuing me from the End of Days?"

"What indeed."

Laurie stepped into the unit. "Tyler was Mr. Ready For Anything," she said. "Always has been. Hard to say why. Maybe that came out of growing up in a dumpy little farm town out yonder on the plains, or maybe from growing up in a family where anything could happen and often did. Small-town version of my own. It's one of the reasons we got along. Who knows. But I'll tell you this: after the shift he spent at the Trade Center, he was convinced that the clock was running down."

"He told me that during a recent argument."

"He couldn't be convinced otherwise. So—" She gestured at the stack of supplies: "—he stockpiled this stuff and was all set to boogie."

"What about his son?"

"Meaning, did Tyler plan to take Jared with him?"

"It's not implausible."

"Look. Tyler loved Jared more than anyone else on the planet. Whatever you say about Tyler, he was a devoted father. Even Gabi would admit that. So, was he going to rescue his son by kidnapping him?"

Frank stayed silent.

"I can't answer that question," Laurie said. "It's possible he'd've done that. It's also possible that despite Tyler's rage at Gabi, he wouldn't've separated Jared from his mother." She fell silent for a while. Before Frank could speak, Laurie said, "You know what I think? I think Tyler knew on some level that he was full of shit. That no matter what he said, he wasn't escaping from the Tribulation after all."

"Then why stockpile this stuff and head for the hills?"

"To escape from his own life."

They looked at the pile of supplies for a moment longer; then Laurie turned and stepped out of the unit.

Frank followed her and lowered the door.

Laurie replaced the lock and clicked it shut. "Done." Then she walked over to the car and let Frank help her into her seat.

He went around and climbed in.

"So—what happens now?" she asked. "Happens to you next?"

"I'll fly to Chicago and talk with people at the Order."

"Get interrogated? Strapped to the rack? Burned with red-hot pokers?"

"It's not like that," Frank said. "They'll be altogether civil. There will be a discussion, not an inquisition. We'll sort things out."

"What do you want to happen?"

"I'm still thinking it through." He paused. "And you?"

"I don't know either."

"Fair enough." Frank went on: "There's one thing I'm sure of. Whatever you call this conversation we're having, we deserve a nicer place than a storage unit. How about some lunch?"

"To be honest, I'm not feeling so great at the moment."

"Of course. I'll drive you home."

V

THE VIEW

Attired in blue surgical gowns, caps, and masks, the surgeon and her assistant flank the patient lying on the table. The patient, Itandehui Acevedo Ortíz, age fifty-two, is scarcely visible. A sheet and a light blanket cover her body; a surgical drape on her face exposes only her right eye. A tray of instruments rests on the stand extending across Nayeli's abdomen in easy reach of both the surgeon and the assistant.

"Okay," says Dr. Jamison, the ophthalmic surgeon. "Let's make sure she's ready."

Frank nods. "Nayeli," he asks the patient, *"¿estás lista?"*

"Sí, Padrecito." Her right eyeball, fully exposed by the lid retractors, the iris widely dilated, is all Frank can see of this woman. He knows little about her. He learned earlier that she is the wife of a farmer, the mother of seven children, and a member of a Zapotec indigenous community somewhere in a rural area of Oaxaca. Just two years into her fifties, she is already almost blind from cataracts in both eyes. She has traveled for a full day in the back of a pickup truck to reach this clinic and undergo her procedure.

"Check on her comfort level," Dr. Jamison says, "then get her consent to proceed."

Nayeli's eye shifts slightly when Frank leans forward to let her see him better.

The view, Frank tells himself. The view, the view. He asks, *"¿Estás cómoda?"*

"Completamente."

"¿Podemos comenzar?"

"Sí, Padrecito. Ándele, pues."

Frank tells the surgeon, "She says she's completely comfortable and tells us to go ahead."

"Great," says Dr. Jamison. "All right, hand me the Feather Keratome scalpel." When Frank selects the instrument from the surgical tray and reaches out, the surgeon takes it with her gloved hand and tells him, "Let's get started."

AUTHOR'S NOTE

Among the many people who have made this book possible, I'd like to offer special thanks to the following:

Paul Zak, who provided generous, indispensible guidance on and insights into a multitude of issues including, but by no means limited to, the nature of campus ministry priests' work.

Sander Schultz, who offered his expertise on EMS issues, especially the complexities of scene management during mass-casualty incidents.

Jared Hanson, who clarified issues of EMS in a variety of settings.

Meredith Sue Willis, Jim Barszcz, Anita Diamant, Jonathan Strong, Marilyn Levy, and Mary Hays, all of whom generously read the manuscript in early drafts and dispelled my wishful thinking about its strengths and weaknesses at those stages of writing and rewriting.

Members of the Maplewood (N.J.) First Aid Squad for their guidance and inspiration during my years of membership among them.

And of course Edith, Robin, and Cory, partly because of their own insights into what did or didn't work well throughout the book, but mostly—and always—because of their patience and loving support of the somewhat OCD novelist living in their midst.

ABOUT MONTEMAYOR PRESS

Montemayor Press is an independent publisher of literature for children and adults. To learn more about our books, visit:

www.MontemayorPress.com

or write for a catalogue at:

Montemayor Press
P. O. Box 546
Montpelier, VT 05601